EDGE OF
MADNESS

EDGE OF COLLAPSE SERIES BOOK TWO

KYLA STONE

Edge of Madness

Printed in the United States of America

Cover design by Christian Bentulan

Book formatting by Vellum

First Printed in 2020

ISBN: 978-1-945410-49-9

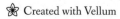 Created with Vellum

ALSO BY KYLA STONE

The *Edge of Collapse* Post-Apocalyptic Series (EMP):

Chaos Rising: The Prequel

Edge of Collapse

Edge of Madness

Edge of Darkness

Edge of Anarchy

Edge of Defiance

Edge of Survival

Edge of Valor

The *Nuclear Dawn* Post-Apocalyptic Series (Nuclear Terrorism):

Point of Impact

Fear the Fallout

From the Ashes

Into the Fire

Darkest Night

Nuclear Dawn: The Complete Series Box Set

The *Last Sanctuary* Post-Apocalyptic Series (Pandemic):

Rising Storm

Falling Stars

Burning Skies

Breaking World

Raging Light

Last Sanctuary: The Complete Series Box Set

No Safe Haven (A post-apocalyptic stand-alone novel):
No Safe Haven

Historical Fantasy:
Labyrinth of Shadows

Contemporary YA:
Beneath the Skin
Before You Break

Audiobooks:
Nuclear Dawn series:
Point of Impact
Fear the Fallout
From the Ashes
Into the Fire
Darkest Night
Edge of Collapse series:
Chaos Rising
Edge of Collapse
Edge of Madness
Edge of Darkness

Much of this story takes place in Southwest Michigan. For the sake of the story, I have altered certain aspects and taken a few liberties with a real town or two. Thank you in advance for understanding an author's creative license.

"Courage is not having the strength to go on, it is going on when you don't have the strength."

— Theodore Roosevelt

1

NOAH
DAY ONE

"We've got a body."

Thirty-year-old Noah Sheridan gripped his phone tighter. The caller's words sent a chill up his spine. "What?"

His friend and fellow Fall Creek police officer, Julian Sinclair, cleared his throat. "A snowmobiler called it in this morning. The vic was found near the river past the trailer park. Caucasian male, early twenties, a known junkie with a beat sheet a mile long. Mostly drug arrests and petty crimes."

"Cause of death?"

"Beaten to within an inch of his life and then some. Dozens of broken bones."

Noah shifted, forgetting he still wore his skis, and nearly fell over. "You think it's connected to the other cases?"

"Too early to tell."

Like any small town, the rural township of Fall Creek in Southwest Michigan had its share of domestic disputes, occasional assaults, and drug busts, but few murders. The last murder was a bar fight gone wrong four years ago.

However, nearby counties had reported a handful disturbing

murders over the last several years. All junkies or known criminals. All found with dozens of broken bones.

None of them had touched Fall Creek—until now.

"Chief Briggs is calling everyone in," Julian said. "On Christmas Eve, no less."

A beat of silence. Noah had taken the day off to be with his son. He always took December 24th off, no matter what.

No one in the department gave him crap for it either. They all knew why.

Today was the fifth anniversary of Hannah's disappearance. Five years since Noah's world imploded, since he watched his life splinter to pieces right before his eyes.

It had taken all these years to piece himself and Milo back together again.

"You don't have to," Julian said quickly, too quickly. Julian Sinclair was Noah's best friend and as close as a brother, the closest thing to family he had left.

They'd been friends through elementary school, played high school football together, and it was Julian who had encouraged Noah to become a law enforcement officer and join the Fall Creek Police Department.

Julian understood what Noah had gone through, had supported him every step of the way.

Noah glanced down at his son, Milo. The eight-year-old stood beside him in his skis, waiting patiently for another go at the Apple Blossom beginner's ski run.

"I'll come in," Noah said.

Milo stared up at him, his eyes big and round with disappointment. Guilt skewered Noah's heart, but there was nothing he could do about it.

"It's the right thing, brother," Julian said, his voice brightening. "I'll work your shift on Christmas so you can get some time with the little man. This is growth, Noah. This is good for you. Time to stop languishing in the past and start living again."

Noah swallowed the lump in his throat. Julian might be right, but he couldn't quite bring himself to agree out loud. He glanced down at his son's pleading eyes. "We're heading back. I'll line up a sitter."

He ended the call and checked the time before slipping the phone into his coat pocket and tugging his leather glove back on. It was 12:10 p.m. At least they'd gotten a few good hours in. They'd spent the morning on the Sweetpea and Apple Blossom runs and practicing at the terrain park.

Early that morning, they'd driven an hour north from their home in Fall Creek to Bittersweet Ski Resort in Otsego, Michigan for their annual father-son ski day. Noah couldn't bear sitting around at home, letting the anniversary eat him up inside.

The day was cloudy and heavily overcast, the cold air stinging Noah's exposed cheeks and nose. He exhaled crystalized clouds with every breath.

Nearly every day in December, they'd suffered record-breaking low temperatures. And another snowstorm was forecast for later tonight.

"We had lots of fun already," Noah said, trying to placate his son. "You did the Birch run like a champ."

"We haven't even had lunch at the cafe yet," Milo argued.

Noah's gaze strayed to the nearest slope, searching in vain for something to make it up to him. More than twenty different runs of various difficulties all circled one large hill, with the lodge at the base near the parking lot.

Several ski lifts carried eager skiers to their next big run. Skiers zipped down the various runs rated from beginner to expert.

The crisp air rang with laughter and happy shouts. "All I Want for Christmas" played from a tinny speaker.

Behind them, the lodge was decked out in Christmas lights. It featured a ski shop, restrooms, bar, and comfort-food style café with specialty hot drinks and giant, fresh-from-the-oven peanut butter chip cookies as large as Milo's head. They were Milo's favorite.

Milo rubbed his reddened, runny nose with the back of his arm and sniffled. "Can we at least ride the Rocket Launcher?"

Noah's gaze snagged on the tallest section of the hill rising in the distance, thickets of pine, maple, and spruce trees fringing either side of the slope. Last year, the resort had brought in earth-movers and created their longest, steepest run, the intermediate-rated Rocket Launcher.

Milo loved riding the lifts as much as the skiing itself. The high-speed quad, triple chair, or double chair—he loved them all.

Noah didn't care for any of them. The rope tow or even the wonder carpet was just fine, thank you very much.

But for his son? He might just have to suck it up. "Okay. Let's do it."

Milo's eyes grew huge. "For real?"

Noah hated heights. That was no secret. Milo, on the other hand, was just like his mother.

Small, quiet, and serious, he looked like the kind of kid who'd be afraid of everything, but he wasn't. He loved roller coasters and the scariest rides at the Berrien County Youth Fair every summer. The taller and faster, the better. It was Noah who did all the worrying.

"Are you sure, Dad?" Milo asked. "You won't be scared?"

Noah's chest squeezed at the thought of his son's tender heart, his childish concern. "Don't you worry about me. I'll be brave, just this once. But we're not skiing down. It's just for the big chairlift ride to the summit. That's it. Then we're riding back down."

"I know, I know," Milo promised, nodding his little head emphatically. "No whining, I pinkie-swear."

"And on the way out, we'll get our hot chocolate and a whole bag of peanut butter chip cookies for the ride home. How does that sound?"

There was that brilliant smile. The eager glee in his eyes. The kid was okay. He'd be fine.

Five minutes later, they were in the chairlift, safety bar lowered, the metal seat freezing Noah's butt and thighs even through his snow pants. The liftie—a guy in his twenties with long blond dreads—waved them on.

They hadn't gone more than forty feet when the chair lurched. A grinding sound came from the loading terminal.

"Oops, hold on," the guy called from behind them.

Noah twisted around, his gut tightening. Two people were riding in the chair behind them, but the lift operator had stopped the line, preventing anyone else from getting on the lift.

"Everything okay?" Noah shouted back.

The liftie gave him a thumbs-up and waved. The chairlift continued moving, but the chairs swinging behind them remained empty.

"Great," Noah muttered as he turned back around, his stomach doing nervous flip-flops. "Just great."

"What's wrong, Dad?"

"Nothing, I'm sure. Just a little glitch they're checking out before they let anyone else on. Once we get to the top, they might close the lift while they fix the problem."

They swayed upward, twenty-plus feet above the ground as they headed toward the summit, skis swinging. He tried not to look over the edge. Tried not to imagine the grip releasing from the cable and their chair plummeting to the hard, unforgiving ground beneath the snow.

The lift operators were trained. They knew what they were doing. The electric engines, bull wheels, terminals, towers—everything was inspected and maintained.

"Look, Dad!" Milo twisted around in his seat, pointing to the base of the slope, where dozens of skiers milling about in their colorful coats and scarves appeared smaller and smaller.

"Can't say I really want to look right now, buddy." Noah gripped the slick safety bar with his gloved fingers, his anxiety building. He was doing this for his kid. Surely, that made it worth it.

Noah tried to keep his mind focused on his kid, but he was already thinking of the hour-long drive home, of how to find a last-minute sitter on Christmas Eve.

He removed his leather gloves, pulled his phone out of his zippered pocket, and searched his contacts database. Maybe his neighbor, Mrs. Gomez, would be home.

The phone rang.

The chairlift jerked to a stop.

Noah gritted his teeth in frustration. *Now what?*

"We stopped." Milo leaned over the metal bar and swung his skis. The chair swayed.

Noah grabbed the back of Milo's coat with his free hand. A vision struck him—Milo toppling over the side and plunging to the frozen ground below. "Okay, buddy, sit back."

"Why'd it stop? Is it broken?"

A wave of dizziness hit him. He closed his eyes for a second before forcing them open again. "I'm sure they'll get it going in a minute."

He glanced down at his phone. It wasn't ringing anymore. The screen was black.

Frowning, he tapped it with the tip of his right finger. Nothing happened. He shook it, swiped it again. Still nothing.

Maybe he'd lost signal up here, but the phone shouldn't be dead.

He shook his phone again. Pressed the power button a few times. Weird. He'd had over 50 percent battery a few minutes ago.

He twisted his wedding ring uneasily. The cold nipped at his bare fingers.

He pulled his gloves back on, tucked his phone in his pocket, and rubbed his hands together. He settled back to wait. Kept his gaze straight ahead. They were almost to the top.

"Just be patient," he said, more to himself than to Milo. "It'll be over soon."

Boom! A loud crash sounded behind them.

Someone screamed.

2

NOAH

DAY ONE

N oah and Milo twisted around in the lift, their legs still
hanging off the front, ski tips pointing toward the sky.
Noah kept one hand on Milo to hold him steady as they looked
back.

In the distance, at the base of the hill, a resort employee
driving a snowcat groomer had apparently lost control of the
vehicle and barreled front-first into a cluster of pine trees.

The front-end was a crumpled mess. Black smoke billowed
from the huge crashed snowcat and spiraled up into the
iron-gray sky.

Guests, Ski Patrol in their red vests, and resort employees
were running toward the scene of the accident. From up here,
they were the size of toothpicks.

"Someone needs to call 911!" a guy yelled from the chair in
front of them.

"I'm sure they already did," the girl beside him said, though
the guy already had his phone out. They were a young Caucasian
couple—both college-aged, decked out in fancy snow gear, with
snowboards dangling from their feet.

"Hey!" The guy shook his phone. "My phone doesn't work."

"Mine either!" said the old man in the chair behind them. A teenage girl with Windex-blue hair and a bored, sullen expression on her face slumped next to him.

She was young, maybe fifteen or sixteen. The old man next to her probably in his seventies. She was a snowboarder—he wore skis.

The girl stared back at Noah. One of her eyebrows was pierced, her eyes ringed in black makeup. Her shiny, stick-straight hair was a brilliant blue and spilled around her shoulders. A swoop of aqua bangs completed her look. Emo—or whatever they called it these days.

She looked familiar. They both did.

"My screen is black," said the college-aged guy. Tufts of bleached blond hair stuck out beneath the beanie covering his head. He had a narrow face still sprinkled with acne and a wispy goatee. "I had a full charge."

"So did I." A small shiver of apprehension streaked up Noah's spine. Usually he had his department-issued radio on him too. But not today. His day off.

"Why aren't we moving?" The girl was as bottle-blonde as her boyfriend and wore a hot pink parka, the fur around her hood dyed pink to match. "What's going on?"

"Maybe something happened with the power," said the older gentleman. His voice was deep and gravelly, and he spoke with an accent Noah couldn't quite place. He looked Filipino, or maybe Vietnamese. "But they've got diesel generators."

"I'm sure they'll get things figured out quickly." Noah projected his voice, kept it calm and steady. He was used to diffusing tense situations, to calming frazzled nerves at car accidents and talking down drunks itching for a fight at the bar. "The generator will kick on, and we'll get moving again. I'm sure the staff are just distracted by the accident."

9

The co-eds in front of him nodded and settled back in their chair.

The smoke from the crashed snowcat reached them, stinging his nostrils. He shivered. The temperature was dropping. Or maybe it just seemed colder up here, above the trees, exposed to the elements.

A strange low fog drifted between the pine trees along the ridge below them. In the distance, a bank of dark clouds roiled over the horizon from the west.

The snowstorm appeared to be ahead of schedule.

"I know her," Milo whispered. "The blue girl. She lives at the end of our street, Dad. I see her getting in and out of a car sometimes. Or mowing the lawn in summer."

Now that Milo had said it, Noah realized he was right. He recognized the girl's grandfather too. He'd chatted with the guy a few times on evening walks with Milo, at the town's single gas station, or in line at the hardware store.

"She's a Riley," Noah said quietly. He didn't know the grandfather or the granddaughter well, but the grown daughter, Octavia Riley, was a troublemaker. He'd gone to high school with her—and arrested her more than once.

Noah studied what he could see of the chairs ahead of them. The next tower was after the college couple in the chair ahead of them, and beyond the tower were six or seven empty chairs and what appeared to be the top of the hill and the terminal.

Behind him sat the Riley girl and her grandfather, and then a train of empty chairs all the way to the loading zone at the bottom of the hill. Whatever they were testing, whatever malfunction they'd been worried about, they'd held off on letting anyone else on the lift.

That didn't seem like a good sign.

"Dad," Milo said.

"Yeah?"

"Look."

There was something in his voice, a hint of apprehension, an edge of fear—that caught Noah's attention. "What is it?"

"There," Milo said simply.

Milo wasn't staring down at the slope anymore. He was craning his neck up toward the sky. He pointed.

To the northeast, beyond the base of the hill, the huge brown lodge with the green roof, the parking lot, and ribbon of highway and woods, a small black object appeared above the tops of the pines.

A helicopter. But it wasn't flying like any chopper Noah had ever seen.

It zoomed low, just barely skimming the trees. It was tilted at a weird angle, rotors spinning lazily—almost slowly—with no accompanying *thump, thump, thump*, no roar of the engine.

"Dad!" Milo cried.

Noah grabbed his hand.

They watched, horrified, as the helicopter spun crazily, drunkenly. It plunged toward the ground. Tiny people fled in all directions, scattering like ants from a kicked nest.

With a cacophonous screech of metal, the chopper crashed into the lodge. It plummeted through the roof, rotors churning, smashing through wood and mortar and glass.

Stunned, Noah stared open-mouthed.

Thick black smoke poured into the sky. Screams and shrieks of pain and terror echoed in the cold air. Flames exploded from the resort's roof as more people spilled out the doors, desperate to escape.

"What just happened?" the girl in the hot pink coat cried. "That helicopter—it just fell! Right out of the sky! It just crashed!"

"Holy crap," the Riley girl breathed.

"I want to go home!" Hot Pink said tremulously, wiping at her eyes. "I want off this thing. Right freaking now!"

"First the chairlift," College Guy said, fear in his voice. "The phones. Then the snowcat. Now that chopper."

"Something's wrong," the Riley girl said. "Very, very wrong."

3

QUINN
DAY ONE

Quinn Riley sniffed and shifted against the freezing metal seat of the chair lift. She shivered, her teeth chattering. She couldn't remember ever being this cold.

Some sixteenth birthday this was turning out to be.

Gramps had brought her out here for nostalgia's sake. Her mother rarely had the money to splurge on stuff like this these days. She splurged on other things, like her next meth fix and her crackhead boyfriend, Ray Shultz.

Which is probably why Gramps had wanted to take Quinn so badly. To make it up to her or something. Quinn was blunt to a fault and wore her feelings on her sleeve, but even she couldn't say no to Gramps when he had his mind set on something.

So here she was, freezing her ass off on a stupid ski lift at a stupid resort in stupid Michigan—instead of spending the day far away from other humans, reading sci-fi novels or painting a mural on her bedroom wall.

But then her old, cracked Samsung phone had stopped working. The enormous groomer machine had smashed into that pile of trees. And the helicopter, crashing into the lodge like that . . .

It was surreal. Like something out of one of her favorite science fiction novels. She read all the classics she could—*I, Robot, Ender's Game, 1984, Snow Crash, Fahrenheit 451*. She'd even read some of those crazy end-of-the-world books from Amazon.

The hairs on the back of her neck lifted. She pushed her blue bangs out of the way and stared back at the lodge—the smoke, the fire, the black and twisted rotors poking out of the roof like scorpion claws—until her eyes blurred.

Her heartbeat quickened. It was almost exciting. Finally, something crazy was happening in her stupid boring life. She'd spent her whole life in Fall Creek, a tiny rural township of less than a thousand people located in the bottom southwestern corner of Michigan in Berrien County.

Fall Creek was surrounded by lakes and rivers, farms and orchards and forests, with the beaches of Lake Michigan only a twenty-minute drive away.

Nothing ever happened here. Nothing interesting, anyway. Fall Creek didn't even have a Taco Bell.

"Maybe it's that thing that destroys all technology," she said loudly, surprising even herself.

"What are you talking about?" College Boy asked dubiously.

"An electromagnetic pulse thing. An EMP. Or a massive storm on the sun that creates a super solar flare. It's called a coronal mass ejection. They both take down the power grid. Permanently."

Gramps put his mittened hand on her arm. "Quinn. Enough of that," he said, stern but gentle. "No need to scare people."

"Maybe they should be scared." Quinn pointed down the hill at the black smoke billowing from the half-collapsed lodge roof. "That's not in my head."

"Let's not jump to conclusions, now," said the dark-haired cop sitting in the middle chair, his little boy beside him. She'd recognized them immediately. They lived on Tanglewood Drive, the same street as Gran and Gramps in Fall Creek. Weird coincidence.

The cop was the husband of that woman who'd gone missing five years ago. She still remembered the woman's name from the newspapers: Hannah Sheridan.

It wasn't every day a woman disappeared in the tiny township of Fall Creek. Let alone disappearing on Quinn's birthday.

She shrugged with a scowl, though she didn't pull her arm away from Gramps. "Just saying. What else would take out everyone's phones? It doesn't make sense. Armageddon could be happening right under our noses." Quinn shot a glance at the kid and grinned. "Maybe they're all turning into zombies down there."

The cop frowned at her. "Let's not scare everyone, okay?"

"I'm not scared," the kid said quickly.

"Look, my name is Noah Sheridan," the cop said. "This is my son, Milo. I'm a police officer with the Fall Creek Police Department in Berrien County. Places like this, they prepare for emergencies. They'll turn on the generator any minute now. Emergency services are already on their way."

Quinn doubted it. The more she thought about it, the surer she was. Her mouth went dry. She wished she'd brought a water bottle with her. "With no way to call them? I don't think so."

Gramps shook his head at her. "Officer Sheridan is just trying to keep us calm. What good will panic do right now?"

Gramps was a good man. She loved her grandfather more than she'd ever let herself admit out loud. He was the soft-hearted one, not tough and snarky like Gran, like Quinn herself. She usually tried to restrain her sharp tongue with him, even though it wasn't easy.

"Okay, Gramps," she said with a reluctant sigh. "I get it. No one ever wants me to be right."

He winked at her. "Certainly not this time."

"My name is Phoebe," said the blonde chick in the pink coat. "This is Brock."

"Dương Văn Dũng," said Gramps proudly, leading with his family name. "You may call me Mr. Dũng. This is my grand-daughter, Quintessa. We call her Quinn."

Quinn didn't wave, just scowled. She hated that name, and she hated them all right now—even Gramps—for dragging her up here on her birthday, of all days.

She squished down further in her seat, trying to get comfort-able. It was impossible. These stupid chair lifts were meant for only a few minutes of sitting, not for hours.

Fifteen minutes passed. Then thirty. They sat in the chairs. The lift didn't move.

The pine trees along the hill rustled slightly. The red flexible fencing snaking the boundaries of the Rocket Launcher run rippled in the breeze. It got even colder.

The skiers at the top of the Rocket Launcher run had all made their way down the hill. She could barely make out the next chair-lift across the slopes through the thickening fog, could just see the Ski Patrol workers surrounding the terminal, working on getting people down from the lift.

Good. It would just be a matter of time, then.

Down at the lodge, the screams and shouts continued, tiny people racing frantically around the lodge. But she heard no shrieking engines, saw no flashing lights.

No vehicles of any kind were moving down there.

Normally, a hundred calls would've gone out to 911 already. Even if everyone else had the same communications problem with their non-working phones, the ski resort employees would have access to a landline phone or a radio.

Even if they didn't, someone would've hopped in a car and driven to the nearest police or fire station. It wasn't like they were in the middle of nowhere.

The weird, nervous feeling in her gut intensified. A blend of uneasiness mixed with a dark little thrill. She didn't want people to get hurt, but this sure wasn't boring.

Blonde Chick—Phoebe—started crying and rubbing her eyes. "What if they've forgotten about us? We need to call for help. We need to make them hear us."

"Good idea, babe," Brock said. His teeth were so white and so straight. It was abnormal.

"Help!" Phoebe shouted.

The others joined in. Even Quinn gave in and yelled a few times. Why not? She was freezing. Her ears were stinging, and her butt was going numb. Beside her, Gramps shivered. He was too old to be stuck out here like this.

The wind snatched their voices. It felt like they were screaming into a white void of nothingness.

"Please!" Phoebe cried. "Will someone please help us!"

But no help came.

More time passed. She couldn't see the sun through the heavy gray clouds, but it had to be well after two, maybe three. She was just guessing.

She didn't wear a watch. She didn't need one with her phone always with her. Until now.

Her stomach grumbled hungrily. The cold snuck beneath her scarf, tunneled its way into her gloves and boots.

"You're a good girl, Quinn," Gramps said quietly, so only she could hear. "You know that?"

She glanced at him. He was shivering harder than she was. She realized suddenly how old he looked—the dozens of fine wrinkles webbing his weathered brown face, the sagging skin around his kind dark brown eyes. He looked tired.

At seventy-three, he'd slowed down considerably since his last heart attack. He wasn't skiing himself but riding the lifts with her, then taking them back down while she snowboarded down.

"You okay, Gramps?"

"Fine, fine." He tried to stop himself from shivering, but she wasn't fooled. "Don't worry about me, *con gái*."

He often called her that—daughter. She spent so much time at their house escaping her own mother, she might as well have been. Her grandparents had an open-door policy for her and even gave her a bedroom to decorate any way she wanted.

Which was more than she could say for the trashy trailer her mother lived in.

She worried at the piercing over her eyebrow with a frown. Her mother was the last thing she wanted to think about right now. She had enough on her mind already.

Like figuring out how to get off this chair lift from hell.

Her grandfather patted her arm. "I think I will just close my eyes for a bit."

"Okay, Gramps," she said, her chest tightening.

4

NOAH
DAY ONE

Noah was bitterly cold. His ears and nose hurt. Milo had to be freezing, but he didn't complain. Luckily, Noah had made sure they were both dressed in heavy layers.

He tightened Milo's hood strings and made sure his scarf covered the lower half of his face.

The wind was picking up, whipping around the trees, blowing the fresh powder and swaying the chairs gently. The cables creaked. To speak to each other, they had to raise their voices.

The unease he'd felt earlier had blossomed into full-on apprehension.

It was eerily quiet. No sounds from the lodge at the bottom of the hill. Only the soft whoosh of the wind, the occasional thump of snow falling from the branches.

This wasn't supposed to be happening. This wasn't how things worked. When something went wrong—a disaster, an accident, a crime—there were dozens, hundreds of emergency-trained personnel ready to jump into the gap.

He knew. He was one of them.

Where was everyone? What the hell was happening?

"Dad, I'm thirsty," Milo said.

From his pocket, Noah pulled the small bottle of water purchased for a ridiculous price at the café earlier. It was three-fourths full. He handed it to Milo along with a granola bar he had in his pocket. He had fruit leather and a baggie of nuts as well.

Once upon a time, he'd been terrible at remembering stuff like that. Not anymore.

Milo drank a bit and handed it back. Noah licked his dry lips. He was thirsty. Hungry, too. But he needed to save it all for his son.

Noah squeezed Milo's shoulder. "Help will be here soon. EMTs will save anybody who's hurt. And Ski Patrol will come get us. We'll be rescued and have a great story to tell Uncle Julian when we get back, okay?"

Milo nodded solemnly, his eyes big and dark in his small face. "How will we get down?"

A few years ago, Noah had taken part in a mock emergency drill at Bittersweet as part of their region's emergency response preparedness protocols. "In a regular power outage, it's pretty easy. They have diesel engines for backup juice. On newer lifts, snowcats can hook into the pulley system and drag each chair slowly down the hill until it's safe to unload."

"What if the snowcats and the back-ups don't work?"

"Well, when Ski Patrol comes to our rescue, they'll start at the top of the lift and work their way down in teams. A patroller will climb the lift tower and secure a rope to the lift cable with some-thing called a T-seat, which is a one-person chair without legs. The patroller will scuttle down the tower rungs and drag the chair to us. They'll secure passengers one by one in the T-seat and lower them to the ground with a relay system. They might use a body harness instead of a T-seat, but they can get everyone down, even when chairs get stuck above precarious spots like we are."

"Okay," Milo said, shivering.

Noah studied Milo, checking his vital signs, looking for symptoms of stress. It was second nature, even though Milo's medication mostly allowed him to be a normal kid.

About a month after Milo had started kindergarten three years ago, he'd started complaining of stomach aches, lost his appetite, and was too tired to play with his friends at school. Then dark patches on his elbows, knees, and the back of his neck had appeared.

When a stomach bug quickly turned into severe vomiting, dehydration, and stabbing stomach pains, Noah rushed him to the emergency room.

The hospital had run a battery of labs on Milo's cortisol, potassium, sodium, and ACTH levels before giving the diagnosis of Addison's disease. Milo's adrenal glands didn't make enough cortisol on their own. Since cortisol regulated the stress response in the body, lifelong treatment to replace the hormone was critical.

Serious complications were more likely when Milo was under physical stress. An accident or illness could quickly escalate into adrenal crisis, a life-threatening situation which could lead to kidney failure, shock, and death.

Milo took hydrocortisone pills three times a day on a schedule mimicking the normal twenty-four-hour fluctuation of cortisol levels in the body. He wore a medical alert bracelet and kept a card on him describing his illness and the schedule and dosing of his medication.

They also kept an emergency dose of injectable glucocorticoid in a fanny pack that was either always with him or in the car. The pack also contained extra pills, snacks high in salt and sugar, and an electrolyte drink since Milo's sodium and potassium levels were affected during stress; both were critical for the heart's electrochemical system.

"Do your arms and legs feel tired or funny?" Noah asked him. "Any stomach pain? Dizziness?"

Milo shook his head. "Just really, really cold."

Noah nodded, relieved. Milo took his pills every day like clockwork. Noah had given him his afternoon dose at noon. "Tell me if you start feeling sick."

Noah checked his coat and scarf again. He was as covered as he was going to get. It still wasn't enough. Noah unwound his own scarf and wrapped it around Milo's head and face, creating a double layer of protection. Only his son's dark eyes peered out at him.

Noah took after his Irish-American father, with dark brown hair but a fair complexion. Milo had inherited the olive skin-tone of Noah's Venezuelan mother, with curly black hair and huge dark eyes that could swallow a person whole.

He looked more like Noah than his mother, and yet Noah saw glimpses of her in his mischievous expressions, in the way he tilted his head or bit his lower lip. His mannerisms were so similar, sometimes it made Noah's chest ache.

A memory flashed through Noah's mind. The last day he and Hannah had ever spent together was at Bittersweet Ski Resort five years ago—the day she disappeared.

He wished he could say they'd been happy that day. But the fight was already brewing between them, Hannah tense and Noah closed off. But they'd been happy for their son. On all those miserable sleepless nights, he clung to that truth.

They'd smiled and laughed and drank hot chocolate and ate warm gooey cookies out of a paper bag, Milo's chubby face smeared with peanut butter and chocolate.

They'd introduced Milo to his first set of skis and the bunny slope called "Babies' Breath," where he'd fallen over and over, his bubbling giggles the glue that held their fragile bond together.

The photo of Hannah—the one he'd snapped on his phone that day, the last one of her ever taken. The one the media had plastered all over the television and internet, the one Noah printed on 'Missing' posters and tacked on every telephone pole for thirty miles.

She had been so beautiful. The snowflakes caught in the chocolate-brown strands of hair framing her delicate face, her cheeks pink from the cold, her emerald-green eyes matching that dark green suede coat he'd bought their first Christmas together, back when she still loved him.

Noah had done his best to build new, good memories over the bad ones, for both himself and Milo. They'd endured five years of hell together—both bereft, lost and unmoored, clinging to each other like drowning sailors.

"Dad?"

Noah clenched his teeth to keep them from chattering. "Yeah, bud?"

"I have to pee."

"Okay, I'll help you."

"And I wanna go home."

"I know, buddy. Soon, I promise."

5

QUINN

DAY ONE

"I —I don't feel so good." Gramps took off his hood and hat with a trembling hand and rubbed his bald head. He didn't put his hat back on.

"Gramps," Quinn said. Gone was her usual snark and sarcasm —her go-to attitude. Real worry strained her voice. "What's wrong?"

The cold grew colder. The gray day turned dark. Snow had begun to fall. It spiraled from the slate-gray sky, falling thicker and faster with each passing minute until it obscured their view of anything down the hill.

They couldn't see the lodge or the fire anymore, couldn't see the crashed snowcat, or any people. It was like everyone had fled the ski resort and simply abandoned them. It felt like being totally cut off from civilization.

Gramps turned toward her, his movements slow and sluggish. His skin had turned an unhealthy gray, his eyes sunken. Gramps pressed both hands to his chest. "I feel dizzy. Like I'm going to lose consciousness. My shoulder and arm hurt."

He'd had three heart attacks already. He was too stubborn to listen to anyone, not even the doctors.

Gram kept insisting he eat better, but he bought candy and chocolate and hid it. He piled butter on his spaghetti and ravioli. He drank too much Mekong whiskey. He'd been raised on little in Vietnam; he always said he loved America so much, he wasn't going to miss out on any of her pleasures—especially food and drink.

"It's your heart," Quinn said flatly.

"It's battering against my ribs a million miles a minute and won't stop."

Quinn let out a string of colorful curses.

Noah clapped his hands over his son's ears. "Language."

She rolled her eyes and didn't bother to apologize. Her own heartbeat quickened. Worry snarled in her belly. "Gramps?"

"It's—hard to breathe."

She glanced back at Noah with accusing eyes. "He has a pacemaker."

She knew that if this electromagnetic pulse had really knocked out her grandfather's pacemaker, that alone wouldn't cause a heart attack. Pacemakers helped keep the heart from beating too slowly, but it wasn't keeping his heart beating.

But combined with incredible stress and the vicious cold . . . his heart was just too weak to handle the strain.

Whatever interest or excitement she'd felt were gone. Anger—and fear—flared through her. She waved one hand in the air, encompassing everything in one fell swoop. "It's real. Whatever it is—it's destroyed everything electronic. Including the thing keeping his heart working right."

"Are you okay, sir?" Noah called.

"No, he's clearly not!" Quinn said sharply. "His skin's all gray, and he's acting funny."

"I'm just gonna . . . sleep awhile," Gramps rasped. His breath was shallow and uneven. "Don't mind me. I'm gonna dream up some tropical beaches, maybe a cruise, some fine ladies in bikinis to keep me company . . . don't tell Gran."

"You'll do no such thing. You have to stay awake."

"I . . . love you, *con gái*. Don't . . . ever forget that."

"Gramps! Stop talking like that! You're scaring me."

He groaned, mumbled something, and his head fell back and thudded against one of the metal bars.

Quinn shook her grandfather's frail shoulders. "Gramps! Wake up!"

He didn't respond. He was unconscious.

"How's his color?" Noah called. "His breathing?"

"His lips are blue. His face is gray. I can't tell if he's breathing."

She looked back at Noah, desperate for him to do something, anything—but the cop was as trapped as she was, stuck twenty-five feet off the ground, and yards away from her or her grandfather.

What was he going to do? What could anyone do? They had no phones. No way to contact anyone. No one coming to get them.

"I can't wake him up," Quinn said in a stricken voice. "I think he just had a heart attack."

6

NOAH
DAY ONE

The sky was darkening rapidly, the temperature dropping with it. The snow fell fast and hard. Noah had to squint to see clearly.

"My grandfather is dying!" Quinn cried.

They couldn't wait any longer. He hadn't wanted to believe it before, but he couldn't deny it any longer. The worst had happened—everyone, even Ski Patrol, had forgotten about them.

The truth was, with the threat of frostbite and hypothermia, none of them would last overnight in a snowstorm and subzero temperatures.

They had to find a way down to the ground.

"I know." Noah tried to keep his voice calm and soothing, tried not to let the anxiety show. "We have to do something."

"There's only one thing to do, man." Brock looked down. "Someone has to jump."

Instinctively, Noah looked down, too. Vertigo plunged through him. He gripped the safety bar and swallowed hard. "Anyone who jumps is likely to break something. It's steep here, at least thirty feet down. Maybe more."

"Then what, man? What else do you suggest?"

Noah eyed the cable above them, tried to measure the distance to the next tower. Each of the towers had a narrow ladder attached for maintenance, repairs, and emergencies.

If they could reach the tower . . . but how? Go hand-over-hand across the cable like monkeys? With their numb, stiff fingers? What if he fell? What if Milo fell?

At least if someone jumped, they'd have more control over the fall, how their body landed. They could go get help and bring a rescue crew back up the hill.

Maybe this was the least-bad option out of several bad choices.

"My balls are freezing off, dude," Brock said. "I'm not gonna sit here while our fingers turn black and our toes fall off. I'm gonna jump."

"I'll do it." Noah was the cop. It was his job to protect everyone. He was the one who should put himself at risk to get help. Even though the thought of leaving Milo up here alone made him feel physically ill. "It should be me."

"No way, man," Brock said. "You've got the little kid you've gotta take care of."

Noah swallowed. Shame pricked him. He'd pegged Brock as a shallow jock. He'd been wrong. "Are you sure?"

Brock nodded, his jaw set. "Man, I got this."

"Make your body loose," Noah said. "Roll when you hit the ground."

Brock lifted the metal safety bar. He leaned down, fumbled with his boot, and snapped off his snowboard.

They all watched it fall through the air. The board dropped to the ground and landed in the snow with a soft thud.

Brock twisted around and lowered himself from the seat, using the crossbar just below the seat to hold onto. With his gloved hands gripping the bar, he hung by his arms.

He still looked a good twenty-five-plus feet above the ground.

"Close your eyes, Milo." Noah unzipped his coat pocket and pulled out the small but powerful maglight he always kept with him, along with a folding knife attached to his keychain. He shone the beam at Brock to give him light.

The chair swayed beneath Brock's shifting weight. Phoebe let out a tiny cry and seized one of the side bars to steady herself. She raised one hand and re-lowered the safety bar to keep herself from falling.

Phoebe started crying, sniffling and wiping at her eyes. "Be careful, babe."

Brock looked up at her. His body swayed gently. "I love you."

"I love you too, Brock Mason."

"Gross," Quinn said, some of the snark returning to her voice. "Just jump already."

Noah watched, blinking against the snowflakes catching in his eyelashes, his hand over Milo's eyes, and hardly dared to breathe.

Brock let go.

The drop took only a moment, a heartbeat, a sucked-in breath.

Brock landed feet-first. He tumbled awkwardly and collapsed on his back in the snow.

An unearthly scream shattered the air.

"Brock!" Phoebe shrieked.

Brock only screamed louder.

Noah leaned against the back of the chairlift and peered over the edge, shining the penlight and squinting in the twilight. The guy lay on his side in the snow, one leg stuck straight out, the other bent inward toward his chest.

"My leg! My leg!"

"What's wrong?" Phoebe asked. "Are you okay?"

"I freakin' broke my leg, man!" Moaning, Brock ripped off his gloves and fumbled for his leg, patting it to search for the injury. "I can feel—the bone! I feel it sticking out!"

Noah cursed under his breath.

Brock howled in agony. Even in the twilight, Noah could clearly see the dark stain spreading across the man's snow pant below his knee. Something poked against the fabric over his shin— the broken bone.

Now what? They couldn't do a thing for him up here. Brock couldn't make his way all the way down to the lodge on a broken leg.

"We have to help him!" Phoebe cried.

"What the heck do you want us to do?" Quinn said. "Pray his leg knits itself back together in the next five minutes? Float down to him like angels of mercy?"

"You don't have to be a jerk about it," Phoebe muttered.

"Can you move at all?" Noah asked Brock.

"No!" Brock's voice was high and strained, cracking in panic. "I can't move! It hurts so much! I can't frickin' move at all. I'm dying! I feel like I'm dying, man! Help me!"

"Don't look at it, okay? Try not to think about it. Take steady breaths. Can you look around for something to splint your leg with to provide you some support?"

Brock turned his head and vomited. He groaned.

"Try to stay calm. You need to lay down and elevate your legs, if you can. Maybe shovel some snow underneath your unhurt leg—"

"I can't breathe!" Brock cried. "It hurts, it hurts so much!"

"He's going into shock," Quinn said.

"Brock!" Noah said. "Calm down. Take slow, steady breaths."

It was no use. Brock writhed and screamed in agony. They could do nothing but watch him suffer in stunned horror. Noah held Milo's head to his chest, covering his eyes and ears to shield him.

The minutes passed with terrible slowness.

Brock's low, anguished moans were snatched by the growing

wind whistling between the tree trunks, branches creaking. The snow came down fast and heavy, making it difficult to see.

Noah forced himself to look down again. "Brock! What are you doing?"

Brock had taken off his coat. He was spreading it over his injured leg. "I'm too hot. I'm burning up. I've got to save my leg, man . . . I got to save it . . ."

Fear spiked through Noah. "You have hypothermia, Brock. You're not thinking straight. You need to put the coat back on. Cover your head with your hood. Find your gloves."

"I'm just . . . so tired, man . . . I'll feel better when I sleep . . ."

"You have to do something!" Phoebe said through hitching sobs. "Please!"

"Don't fall asleep!" Noah shouted. "Stay awake! Stay with us!"

But Brock didn't appear to be listening. His scarf had fallen off, exposing his face and throat. His head was bare. Without his coat to protect his core, his body temperature would drop to critical levels incredibly fast.

Brock's eyes rolled back in his head, and he flopped on his back in the snow like a fish.

He'd passed out from the pain. Or succumbed to the cold. Either way, it was bad.

"Brock!" Phoebe stared down at her boyfriend in the twilight, tears streaming down her cheeks. "He's dying! Brock!"

Arms extended, his bare hands stretched out like he was making a snow angel. Brock didn't answer. He didn't move.

7

NOAH
DAY ONE

Dread and dismay tangled in Noah's gut. He never should have allowed Brock to jump. It should have been him. It should have been Noah.

The wind howled through the trees, whipping the heavily falling snow into a frenzy. In only a few minutes, it would be completely dark.

The fear rose up in him, the old familiar terror of high places, of falling. That familiar sickening lurch in his gut, the wave of vertigo.

It didn't matter how afraid he was, how much he dreaded what was coming. Milo was so young, so small, so vulnerable. For his son, he would do anything.

He shimmied forward, leaned far over the safety bar, and unclipped first one boot, then the other. His skis fell away into the darkness. He unclipped Milo's skis as well.

Slowly, he pushed himself into a kneeling position, grasping the nearest bar with his left hand. The chair wobbled. The lift creaked and swayed beneath his shifting weight.

"What are you doing?" Quinn asked.

"I'm going to get down and get us out of here."

He couldn't see her in the dark anymore. "Using the cable?"

"I just have to shimmy down to your chair, past it, and then to the tower. From there, I can climb down the ladder. It can't be that hard, right?"

Quinn didn't bother to answer. Her skepticism screamed loud in her silence.

A gust of wind blew down the hill, whipping stinging snow into his face. He blinked against the onslaught. His lungs burned with every breath, his nostrils stinging.

The cold burrowed into his bones.

He handed the flashlight to Milo. His fingers felt stiff and awkward. He opened and closed his fists, working out the stiffness, willing feeling and warmth to return to his hands.

"Your job is to work the light, okay buddy? It's an important job. You think you can handle it?"

Milo nodded solemnly.

"You feel okay?"

"I'm okay, Dad. Don't worry about me." Milo hesitated. "You can do it, Dad."

Phoebe's sobs had quieted to sniffles and hiccups. Quinn said nothing, but he knew she was watching his every move.

They were depending on him. Milo was depending on him.

He stood cautiously, shakily. The chair wobbled and lurched beneath him. His boots were slick on the metal. His feet threatened to slide right out from under him.

He grasped the center pole with both hands and craned his neck, examining the apparatus he was about to climb. The center pole above his head curved into an attachment to the thick steel cable, locking each individual chair into place. If he stepped onto the top of the chair back, he could reach the grip and the cable.

He would travel along the cable down toward Quinn and her grandfather. It was a longer journey, but gravity would be on his side. That was the hope, anyway.

Snowflakes collected atop the thick steel cable. The metal glinted in the beam of the penlight. It would be slick and hard to grasp.

If he removed his gloves, his skin would stick to the freezing metal, might even tear chunks off his palms. He glanced down at his hands. His gloves were leather, a definite advantage over nylon or some other synthetic, slippery material.

Noah was six-foot-one, a hundred and ninety pounds. In high school, he'd played varsity wide receiver and took the Fall Creek Wolves to the state championship two years in a row. Maybe he'd gained a little pudge around the middle in the last few years, but he kept himself in shape with weights, jogging, and twice-weekly racquetball.

Still, he hadn't scaled a rope since high school gym class. He was athletic, but this required a different skill set.

He inhaled a frozen breath, preparing himself.

"Good luck, Dad," Milo said.

Noah kissed the top of his son's head. He would need all the luck he could get.

His heart in his throat, Noah stepped onto the thin metal lip of the chair back and grasped the center pole for balance. His boots started to slip immediately, but he was already using his arms to clamber up over the T-bar.

He reached up and grasped the top of the grip. His fingers slipped, but he adjusted his hands until he found a better purchase.

He leaned forward, seized the cable with both hands, and hung there for a moment, his arms at right angles to keep the strain of his weight off his fingers. Using all his strength, he swung his legs up and attempted to fold them over the cable at the knees.

He missed. His right boot scraped the cable, sending a jolting thrum through his hands, his left leg missing altogether.

"We're doomed," Quinn said.

8

NOAH
DAY ONE

"No, we're not." Noah tightened his grasp on the cable, legs swinging freely. He sucked in a deep breath, ignoring the aching burn in his lungs, the swirl of nausea in his gut.

His biceps already straining, swung his body a second time, using his abs, putting everything into it. This time, the back of his knees hooked over the cable, one on each side.

"Now scooch," Quinn called.

"I know what to do." Though he didn't, not really. He was figuring it out as he went. He recalled some swat-style training Julian had dragged him to a few times, a style of horizontal rope climbing similar to a crab crawl.

If he could pull himself up on top of the cable, he could lay on top and hook his boot to push while he pulled. It would hopefully stave off the exhaustion of hanging upside down and forcing his limbs to support all his weight.

After several tries, he pulled himself on top of the cable and settled himself. Then, pulling with his arms, pushing with one leg while using his hanging leg to balance, he began the methodical descent on top of the cable.

He shut out Phoebe's plaintive crying, Quinn's snark, even Milo shouting encouragement. His attention narrowed to an absolute focus.

Snow pummeled his face and stuck in his eyelashes. His fingers were stiff and going numb. The cable thrummed below him with each movement, wet with snow, threatening to dislodge him.

Fear was a hook in his throat. It trembled through him, colder even than the air, a deep and unknowable terror. He moved because he had to. Because he had no choice.

Don't fall. Don't look down. Don't fall.

One hand in front of the other. His arms shook from the strain. His hands were aching. He could've gone five feet or twenty. He had no idea.

Inch by inch, he scooted, just a little further along the perilous journey across fifty feet of cable.

One hand after another while pushing with his leg. One slow painful slide after the next. His muscles taut and aching, the cable scraping across his torso.

He thought only of Milo. Of getting him safe. Getting him home.

The wind in the dark gave a low-pitched moan as it eddied around the trees and the lift towers. Snow was falling in opaque sheets.

His outstretched hand struck something. He flinched, startled.

"The top of my chair!" Quinn yelled over the wind. Her voice was far closer than he'd expected. "You reached us!"

Carefully, he unslung his legs, lowered his arms, and hung for a moment. The next chair swayed only a couple feet in front of him.

The old man slumped on the right side of the chair, unmoving. Quinn was on her knees on the left side, one gloved hand gripping the safety bar, her other hand outstretched toward him.

He lowered himself with shaking arms into the chair. It swung dangerously beneath him, but Quinn grabbed his legs. He wrapped his arms around the center pole to steady himself.

It would take energy to climb back up again, but he desperately needed a few minutes' rest or he would fall. He knew it.

There wasn't much room; he remained standing. He glanced backward over the space he'd traveled. In the glow of the Maglight, Milo was a small dark shape barely visible through the swirling snow.

He couldn't see or hear Phoebe anymore. A shiver of unease passed through him. He needed to hurry.

He shook out his arms, clenched and unclenched his aching hands, always keeping one arm encircling the pole. Every muscle in his body ached. The fear shuddered through every cell in his body.

He had to keep going. He had another stretch to go. It was hard to judge distances when he could barely see. Thirty feet? More?

"Th-the storm's getting b-bad," Quinn said through chattering teeth. The flashlight beam barely reached this far. She was a shadow. He couldn't make out her features or check for blue skin or frostbite.

"I know."

"W-we can't wait up here. We all have to get d-down now."

"What about your grandfather?"

A beat of silence. Then she said, "H-he's dead."

Dread squeezed Noah's heart. He didn't say, *are you sure?* He didn't want to belittle her or her grief.

He had nothing worth saying, no comfort to give her.

"W-we have to get down," she repeated.

"I'll go for help—"

"No time. I can f-feel it. It'll take too long."

His lungs constricted. She was right. "Milo can't do this climb. He can't. It's impossible."

"I-I watched what you did," Quinn said. "W-we get down, then we figure it out. I'm coming with you."

"No, you aren't."

"I wasn't asking your p-permission."

He didn't have the energy to fight her.

Two minutes later, Noah was precariously balanced on the cable again, every muscle in his body burning as he worked through the freezing darkness and the driving snow.

Quinn followed him. He craned his neck to glance back to check on her.

After a last hug for her dead grandfather, she'd managed to scurry up the pole, get her hands on the grip, and swing her legs up and over the cable.

She locked her knees and slid herself forward, moving hand over hand, her leg balanced behind her. She was surprisingly quick and agile.

"Be careful," he called.

She only grunted.

He kept going, hoping she was following, but unable to see her behind him.

Concern for Milo dug into his brain. What if he got scared, moved around, and fell out? Noah would never forgive himself.

He forced himself to focus on the cable, on not slipping or losing his grip and plummeting to the hard ground below. The seconds passed, then minutes.

After what felt like an eternity, he reached the edge of the tower.

The shallow, narrow ladder hugged the side of the tower. He tightened his grip on the cable, unslung his legs, and stretched for the ladder.

His boot hit the narrow rung and nearly slid off. Arms straining, he scooted closer until he could balance both boots on the rungs. He swung his body forward and seized the side rails.

He'd made it.

9

NOAH
DAY ONE

N oah allowed himself two relieved breaths. He wasn't safe
yet. Milo and Phoebe were still trapped.

They were all half-frozen and threatened by frostbite, hypothermia, and death.

His brain felt thick and foggy. He could feel the numbness setting in, the fuzzy thinking that signaled danger.

They had to move. He had to get them all down and out of this blizzard.

He wedged his boots through the rungs, made sure he had a steady grip on the slick metal, and turned squinting toward the cable. "Quinn!"

"I'm here!" Quinn shouted over the wind. The girl was a dark shape clinging to the cable several feet behind him.

Noah could hardly see with the snow driving into his face, the dim flashlight barely reaching through the thick, spiraling darkness.

"Reach for the ladder!" he called. "Be careful!"

Quinn moved slowly, painstakingly closer to the ladder. Noah watched, his pulse a roar in his ears, unable to help or do a thing. It was all up to her.

Her leg slipped off the cable. She fell back, nearly losing her grip.

Fear stabbed him. "Quinn!"

Quinn hung from the cable by one hand. Her right hand flailed uselessly, her feet dangling.

Noah's frozen breath caught in his throat. One hand wrapped around the ladder, he stretched out for her. "Give me your hand."

She got both hands on the cable and hung there, only four feet away.

He reached as far as his arm would allow him, fingers outstretched. His boots slick on the metal rung, barely holding on. "You can do it, come on."

"S-shut up so I can concentrate."

He shut up.

With a grunt, she swung hand over hand the last two feet until she was close enough for Noah to snag her coat. He got his arm around the waist and pulled her into the tower. She clung to him, shaking.

"You okay?"

"Just get us the hell d-down."

"You need help?"

"Just go!"

There was little room for them both. Noah hurried down, rung after rung, pressing himself tight against the tower as the wind and snow buffeted him. Quinn followed.

He jumped the last few feet, his boots sinking up to his shins in the snow.

He held out his hands, ready to catch her if she fell, but the girl didn't need him. She clambered down with ease.

Noah followed the beam of the flashlight, staggering uphill

through the snow, Quinn close behind him, holding onto the back of his coat.

When he was directly beneath the chairlift, he shouted for Milo to drop the flashlight, which he did. Noah picked it up and hurried to Brock's fallen form. The man was nearly covered by fresh snow. He wasn't moving.

Noah knelt in the snow and brushed the flakes from Brock's face. "Brock!"

He didn't answer.

Noah ripped off his gloves. He pressed his fingers to Brock's neck and searched for a pulse. Nothing.

His skin was ice. It didn't feel human anymore. His open, blank eyes were crusted with ice and snow.

Noah's gut twisted. The man was dead.

Behind him, Quinn mumbled a curse. "Screw this noise. We've got to get out of h-here."

Noah climbed to his feet and tugged his gloves back on. He could barely get them on over his stiff fingers. "There's no w-way Milo can do what we did. Or Phoebe. We have to get them down ourselves. Somehow."

Quinn turned toward him. He couldn't read her features in the dark. She was shivering, teeth chattering, but she wasn't panicky or frantic. "I have an idea."

"What?"

"We use t-that." Quinn pointed toward the tree line Noah could barely see in the snowstorm.

He pointed the flashlight. The beam highlighted a flicker of red through the snow. The red boundary fencing separating the trees and the Rocket Launcher run.

"The fence is soft and flexible," Quinn said. "It's s-some kind of fabric. We can use it as an improvised trampoline to catch them."

She was right. The thick netting just might work.

Side by side, they trudged toward the trees. Ten minutes later, Noah had used the pocket knife on his keychain to cut a ten-foot section of the flexible fencing, which was attached to a thin metal post on each end.

Quinn took one side and Noah the other. The flashlight between his teeth, Noah positioned the improvised trampoline beneath Milo's chairlift. He gazed up at the swinging chair so high above them.

"We'll c-catch you," he shouted into the wind. "I've got you, son. Don't worry."

Concern ate at him. What if Milo was too scared to jump? What would Noah do then? He could hardly bear to contemplate it.

"I'm not worried, Dad," Milo yelled.

Milo, his brave little son, didn't hesitate. He jumped.

10

NOAH
DAY ONE

Milo pushed himself off the chairlift and jumped, arms and legs flailing. For a heart-stopping instant, Noah watched him falling, falling, falling.

His little body hit the center of the fencing. The weight of him barely registered. The fencing wasn't as stretchy as a trampoline, but it worked well enough to absorb the shock of his fall.

Noah dropped his end of the fence pole and ran to his son. He knelt and wrapped him in his arms. His heart nearly burst. He didn't know what he'd done to earn such total trust, but he was eternally grateful for it.

"Are you okay?" he asked. "Are you all right?"

"I'm f-fine, Dad," Milo mumbled against his chest. But he was cold, so cold. Of course he wasn't okay. Noah had to get him out of this storm. He had to get them all out of here.

"Stay right here. We're going in one minute. Just as soon as we get Phoebe down." He turned Milo away from Brock's body. "Don't look over there. Here, help us with the flashlight. Just point it at whatever we're doing so we can see."

"I-I can do that, Dad."

45

Noah and Quinn grabbed the improvised trampoline again and positioned themselves beneath Phoebe's chair. Milo pointed the flashlight.

Snowflakes dove and churned in the cone of light. Outside the light, the entire world was a rush of darkness and snow.

"You need to jump!" Noah called up to Phoebe. His voice was hoarse, his throat and lungs raw from the burning cold.

Phoebe only clung to the chair harder. "I can't! I can't do it!"

Noah cajoled and pleaded and encouraged. The woman wouldn't move.

He didn't want to leave her behind. He was a police officer. It was his job to save everyone he could.

He'd already lost two people. He couldn't lose any more.

He felt every second ticking by, felt the tension of his choices tearing him apart, inch by inch. He couldn't abandon a civilian, but he wouldn't allow his son to suffer any longer, either.

"Lady, get the hell down, or we'll leave your ass behind!" Quinn shouted. "We're not dying for you. You have five seconds!"

That seemed to get through to her. Somehow, the threat from Quinn seemed more real. The only thing more terrifying to her than jumping was remaining in the chairlift alone.

She unclipped her snowboard. Quinn and Noah moved out of the way as it fell.

Phoebe pushed herself off the chair and hung for a moment like Brock had, moaning softly. Finally, she dropped.

Her weight struck the fence. The pole threatened to slip from his fingers, but Noah tightened his grip. She dropped to the snow, but at least the fence had cradled her fall.

She pulled herself to her feet, sniffling and rubbing her side.

"About damn time," Quinn muttered.

"Anything broken?" Noah asked.

She wiped the snow from her face. "My back and shoulder hurt, but I don't think so."

"Good." Noah turned his full concentration to Milo. He handed Quinn the flashlight and hoisted Milo to his chest; the boy's legs wrapped around his waist, Noah holding him in place with one arm. Hopefully, he wouldn't need his hands too much. "Hold on, buddy. Almost there."

Phoebe turned toward Brock's body. "I need to see him."

Quinn seized her arm. "Phoebe. You can't."

"We'll come back for him," Noah said. "But we have to go now."

Phoebe didn't fight them. She had stopped crying. Her chapped face had a dull, stunned look. She said nothing, simply followed closely behind Noah, Quinn right beside her.

The slope here was steep, pocked with trees, and ungroomed. Noah didn't have the skills to ski back down, and Milo certainly didn't. He doubted the others did, either. With the cold numbing their extremities, they didn't have the dexterity.

"You two w-walk in my footsteps," Noah instructed. "It'll be easier."

His nostrils stung with each inhalation. His fingers were numb, so were his cheeks, his ears. His thoughts came slow and jumbled.

Hypothermia would be setting in soon if it hadn't already.

Get down the hill. They just had to get down there. He couldn't think beyond this task. *Just get down.*

The long slog down the hill was both tedious and dangerous. They could see little in the driving snow. There were no lights to lead them, only the red smudge below them that occasionally appeared and disappeared between the trees—the burning lodge.

They needed to watch their every step to avoid twisting an ankle or pitching forward and tumbling down the slick hill. Their ski boots made walking difficult and cumbersome. Milo was awkward and heavy. Noah tripped and nearly fell a few times.

Together, they slowly and painstakingly made it to the bottom of the hill.

They slogged past the chairlift terminal, silent and empty, the domed roof covered in snow. They couldn't see any of the other runs. They reached the Sweet Express lift tower with the green canopy, then the patio, and finally, the lodge.

The once-impressive lodge was flickering embers. Flames still danced here and there, hissing and sizzling beneath the onslaught of snow. Several walls had collapsed, the cafeteria side of the building caving in on itself.

In the dark, they couldn't see the wreckage of the chopper.

The wind howled mournfully. Snow blew swirling tornadoes around their legs, stinging their faces. The frigid cold sucked the life from them, degree by brutal degree.

"K-keep going," Noah said.

With the fire to orient themselves, they made their way around the east side of the lodge to the parking lot.

Quinn stopped so suddenly that Noah nearly barreled into her.

"What? What is it?"

Quinn swept the light across the parking lot. The lot was overflowing with parked cars smothered in a thick blanket of snow.

Hundreds of cars, but no people.

No guests in parkas lugging skis, no staff members or lifties or Ski Patrol in their red vests. No EMTs, no police officers, no firefighters.

Not a single soul.

11

NOAH

DAY ONE

"Where did e-everyone go?" Milo asked.

"They left all their cars," Phoebe murmured. "Why did they leave their cars behind?"

Quinn shone the flashlight beam in slow looping circles, like maybe they'd missed something the first time and help would materialize before their very eyes.

It didn't.

Apprehension knotted in Noah's gut. The whole scene was eerie and disconcerting.

Hundreds of vehicles sat in the same spots they'd parked in that morning. Back when it was Christmas Eve and everyone's thoughts were focused on holiday fun, on the thrills of skiing and snowboarding, on presents and hot chocolate and family.

Before everything had to gone to hell.

How had it even happened? What was really going on?

He swallowed. "I don't know."

Quinn brushed the flakes collecting on her bangs and eyelashes from her face. "Cars have electronic stuff running everything now. Haven't you been listening to anything I've said? Nothing with electronics or computers will work."

Were Quinn's science fiction theories actually correct? Faced with everything that had happened today, coupled with the stranded vehicles—he was beginning to believe that it might be true.

Did this eerie power outage thing affect only southwest Michigan? The whole state? Or possibly the entire eastern seaboard? Or was it even worse?

What did it mean for the future of Fall Creek? The state? The entire country?

Noah's mind ran in panicked circles. He forced himself to shake the frantic thoughts from his head. Thinking like that wasn't going to help anything.

He needed to stay focused and positive, remain clear-headed. Just because they were out of one mess didn't mean they were out of danger.

"I'm going to check my car. It's a 2008 Kia Rio."

"It won't work," Quinn said.

"It's worth it to check. Phoebe, what about your car? Can we check it?"

"W-we came together." Phoebe's shoulders hunched like she'd been punched in the stomach. "Brock has the keys."

"It's okay," Noah said quickly, guilt pricking him.

He struggled to remember where he'd parked the Rio. It didn't help that it was white, and every vehicle was covered in a thickening layer of white powder.

A few freezing minutes later, he found it. Phoebe and Quinn trailed after him. He set Milo down, fished his key fob out of his pocket and used the key to open the door.

The engine wouldn't start. The radio didn't switch on. The Rio was as dead as Quinn said it would be.

His stomach sinking, he grabbed the fanny pack on the

passenger seat that contained Milo's syringe and stress dose vial of glucocorticoid and clambered out of the car back into the freezing wind. "I'm sorry, it doesn't work."

Phoebe spun in a slow circle, rubbing her temples frantically with both hands. "H-how are we going to get out of here?"

"Otsego is about three miles east," Noah said. "That's the closest town."

"I feel like I'm dying," Phoebe said. "I can't walk three miles! We're going to freeze to death!"

"We need to stay calm," Noah said, though he felt anything but calm. He could barely move, he was so numb and frozen. His thoughts were coming slow and sluggish. He picked up Milo and handed him the fanny pack. Milo buried himself against Noah's chest.

Abruptly, Quinn turned and strode away, striding between two parked cars deeper into the parking lot, toward the road.

"Where are you going?" Noah called after her.

She didn't answer, didn't even show she'd heard him. Maybe she just needed a minute to herself to pull herself together.

"What are we going to do?" Phoebe wailed.

Noah looked around, scanning the parking lot in growing desperation. "We can hunker down in the Rio to get out of the wind for a few minutes while we figure out a game plan. It'll still be cold, but without the wind chill. Walking miles in a blizzard is not a good idea. Lots of ways to get lost or hurt. Maybe we need to break into a few vehicles. Some people will have some extra sweatshirts, a jacket, or even a few blankets stashed somewhere."

Phoebe turned to face him. "You want to break into cars? Aren't you a sheriff?"

"A police officer," he corrected. He felt guilty even saying the words, but Milo was now his greatest priority. "Our survival is more important than protecting private property. I'm sure these people will understand. And insurance will cover what we damage."

"What about Brock? And Quinn's grandpa? We can't just leave them up there like that."

"I'll come back first thing in the morning. I'll make sure the county picks them up and we contact you and the next of kin. I'll take care of it."

She nodded dully.

"Where do you live?"

"I'm home for Christmas break, visiting my parents in Dowagiac. It's like, almost an hour from here."

"I know. It's close to Fall Creek. That's where we're from." He patted her shoulder. "We'll get you home. I promise."

An engine growled to life.

After so many hours of silence, the sound was jarring. Noah and Phoebe whipped around. Noah tightened his grasp on Milo, his adrenaline spiking.

A pair of headlights lit up the night several rows in front of them. A truck. It was so covered in snow that Noah couldn't discern the make or model, just the general shape of it.

The driver's side door swung open. Quinn's bright blue head poked out. "You guys coming or what? You've got two seconds before I leave your sorry asses behind."

12

QUINN
DAY ONE

The truck ran perfectly, the tank still three-quarters full. Just like Quinn knew it would. Gramps had let her drive here with her permit; luckily, she'd still had the keys in her coat pocket.

The others piled in, Phoebe and Milo in the back, Noah easing hesitantly into the passenger side. He didn't look pleased to be relegated to passenger, but it wasn't his truck.

"This baby is a bright orange 1978 Ford F150 Super Cab we call Orange Julius," Quinn explained. "Old as hell, but it still runs. Four-wheel drive. Snow tires. Gramps keeps it in pristine condition. He's always tinkering with it in his garage. He—"

Grief struck her like a punch to the chest. Stricken, she stilled. For a second, she couldn't breathe, couldn't suck oxygen into her raw lungs, her burning throat.

Gramps was still up on that desolate hill. He was dead.

It hadn't seemed real until this moment. His truck still smelled like grease and his favorite pho soup—it smelled like *Gramps*. She'd never hear his soft chuckle again, never eat *bun cha* dipped in fish sauce with him, never sit in the garage while he puttered with the engine and told her stories of his boyhood in Vietnam, his experiences as a Vietnamese-American soldier.

She couldn't think about any of that now, couldn't let the sorrow in. She swallowed, forced herself to focus. "He did, I mean."

"I-I'm sorry, Quinn," Milo said.

Her throat thickened. "Not your fault, Small Fry."

She cranked the heat all the way up and switched on the defroster. She could barely see through the frost creeping across the windshield. At this point, she was willing to drive blind as long as they got the hell out of here.

She put the Orange Julius into reverse and gunned the engine. The truck didn't move.

She cursed, banged the steering wheel, and tried again.

The tires spun uselessly in the snow.

"We're screwed," Phoebe said.

"We're stuck, not screwed," Quinn corrected. "Gramps keeps —kept—a shovel in the back. We have to shovel our way out."

"You guys stay inside where it's warm," Noah said. "I'll do it."

Quinn glanced behind her. The little boy was huddled in the backseat against Phoebe, who sagged against the window. The cab wasn't exactly warm, but it was getting there.

Bracing herself against the wind, Quinn clambered out of the truck after him. She slammed the driver's side door and trudged to the rear of the Orange Julius.

"I'm not scared of work," she huffed when Noah shot her a questioning look.

He managed a tight smile. "Good."

There were two shovels in the truck bed. Gramps had added the second shovel when Quinn started driving with him.

She pointed at the supplies tucked into one corner. "Gramps and Gran always keep a sleeping bag, flares, a flashlight, toolbox, shovel, trail mix and water, and a battery-operated lantern in their cars. Oh, and kitty litter. Luckily, Gran always has extra with her five freaking cats."

"Thank goodness," Noah said in relief. "We can wrap Milo in the sleeping bag."

Quinn took one side, Noah the other. They quickly shoveled snow from behind the tires. Their breaths puffed out in white clouds. Quinn's heart thudded in her chest, her ears.

Her stiff, freezing fingers fumbled several times. She dropped the shovel and had to pick it up to keep going. She refused to quit. The exertion sharpened her senses, kept her emotions safely at bay.

Finally, they cleared enough space. Quinn sprinkled the kitty litter for the wheels to grab traction. Quinn tossed the shovel in the truck bed as Noah reached in for the sleeping bag.

Instead of climbing back inside the Orange Julius, she hesitated.

The snow and the dark made everything look the same. She hugged herself, shivering, strands of blue hair whipping around her face. Her metal piercings felt like they'd frozen into her skin.

Noah put the sleeping bag inside the truck and came up beside her. "You okay?"

She felt shaken, rattled, and on edge. "Stellar," she snapped. "Never better."

"Okay, okay. Stupid question. Sorry." He cleared his throat. "Are you okay to drive the truck? I know today has been . . . rough for all of us."

"That's one way to put it." She chewed on her lower lip. "It's not my truck. It's Gramps's truck. He loves—loved that decrepit old thing. He never let anyone drive it, not even Gran."

Except for her. He'd taught Quinn how to drive in that ancient rattling beast. She paused, sucked in a deep, searing breath. She almost choked as her lungs contracted. "It feels . . . wrong."

She didn't know why she was saying this out loud. She hadn't spoken five sentences to Noah Sheridan before today, even though she'd known who he was for years. He was basically a stranger. But after the last several hours, he didn't feel like one.

"I'm sorry we couldn't save him. I really am."

"I know."

"I'm happy to drive," he said. "It's an hour to Fall Creek. We'll drop Phoebe off on the way."

He didn't say he'd be a better, more experienced driver, especially in these conditions.

He was giving her an out. His next question would be to ask how old she was, if she had her license. She knew it, he knew it. Technically, she didn't have her license, just her permit, though she'd driven with Gramps a thousand times.

She nodded and kicked defiantly at a snowdrift. She stared through the snow at the rows of vehicles like giant white boulders.

Something moved inside one of the cars.

13

NOAH
DAY ONE

"What is it?" Noah asked.

Quinn pointed silently at a car parked a few spots from the Orange Julius. Noah stooped and wiped snow off the driver's side window of a dark-colored sedan.

A man slumped in the driver's seat, shivering and gripping the steering wheel with both hands, like he was expecting to drive off into the sunset any minute now.

Noah's hand instinctively strayed to his service weapon at his side beneath his coat. He knocked on the driver's side window.

The man flinched. He turned toward Noah, mouth hanging open, eyes wide and bloodshot through the frosted glass.

Noah and Quinn stepped back as the guy opened his door.

He stared up at them, incredulous. "Where the heck did you come from?"

"From the chairlift, you idiot!" Quinn jabbed her finger at the Bittersweet Ski Resort staff badge emblazoned on his ski parka. "You left us up there!"

The guy blanched. "What?"

"We got stuck on the chairlift at the Rocket Launcher," Noah explained, trying to keep his own voice calm, though the frustration, stress, and trauma of the day were taking their toll.

"No one came for us!" Quinn's voice rose in fury. "My grandpa is *dead*!"

Beneath his straggly beard, the guy's pale, acne-scarred skin was bluish. He looked to be in his late twenties, a granola-eating new-age hippie type. The whole car reeked of weed.

He raised his hands, palms out in a placating gesture, a joint tucked between the fingers of his right hand. A thin swirl of smoke spiraled toward the ceiling. "That makes no sense. That doesn't happen."

Noah gritted his teeth. "It *did* happen."

"Patrol spent hours clearing the lifts. We had to go old school and use haul ropes and harnesses, do it all by hand. We-we've got safety protocols . . ."

"Not today, you didn't," Quinn snapped.

His eyes widened. "You're serious?"

"Where the hell do you think we just came from?" Quinn rolled her eyes. "You think we fell from the sky?"

The guy stared at her, bleary-eyed. He'd probably smoked every joint he had. Dismay—and chagrin—finally filtered into his features. "I'm so sorry." He shook his head. "I . . . I guess I'm really out of it. Today, man. I've never experienced anything like it."

"You?" Quinn sputtered. "You think you've never experienced—*WE* were the ones trapped thirty feet off the ground in a freezing snowstorm! My grandpa had a heart attack. One guy even jumped, he was so desperate! He's dead, too!"

"More people died?"

"Brock snapped his tibia," Noah said. "He went into shock and we . . . there was no way to save him."

The man licked his chapped lips. He took a drag off his joint with quivering fingers. "Oh man, oh man. I didn't know. We didn't know. I swear. We had nineteen people die on us down here. Nineteen! It was so intense, just b-beyond anything . . . with the fire, the helicopter crashing . . . everyone was panicking. We had people burned, their limbs busted in the crash. It was chaos, man.

"And then when people tried to drive away and their cars wouldn't work . . . I sent Tim and Max to clear the lifts. I assumed they did. One of 'em must have cut a corner, did a visual check instead of hiking all the way up the hill. Sam said the Rocket Launcher lift was malfunctioning. We only had one working snowmobile. A junker we should've trashed years ago. Nothing else was working. It was like God Himself just flipped a switch, and bam. No lifts. No electricity. No snowcats or cars."

His gaze briefly met Quinn's furious eyes and flickered away. "I didn't know."

"How could you not—" Quinn started, still enraged, but Noah interrupted her.

"What's your name?" he asked.

The guy blinked rapidly. "C-Chris. Chris Doenges."

"How did everyone get home, Chris?" Noah asked.

Quinn glared at him, but he ignored her. Screaming at this poor shmuck would do nothing to change this night's events. Nothing could undo the terrible hours they'd just endured.

"A few hours ago, they brought in buses, old diesel school buses. Justin drove the Ski-Doo into Otsego to get help. Everyone's freaking out, but they came. A few deputies, firefighters, EMTs. They're going around rescuing stranded people all over the county. They were talking about working out a rotation with the snowplows that still function to keep the main roads clear."

"Why are you still here all alone?" Noah asked.

"The last bus was too crowded. They couldn't fit another human body in there and I . . . guess I kinda panicked, you know? Don't like enclosed spaces." He waved his arm feebly. "That's why I work here, right? No cubicle, man. Just open sky and fresh powder."

He stared off into the darkness, working his jaw like he was going to say something else, but he didn't.

"We're headed south to Fall Creek," Noah said.

Chris's gaze shifted past them. "You've got a car that works?"

"You didn't hear the truck's engine? You didn't notice the headlights?" Quinn asked, incredulous.

"Tell us where you live," Noah said evenly. It didn't matter how he personally felt about this useless pothead. As an officer of the law, he couldn't just leave him behind to freeze to death. "We'll take you, too."

Chris nodded gratefully. "Thanks, man. I was totally starting to think I was gonna die out here."

"So did we," Quinn said.

Ashamed, Chris dropped his gaze to his lap and said nothing.

"Let's go," Noah said, "while we still can."

14

NOAH

DAY ONE

Noah leaned forward, his hands gripping the old Ford's steering wheel, every muscle tensed, his heart thudding against his ribs. The truck drove at a crawl.

The snow was thick, the roads slick and slippery, a steep ditch on the left Noah could barely see but knew was there, just waiting for him to make an error and slide over the edge. It was difficult to drive in ski boots, so he'd removed them and drove in his socks.

They headed home on M-40 S and I-94 W in absolute darkness. No stars. No moon. No streetlights, no glow from towns or cities, no lights from passing cars. No passing cars, period.

They'd already dropped Phoebe and Chris off at their respective homes—Chris in Plainwell just southeast of Otsego, and Phoebe in Dowagiac, about fourteen miles east of Fall Creek. The neighborhoods were dark. Everything was dark.

Their headlights were the only lights anywhere. Two yellow cones pierced a veil of black slashed with diving, spinning swirls of white. He couldn't see the farmland interspersed with woods and occasional houses and businesses—warehouses and used car lots.

He couldn't see anything but a few yards directly in front of him.

Here and there, the truck's headlights haloed great humps of snow-covered metal—cars and SUVs and trucks, all stalled and abandoned on the side of the road. Several times, he had to swerve around pile-up accidents of two, three, or more cars.

Quinn huddled in the passenger seat beside him, just a dark shape in the dimness of the cab. Her knees were drawn up to her chest. She held her hands in front of the heater to warm her fingers as she stared dully out the window.

Milo slept soundly in the back seat, curled up like a puppy inside the sleeping bag. Noah kept glancing nervously at the rearview mirror to check on him, occasionally flicking on one of the overhead lights. His skin tone seemed okay. His chest rose and fell steadily.

His vitals were strong. Still, Noah worried.

The boy had endured an incredible amount of stress tonight. It was too much for an adult, let alone a child. What toll had that taken on his adrenal glands? Was his medication enough to protect him, or was his body already turning on itself like a silent, invisible poison?

Before they'd started the drive home, Noah had given Milo his evening pill. For a cold or flu, he usually bumped Milo's dosage for three days. Beyond that, it was a visit to Dr. Prentice.

Anything serious, and they doubled or even tripled his dose for a longer period, constantly monitoring his hormone levels.

Milo was a strong kid, brave and resilient. He'd survived losing his mother in the most horrific manner imaginable, hadn't he?

He'd be okay. He had to be.

Noah shifted his grip on the steering wheel and winced at the bright throb of pain. The heat in the cab had finally thawed his extremities. His fingers, ears, and nose hurt almost like they were burning.

It meant he had frostnip probably, but no frostbite. Pain was a good thing.

"I know who you are," Quinn said after a long silence. "I remember Hannah Sheridan."

He glanced at her, startled. "What?"

"It's my birthday today."

Noah's chest clenched. "I . . . see."

"I remember that day. The day she disappeared." Quinn kept her gaze out the window. "It wasn't like there was a big party planned or anything. Not on Christmas Eve. Octavia—my mother —she usually forgets. But that year, she managed to get me a cake. My Gran wrapped a few presents, painting supplies mostly. A cheap drawing pad from Walmart. It was an okay day, I guess. My eleventh birthday. It wasn't anything special.

"But I remember the red and blue lights flashing through my window the next day. She'd disappeared on my birthday . . . I'd seen her a bunch of times. Like, just living her life. She liked to jog early in the morning with the baby in the stroller, always with her headphones on. Sometimes she would sing out loud to whatever she was listening to. Aerosmith or Pink Floyd or whoever. She would stop and wave to me, every time."

"I remember." He sucked in a breath so sharply it seared his still-aching lungs. "Hannah was always kind."

He normally didn't like to talk about this stuff, but he didn't have the heart to shut her down. This strange, sarcastic teenage girl was rattled, just like he was.

She'd lost a family member on top of everything. She was just a kid, really.

"I don't know. It just . . . hit me hard, I guess. Not like what you and Milo went through. Nothing like that. But I just . . . I googled the case every single day. I paid attention. When they arrested you, for a while I really thought you'd done it."

"So did most of Fall Creek," he said. "The whole county did, really."

He hated thinking about those days. The suspicious stares and mistrust from friends and neighbors. The sense of isolation. The loneliness.

They'd never found any evidence implicating him. The most damning fact was simply that he was her husband, and statistically, most women were killed by the men closest to them.

The masses had been trained by glossy cop shows on TV to believe a trail of DNA evidence littered every crime scene. The reality was much different.

After a while, the case simply ran cold. That night's snowfall had erased any tracks that might have been left. They had nothing to go on. No leads, no witnesses, no hairs or fingerprints. No other suspects. Just a car abandoned on the side of a highway.

Rosamond Sinclair, Fall Creek Township superintendent, had been vocal in her support of Noah's innocence. Her faith in him had never wavered. Chief Briggs had eventually believed in him, too. Over time, the town's suspicions had faded.

Noah was never exonerated. He was never convicted, either. People harbored their opinions based on hearsay, rumor, grudges and long-held loyalties.

A few people suspected—and maybe still did—that Noah had hurt Hannah rather than allow her to leave an unhappy marriage. Some people believed she'd left him and Milo and hitchhiked to California, choosing to unburden herself of her family completely.

Others thought that there was someone else out there. A predator who'd stumbled across an opportunity and gotten away with murder. The FBI estimated that between twenty-five and fifty active serial killers stalked the United States.

Noah didn't believe she was still alive. He wished she'd run away to California. But she never would have abandoned Milo. He knew that like he knew his own name.

He'd never intentionally hurt Hannah, but he still lived with tremendous guilt. He'd done nothing more damning than failing to love his wife enough.

In the end, that was all it took to lose the things that mattered most.

Quinn shrugged, shifted uncomfortably. "I'm just . . . I remember Hannah, is all. I remember what day it is for you, too. And I'm sorry."

He closed his eyes, blinked back a sudden wetness. Grief had a way of walloping you when you least expected it, even years later. "Thank you," he said, and meant it.

The snow fell harder, grew deeper. Soon, it would be too deep to drive if the plows didn't get out to clear the roads. If there weren't enough of them that still worked.

The dashboard analog clock read 9:17 p.m. With every passing minute, dread and anxiety snarled tighter and tighter in his gut. The further they drove into this eerie, silent world, the stronger his dread grew.

More darkness where there should be towns and cities. Humps of snow-smothered vehicles rearing suddenly out of the blackness like crouching gargoyles. And always, the endless swirling snow.

They could have been driving off the edge of the planet and wouldn't even know it.

"What the hell is happening?" Noah breathed.

"I told you," Quinn said, but there was no triumph or glee in her voice, only a broken resignation. "It's the end of the world as we know it."

15

NOAH
DAY TWO

"**D**ad? The electricity is still broken."

Noah groaned and dug deeper beneath the pile of blankets. The cold was brutal.

He rolled toward his son and opened his eyes. It felt like his eyelashes had been glued shut. His head ached. His whole body ached, his muscles clenched tight like a fist.

Milo was already sitting up and rubbing his face with his little fists. "Merry Christmas, Dad."

The events of yesterday came rushing back with a vengeance. The hours enduring the freezing cold, the fear and the panic, the struggle to keep Milo or himself from succumbing to hypothermia. The dead bodies.

Noah yanked himself to a seated position, pushing aside the couch cushions they'd stacked around themselves the night before.

Gray morning light streamed into the room. Last night, he hadn't had the energy to block the single window with a blanket, and the blinds did nothing to keep out the cold.

Noah had picked the warmest room—or more correctly, the

least freezing. His office was the most interior room of the house, with the fewest windows.

They had a fireplace in the living room, but they'd used the last of the firewood over the past week, enjoying pre-Christmas fires complete with roasted marshmallows, s'mores, and late-night bedtime stories.

He'd tried to make it fun for Milo. Using the small flashlight to see, they'd quickly made a fort of pillows and cushions they'd stolen from the couch, spread a blanket above them, and shoved in as many sleeping bags and comforters as he could find.

The "fort" trapped their own body heat as they snuggled together and passed out. They were both still wearing their winter coats from last night, though Noah had made them remove their boots and damp socks and put on fresh ones.

"Merry Christmas, bud," he said, though it felt anything but merry. "How do you feel?"

As soon as they'd gotten home last night, Noah had checked him again for symptoms: fatigue, muscle weakness, dizziness, nausea.

Milo had seemed okay. He seemed okay this morning, too.

Milo tried to wriggle out of his grasp. "Fine, Dad. I'm fine."

"Let me get a good look at you." Noah examined Milo's cheeks, nose, and ears. They were red and chapped.

"Can you feel this?" He poked Milo's nose.

Milo made a face. "Ouch. That hurts. My fingers hurt too."

"That's a good sign, son."

The anxiety in his gut lessened as he took the boy's hands and turned them over, stripping off his gloves. The tips were pale and white, but the rest of his hands and fingers looked okay. "Some frostnip, but no frostbite. We got lucky."

"'Cause you saved us."

Noah's chest warmed. "We saved each other."

Milo played with the medical alert bracelet on his wrist. "I'm hungry."

Hunger was a great sign. The first symptoms Dr. Prentice had told Noah to watch for were lack of appetite, nausea, and fatigue.

"What about pancakes?" Milo asked.

The last time they'd missed Christmas pancakes was the morning Hannah didn't come home. Noah closed his eyes, opened them. "Great idea. I think I've got a camping stove in the basement. Let's whip some up."

They emerged from the cocoon of the fort. Noah shivered. One day without heat, and the house already felt like an icebox.

"Pancakes with chocolate chips, Dad? And peanut butter?"

"Yes to chocolate chips, buddy! Of course."

Noah got a larger flashlight from the coat closet and switched it on. Surprisingly, it worked. Whatever this electromagnetic pulse thing was, it appeared to spare small objects without too many electronics or circuits.

He didn't overthink it. He headed down to their "Michigan basement," an earthy, damp basement with ceilings so short that adults couldn't stand up straight. The walls were exposed cinder block; the floor, packed dirt. Moisture, water leaks, and structural integrity were constant concerns.

He scrounged through boxes and totes stacked on a couple of metal shelves for the camping supplies. The camping stove was in a large plastic container labeled in Hannah's beautiful cursive script. Next to it, another tote labeled "propane canisters." She'd always been organized like that.

He and Milo hadn't gone camping since Hannah had disappeared. She was the one who lived for the outdoors, who'd wanted to teach Milo cross-country skiing as soon as he was old enough to stand upright.

He pulled out two propane canisters. They had fourteen left. Back upstairs, he set up the stove on the counter and opened the kitchen window for the needed ventilation, even though the air wafting inside was shockingly cold.

His gloves on, he whipped up a pancake breakfast worthy of a king, with orange juice, sausage links, and hash browns, the chocolate chip pancakes spread with Jif peanut butter and topped with swirls of whipped cream—Milo's favorite weird concoction, which he'd loved since he was two.

Normally, the veggies, cheese and milk, and leftovers in the fridge would go bad without power, but considering it was colder than a refrigerator inside the house, Noah figured everything would be fine. The food, anyway.

He and Milo were a different matter.

They were both cold and shivering, hunched over their plates and barely able to hold their silverware. Noah needed to block the windows and get his hands on as much firewood as he could.

The hardware store stocked a supply, and the owner of the local gas station, Mike Duncan, also sold firewood from his fifty-acre wooded lot across the bridge.

Seasoned firewood would be a hot commodity for the next few months—literally. And if he couldn't scrounge up enough to keep himself and Milo from freezing, then they were in serious trouble.

With Milo's condition, he couldn't risk stressing his son's vulnerable system.

Worry twisted his stomach. He'd lost his appetite. He sat and watched his son eat, his mind cycling through the possibilities, none of them good.

After he'd stuffed himself—peanut butter and whipped cream still smeared across his mouth—Milo's gaze shifted to the darkened tree in the living room, and the half-dozen Christmas presents piled beneath it.

His eyes lit up. "Can I open my presents yet?"

Noah forced himself to swallow a bite of pancake and washed

it down with orange juice. "Let me check and see if Mrs. Gomez can watch you for an hour or two first."

Milo pinched his lower lip between his teeth—just like Hannah used to—and frowned. "But it's Christmas."

Regret pierced Noah's chest. He hated being a single father. Hated all the pressure and obligations always pulling at him from every side.

He wanted nothing more than to spend the entire day with Milo like they'd planned.

He rose and put their plates in the sink. He turned on the faucet and watched the water pour from the tap. Without power, the water would stop, sooner rather than later. He hadn't even thought about it when he'd measured water for the pancake mix.

So many things to get used to, to mentally adjust.

He moved the faucet to the clean side of the double sink, set the stopper, and filled the basin. By the time it was full, only a few droplets dripped from the tap. He needed to fill the bathroom sinks and as much of the bathtub as he could before the pipes emptied.

Trepidation churning in his gut, he turned and squatted in front of Milo's chair. "You know how I'm a police officer, and it's my job to keep people safe?"

Milo nodded soberly.

"You remember being trapped on the ski lift, how most electronic things stopped working? I believe it happened here, too, and maybe other places as well."

"People need help."

"Yes. It's very important that I check in with Chief Briggs and the town council to make sure everyone in Fall Creek is okay. I know it's Christmas, but we've got to make sure everyone is safe."

Milo's face clouded over, but he didn't protest. "I know, Dad."

The swiftness with which he put his own wants and desires aside for the needs of others made Noah's heart ache. The boy already got only the scraps left over after Noah's long days. He was already a motherless child.

And he'd watched two people die yesterday. Noah needed to talk to him about that later, make sure he was okay.

"Can we check on Quinn, too?" Milo asked.

"Of course." He patted Milo's head. "And we'll do presents tonight, I promise."

He pulled his phone out of his pocket and checked it. Still dead. He'd tried his radio last night. It was fried, too.

A heavy sense of foreboding settled over him. He hoped it wasn't as bad as he feared. What if Quinn was right, and the power grid was down for months—or even longer? What were they going to do?

16

NOAH
DAY TWO

"Get your boots on," Noah said to Milo. "And fresh gloves and your blue hat."

While Milo complied, Noah went to his bedroom and paused for a moment in front of Hannah's dresser. His hands hovered over the top drawer handle.

He hadn't opened the drawer in years. He'd finally emptied out their shared closet two years ago, but he hadn't touched the dresser. The top still held her mirror and compact and jewelry tree.

And inside her sock drawer, tucked into an unused pair of fuzzy Christmas socks, the two hundred dollars in cash she'd insisted they set aside for emergencies.

They'd argued over that two hundred dollars. When money was tight, they'd had to choose between using the emergency cash to pay the electric bill or eating ramen for a week to make it to payday. She'd made them eat ramen.

He'd been mildly surprised she hadn't taken it with her the night she'd stormed out, vowing they were over for good this time. But of course, she hadn't taken Milo either.

Which meant she was coming back. She never would've left Milo. And certainly not on Christmas Day.

She just needed a few hours to let off some steam, to vent and drink it off with a girlfriend. That was all.

Or so he'd thought. That was why he hadn't notified anyone until the morning after. Didn't call her best friend, Carly. Didn't even go out to look for her himself.

Maybe if he had, Hannah's angelic voice would be filling their home right now as she laughed and sang Christmas carols and classic rock songs with Milo. Maybe the house wouldn't seem so cold, with or without electricity.

He could have won her back. He liked to think that he would have if he'd only had another chance.

Noah shook his head. He'd lost himself in the spiraling vortex of self-recrimination and what-ifs a thousand times. It did nothing but drag the misery of the past into the present.

He'd fought hard to make a life for himself and Milo, to create joy where it wasn't deserved—not by him, anyway. He wasn't going to let the specter of his own regret take that away from him, from Milo.

Noah opened the drawer, found the socks, and retrieved the cash. If this event was widespread, stores wouldn't be able to accept credit cards. Banks wouldn't allow transactions since everything was computerized these days. Cash would be king.

The money would get him some groceries to last them another week or so. And firewood. After he checked in with Chief Briggs, he'd run to Friendly's Grocery and stock up on as many supplies as he could.

If he could get there, anyway. His stalled Kia was still in the Bittersweet parking lot sixty miles away.

And then what? What happened when the cash and the food ran out? He didn't have an answer.

He paused in front of Hannah's dresser a moment more and

closed his eyes. His hand strayed to his wedding ring beneath his leather glove. The wedding ring he couldn't bear to remove.

"I don't know how to do this," he said aloud. "I don't know if I have what it takes to protect him."

Only silence answered him back.

What did he expect? Sometimes he felt like she was watching over them, a benevolent presence keeping Milo safe. Now, he felt nothing.

He was utterly alone against a faceless challenge bigger than he was, so big he couldn't even imagine the far-reaching consequences.

The sense of foreboding didn't leave him as he quickly put on his uniform, checked his service weapon—a Glock 19—and holstered it across from his department-issued Taser.

The hour or two he'd promised Milo might stretch much longer. If he needed to do anything in an official capacity, he should be ready.

Within a few minutes, he and Milo were out of the house and trudging through the snow, Milo so bundled up that Noah could hardly see his face. The temperature hovered around ten degrees. The storm had ended last night, but snowflakes still drifted softly from the gray sky.

Their neighborhood was older, the houses mostly brick ranches, split levels, two-story cape cods with dormer windows, and some colonials. Like many of the homes in Fall Creek, each house was set on its own one- or two-acre lot with a septic system and well.

Noah's house included. He had water in his well, he realized. He just didn't have any idea how to access it. Another item to add to his growing list.

All the to-dos piling up in his mind made his head hurt.

Noah knocked on Mrs. Gomez's burgundy front door, Milo

standing beside him. He waited a beat, then knocked again, louder. Mrs. Gomez was a bit hard of hearing.

"Mrs. Gomez!"

No answer. A bright red cardinal hopped on a bare maple branch and chirped at them.

He banged louder. It didn't make sense for her to not come to the door. Her hunter-green Dodge Caravan was still in the driveway beneath a blanket of snow.

No footprints marred the pristine yard and driveway other than their own.

"Why isn't she answering?" Milo asked. "Maybe she's not home."

"I don't know why she wouldn't be."

Milo rubbed his mittened hands together. "We should check on her. Maybe she fell down the stairs again."

"I think you're right."

He pulled on Noah's hand. "What about her oxygen tank, Dad? She keeps it plugged in. What if something happened to it yesterday?"

Noah's stomach tightened. The memory of Mr. Dũng's death after his pacemaker failed was fresh in his mind. Mrs. Gomez was seventy-seven and suffered from severe COPD. This last year, she'd carted her tank around with her everywhere.

Despite her medical limitations, she loved Milo and spent hours putting intricate puzzles together or playing Legos with him, reading to each other, and teaching him poker and other inappropriate card games.

Noah pulled out his keyring. He'd had a key to her house since she'd first started watching Milo, shortly after Hannah disappeared. "You're right, Milo. We should check."

The house was as dark and cold as their own. He could barely make out the floral wallpaper, the oil lamps and doilies decorating her coffee table, end tables, and fireplace mantel.

The living room smelled like potpourri and something medicinal.

"Sit on the couch and wait for me," Noah said to Milo as he flicked on his flashlight. Milo obeyed.

The silence pressed in on Noah as he made his way down the hallway to Mrs. Gomez's bedroom. He shone his flashlight over the slight lump beneath the ruffled bedspread.

The oxygen tank sat beside the bed. Clear tubes snaked beneath the covers.

"Mrs. Gomez? Are you okay?"

The shape didn't move.

Gently, he moved back the covers. Mrs. Gomez lay curled beneath the blankets in a lacy white nightgown, her gray fluff of hair spread across the pillow. Small tubes from the portable oxygen machine beside the bed crept around her slack, waxen face and fed into her nostrils.

She was stiff and far too cold. His stomach sinking, he checked her pulse to confirm his suspicions. Mrs. Gomez was dead.

He always told Milo that things would be better in the morning. However terrible a day had been, a good night's sleep solved a world of problems.

This time, he feared he was wrong.

Things weren't better this morning. They were far worse.

17

NOAH
DAY TWO

"Dad!" Milo called from the living room. "Someone's outside!"

Noah snapped off the flashlight and hurried back to the living room. He glanced out the window. A snowmobile idled in his driveway.

Julian Sinclair climbed off, removed his helmet, and lifted his snow goggles to his forehead. He waved.

Noah moved toward the front door.

"Is Mrs. Gomez okay?" Milo asked.

Noah cringed. He had no idea what to say to his son, who loved the old woman as a surrogate mother. Milo had watched two people die yesterday. What did that do to an eight-year-old kid's psyche?

Another dead person might be too much for him to handle. It felt like too much for Noah to handle.

"She's out," Noah lied. He'd figure out the right words later. "A friend must have picked her up for the day so she wouldn't be alone on Christmas."

Milo smiled. "That's nice."

"I think so, too. Come on, let's say hello to Uncle Julian."

"Hey, Little Man!" Julian called as they exited the house and trudged toward him. He turned to Noah. "Merry freakin' Christmas. Can you believe this mess?"

"So it's that bad then?"

"It's bad. What happened yesterday? You said you were coming in. Figured you got stuck without a working car like the rest of us."

"We got stuck on a ski lift." Noah didn't feel like rehashing the specifics, not in front of Milo. "It sucked."

"Damn. I guess so." Julian ran a hand through his short blond hair. He was tall and fit, charismatic and handsome, with a charming smile that ladies loved—although he could never commit to one long-term.

Noah leaned in close and lowered his voice so Milo couldn't hear. "What about the vic found yesterday? Any leads or evidence?"

Julian rolled his eyes. "I told you. Just another junkie. We'll figure it out later. The vic is on ice at the morgue in St. Joe. Hope their generator is still working. He's not going anywhere, at any rate. We've got much bigger problems now, brother. Come on. We gotta go."

"Go where?"

"The old courthouse. They're waiting for us. My mother wants the cops there. The sooner we get through this emergency council meeting, the sooner we get back to doing our jobs."

Julian Sinclair had an impatient streak. He was a man of action. He hated meetings and committees; he'd much rather be doing something, anything, other than sitting around. Still single and without the responsibilities of a family, he spent his time downhill skiing and snowmobiling, hunting, and gambling.

"I have Milo." Noah cleared his throat. "His sitter is . . . unavailable."

"Just bring him. It's important." Julian rolled his eyes. "Besides, he's a good kid, and you know my mother won't mind."

Fall Creek was governed as a charter township, with a board of trustees who served on the township council. Rosamond Sinclair, Julian's mother, was the township superintendent; she acted like a mayor, though that wasn't her official title.

She liked Noah—and doted on Milo. He was the grandson her own two sons had never given her.

Rosamond was a busy, high-powered woman who didn't have time for visits to John Ball Zoo or baking homemade cookies, but she never forgot his birthday or Christmas, always bringing by a bottle of wine for Noah and an elaborately wrapped gift for Milo —a new bike or extravagant Lego set.

It was more than his own parents had ever done.

Julian patted the seat of the snowmobile—an ancient Kawasaki Interceptor 550. "Come on. This is a two-seater, but Milo is small. He can fit between us."

It was only three miles from Noah's house to the town hall. Noah hesitated, unsure, but quickly gave in. He was out of options.

He helped Milo on. "We don't have helmets. Go slow." Julian didn't know the meaning of slow. "I mean it."

Julian chuckled. "How fast am I gonna go on this rickety old thing?"

"Where did you even get it?"

"Only old stuff works now. Weird as hell, right?"

"How widespread is this thing? Is it affecting the whole state? The entire Midwest?"

"Hell if I know. My mother said she found someone who can tell us more."

Julian started the engine, and it coughed to life with a throaty growl, drowning out any response Noah might have given.

Noah straddled the seat tightly and held on to Milo to make

sure he didn't fall off. They crossed the bridge over Fall Creek, which was not really a creek but a wide, deep river.

The river almost circled the town in a wide, serpentine C-shape before feeding into the St. Joe River to the north and eventually emptying into Lake Michigan about fifteen miles to the northwest. Several miles to the south, a dam separated Fall Creek from Lake Chapin, a popular recreation destination for fishing, boating, waterskiing, and jet skiing in the summer.

It was a short, cold drive into town. "Town" was a generous term. Most of the businesses were clustered along Main Street, with Friendly's Fresh Grown Grocery just across the bridge on the southern end. The Fall Creek Inn, perched along the riverbank, bookended the town on the north end.

Though it was Christmas day, a few dozen people dressed in winter gear were lined up outside Friendly's Grocery. It was the same with Vinson Family Pharmacy across the street. Folks milled about outside, anxious to fill prescriptions even with the computer systems down.

Past the grocery store, the sidewalks were mostly empty, the Christmas wreaths decorating the light poles swaying in the light breeze. Occasional cars and trucks had stalled in the middle of the road, though many had managed to pull off to the shoulder.

They passed a few fender-benders, but nothing too serious. Everything was smothered in at least a foot of fresh snow, not counting the foot they had already had. Except for the grocery store and pharmacy, the stores were all dark. The gas station. The Pizza Palace and Patsy's Cafe. Gundy's Auto Repair and the Clothesline laundromat.

The single stoplight was dark, too. To the east stood Main Street Apartments and a section of neighborhoods. To the west was the high school and combined elementary/middle school, Tresses hair salon, the Brite Smiles dentist's office, and the post office.

Julian roared into the old courthouse parking lot located in the center of town, just left past the stoplight. The historic Greek revival building featured large white columns inspired by ancient temples. It was built in 1846 and served as the county courthouse until a new courthouse was appointed in the nearby town of St. Joe in the mid-twentieth century.

These days, half the building served as a museum and heritage site for local school children to tour, the other half was used for town hall and township board meetings.

Noah helped Milo clamber off the snowmobile as Julian switched off the engine. He could just make out Crossway Church a few blocks north, along with Fuller's Hardware, the bank, and Fireside Tavern.

Noah turned to Milo. "Remember the museum area with the old-fashioned tables? You can sit out there by one of the windows and read some books on Michigan history. Fun, right?"

Milo made a face. "Eww, no."

Noah managed a tense grin. "I know, son. I know. I have a lot to make up for."

Milo perked up. "Peanut butter sundaes?"

"I make no promises, but I'll see what I can do."

Five minutes later, he had Milo situated inside and was following Julian down a narrow hallway toward the main council room. The hallway was bright, the fluorescent lights buzzing overhead. Noah blinked. "It's not as cold in here. And the lights are on."

"The generator is still working. Fall Creek Inn still has their generator as well. So does Friendly's and Vinson Pharmacy. Lots of other generators don't, though."

Noah nodded as they entered the board room.

"Welcome to the 'End of the World' Club," Chief Briggs said dourly. "Since that's apparently what everyone thinks this is."

18

QUINN
DAY TWO

Quinn shifted her position. The oak tree's bark scraped against her chilled cheek, but she barely noticed.

With her legs wrapped around the thick tree branch and crossed at the ankles to hold her in place, she leaned forward along the branch, twigs poking and scratching her belly as her coat rode up.

She leaned down precariously, focusing all her concentration on the slingshot in her hands, the bands pulled taut as she drew to her right cheek, her anchor point, and aimed at the squirrel perched on the oak branch twenty feet away.

She settled her breathing, focused herself as she canted the fork at a forty-five-degree angle, the pads of her finger and thumb pinching the ammo ball inside the pouch. She reached her max draw length and released the bands.

The three-eighths-inch steel pellet shot toward her target at around two hundred feet per second. It struck the squirrel in the side of its head below the ear, punched through its skull, and pierced its brain.

The animal didn't make a sound as it fell from the fifteen-foot-high branch and tumbled tail-first into the snow. A soft *pfft* broke the muted stillness.

Quinn didn't scurry down from the tree immediately. She lay still, breathing shallowly, watching the puffs of her breath cloud the frigid air. The cold buried itself into her bones.

It was late morning. The lethal cold hovered just above zero, the day overcast like every day before it, but at least the epic snowstorm from last night had subsided.

Little creatures scurried through the underbrush—chipmunks and squirrels, mice and rabbits. A crow cawed from somewhere nearby.

She should go inside. And she would, in just another minute. There was something about winter the artist in her had always loved. The stillness. The whiteness.

Everything perfect and beautiful and unbroken, even if putrid, rotting things lay beneath. For a little while, one could almost forget the ugliness just beneath the surface.

Behind Gran's property was a thick tangle of woods that lay between their street and the village proper and Main Street. The river wound a few hundred yards to the east.

The engine of an ATV broke the stillness—coughing and rattling like it was on its last legs.

Quinn heaved a sigh. She could get used to a world without the rumble of engines and machinery. To be fair, she only thought that when she didn't have somewhere she wanted to go. Skiing and snowshoeing everywhere would royally suck.

Thank goodness for the Orange Julius. Though it would run out of gas eventually. Good thing Gramps had stored a few jerrycans of fuel in the shed.

Quinn thrust the slingshot into her coat pocket. She gripped the branch with both hands, uncrossed her ankles, and swung down, letting her legs hang beneath her.

The drop was only four or five feet. Nothing she hadn't done a hundred times. She breathed in, breathed out, the hairs in her nostrils stiffening from the cold, her throat raw.

She closed her eyes for a second, remembering last night. The chairlift. The driving snow and brutal cold, the anxiety and fear. How those twenty-five feet had felt like a thousand.

How her grandfather had looked frozen. His eyelashes crusted with snow and ice. His opened eyes glassy as marbles. His whole vibrant life drained away in an instant.

She snapped her eyes open and dropped to the ground, her boots sinking deep into the snow, her bent knees absorbing the impact. She straightened and trudged to the fallen squirrel.

Once, she'd been squeamish about death, hated killing living things.

She still hated killing, but she did it because she had to know that she could. Because Gramps and Gran had taught her how to be a survivor.

And she'd needed that in more ways than one.

Don't ever kill for fun, Gramps had instructed her. *Then you deserve that shame. But killing to sustain life is part of nature. Always respect life. And death.*

A savage ache swelled in her chest. The loss of Gramps was so enormous, she hardly knew how to quantify it. Tears started in her eyes and immediately froze. She brushed them away fiercely.

She'd never seen Gran cry before. Not once. Not until last night.

After Quinn had returned late last night on Christmas Eve, half-frozen and numb with grief, they'd sat in the kitchen beside the crackling woodstove, Gran weeping and Quinn heartbroken, Gran holding her like she hadn't done since Quinn was little.

This morning, the old woman went about her business mechanically, barely speaking, slow and precise like if she made an error, her heart would crack open, and all her sorrow would pour out in an endless flood.

Quinn felt the exact same way. The women in her family were aces at anger and irritation, peevishness and snark. Not so much with the hard emotions. The real ones.

Not like Gramps. He was the one who kissed skinned knees and mended hurt feelings. Those rough and calloused but gentle hands, always ready for a hug or tender shoulder-squeeze.

The ATV grew louder. Quinn's stomach knotted in apprehension. She couldn't see it roaring up the road, but she didn't need to. She could already picture it in her mind's eye: an apple-red 1988 Honda Fourtrax 300 4x4, grimy with dirt and snow.

It was Ray Shultz's four-wheeler. Her mother's boyfriend. But Octavia drove it as often as he did.

The engine switched off. Her mother's familiar voice shrieked, "Quinn! I know you're here! Get the hell out here!"

Quinn grabbed the squirrel by its tail with one hand and swiped chunks of snow, shards of bark, and broken twigs from her insulated snow pants and the front of her coat with the other as she entered Gran's house through the rear door.

The kitchen was empty but for the cats. Thor and Odin were curled up on the rug in front of the woodstove, sleeping. Loki, the naughty tabby cat, was perched in the middle of the table, licking his paws. He tilted his furry head and gave Quinn a smug look, like he wasn't even sorry he'd gotten caught.

Quinn motioned at him. "Git! Before I make you regret it!"

Loki gave a disgruntled meow, flicked his tail dismissively, and took his sweet time strolling to the table's edge and hopping down. Quinn rolled her eyes.

Gran was out behind the shed, working on the winter garden where she grew hardy vegetables like turnips, carrots, cabbage, cauliflower, onions, garlic, and Swiss chard. She grew everything in cold frames—portable wooden frames with clear, rigid polycarbonate covers.

They were unheated but captured solar energy and sheltered

the crops from the elements. The insides were lined with aluminum foil to boost light and heat retention. That morning, Quinn had helped Gran brush the snow from the frames to prevent ice buildup.

Hopefully, Gran stayed out there. On top of everything else, she didn't need to deal with Octavia, too.

Quinn set the squirrel on the newspaper-covered counter. The fire crackled and popped in Gran's woodstove. The kitchen was warm. Too warm. Heat prickled her chilled skin.

She unzipped her coat, took off her hat and gloves, and stuffed them in her pockets. Gran had both a fireplace in the living room and the old woodstove in the kitchen. The woodstove gave off more heat, so they'd been staying in the kitchen as much as possible.

Quinn's mother strode into the kitchen from the living room, the front door still slightly ajar. Her clomping boots trailed clots of snow behind her. "What the hell do you think you're doing?"

Trepidation filled her, but she kept her chin high, her eyes hard. "Nothing."

Octavia Riley was all raw agitated energy and wild eyes. She was painfully skinny, with long knobby limbs, gaunt cheeks, and ratty hair. Quinn had hardly any memories of her mother other than as a strung-out junkie.

Octavia leaned against the fridge, smoking a cigarette with a shaky hand. "You didn't come home last night. I didn't even know where you were. We were worried sick!"

Octavia hadn't even bothered to remember that yesterday was Quinn's birthday. Anger and hurt blazed in her chest. "No, you weren't. You just wanted someone to clean up after you."

Octavia's dark eyes flashed. She took an aggressive step toward Quinn. Her hands were shaking. Her entire body was humming with tension and *need* like a struck wire.

Quinn didn't flinch. She'd learned not to flinch long ago.

Her mother was mostly piss and vinegar, all bark with little bite. Just an occasional slap or yank of Quinn's hair. She was strong and frenzied when she was high, but Quinn was usually faster.

The boyfriend, on the other hand, was another matter entirely.

Quinn crossed her arms in front of her chest. She was tired of this. Sick of the same twisted, toxic dance. Her grandfather was dead. The grid was down. Everything had turned inside out and upside down.

Everything else had changed, but Octavia was still the same pathetic, hurtful, loser addict she'd always been. Not even the end of the world could change that.

19

QUINN
DAY TWO

"In case you haven't noticed, everything's going to hell," Quinn said with more sass than she felt. "I'm taking that as my notice to quit."

"Don't you talk to me that way!" Octavia jabbed her cigarette at Quinn's face. Her features contorted in seething contempt. "Don't you dare. You ungrateful little brat!"

It had hurt, once upon a time. All the screaming and name-calling. Quinn told herself it didn't hurt anymore. She wouldn't let it hurt anymore. She'd built her walls to be thick and impenetrable—and they should be. They were constructed of scar tissue.

She stared her mother down, meeting those hard, red-rimmed eyes head-on. Octavia looked like she hadn't bathed in weeks. The smell of smoke didn't cover the unwashed stink emanating from her ratty clothes.

Octavia blinked first. She shoved her lank, greasy hair behind her ears with a trembling hand and took a drag of her cigarette.

"What do you want?" Quinn asked sharply. "What are you even doing here?"

"We're starving! What do you think? We need food. And we

need stuff to trade." To exchange for more drugs, but Octavia didn't need to say that. It was a given.

She strode over to the pantry and flung open the doors. Home-canned applesauce, peaches, freeze-dried fruits, and sealed containers of flour, beans, and grains lined Gran's well-stocked shelves.

Octavia moved to the sink and crouched to open the cabinet underneath. She yanked out a couple of large trash bags. "Help me, baby girl."

Quinn didn't move. Of course, Octavia wouldn't have any food after just a day. She never bothered to go to the grocery store. It was Quinn who always had to scrounge for a meal.

"What are you doing? Get over here."

"Hell, no. No freaking way. I'm not helping you steal from Gran."

Octavia rolled her eyes and started stuffing jars into the trash bag herself. She was careless. The jars clanked against each other, nearly breaking. "What's all this flour and bags of beans nonsense? I can't eat that. Where's the rest?"

"The rest of what?"

"Don't sass me, girl! Where's all the food? I know how much Mom and Dad have hidden away. Don't try to hide it from me." Octavia's face twisted with loathing. "Mom always did like to keep everything to herself and leave the scraps for me."

"That's not true."

"They still have you wrapped around their little fingers, do they?" Octavia gave a malicious grin, revealing her rotting teeth, and waved the cigarette around, spreading the smoke she knew Gran hated. It always made Gramps cough and irritated his lungs.

Quinn's chest constricted. Gramps wasn't here anymore. He was still stuck at that stupid ski resort he'd insisted on, a frozen popsicle.

He was no one's priority now, not with the world going to hell in a handbasket. It was one of his favorite phrases. And now it might actually be true.

"Octavia."

Her mother ignored her.

"Octavia!"

Finally, she looked up in exasperation. "What!"

"Gramps is . . ." The words tore at Quinn's tongue like barbed wire. Just saying it out loud hurt. "Gramps is dead."

That finally reached Octavia.

She went rigid, her twitchy hands lowering to her sides. Smoke from her cigarette swirled lazily toward the ceiling. "What?"

"His pacemaker stopped working when everything else stopped. He was stuck outside in the cold. It put his body under a lot of stress. His heart just . . . failed."

That was only part of it, but it was the only part that mattered.

Octavia's gaze skipped frantically around the small kitchen as if searching for something to anchor herself, something to hold on to. Her reddened eyes grew shiny. She scrubbed at her face, nearly burning her cheek with the cigarette. "I—I didn't know that."

Quinn didn't pity her. She had no pity left. Grief and resentment and anger took up all the space in her chest, expanding until it was hard to breathe. "You didn't even ask how Gramps or Gran was. You don't care. You've never cared!"

Octavia flinched. She stubbed the cigarette out on the newspapers covering the counter and left the butt next to the dead squirrel. She stood there, trembling, just staring down at the squirrel.

In that moment, the ravages of her drug habit fell away. She looked years younger. Lost and vulnerable.

From old pictures, Quinn knew Octavia used to be beautiful, her ratty hair once long and black and glossy, her patchy skin a healthy olive tone, her yellowed and decaying teeth once straight and white when she smiled, her dark eyes that matched Quinn's own shining and healthy.

Octavia and Quinn had both taken after Gramps' Vietnamese heritage, though their skin was lighter. Quinn's father was a Chinese-American adopted by English parents as a baby, so she looked more Asian than her mother did.

Quinn had very few pictures of her father, and zero memories. He'd stuck around long enough for the one-year marriage to end in fiery disaster, decided parenthood wasn't his thing, and took off to work oil rigs in Alaska.

Quinn had his last name and not much else. No one in Fall Creek had heard from him since. And his parents—her biological grandparents—had moved away soon after.

The only family Quinn had left was her mother and Gran. And Octavia barely counted.

Tears leaked down Octavia's face. "I—I should have been here. I didn't even get to say goodbye . . . I—I'm sorry. I'm so sorry . . ."

Quinn let the anger flare through her, let it drive out the grief and sadness. Octavia was sorry now? Of course she was. It was far too little, far too late.

Her expression hardened. "That's the problem, isn't it? You never think. And you're never here."

Not that Quinn wanted her around. Octavia's presence made her edgy and tense. She always counted down the seconds until she could escape her mother and the ridiculous pretense that they loved each other or were any semblance of a family.

And yet, an inexplicable mix of resentment and longing tangled in her gut. What she wanted was the mother Octavia was supposed to be, not the piss-poor version she'd been stuck with.

Octavia snapped out of it. Whatever she'd been feeling—sorrow, remorse—it was gone in an instant. Her eyes dimmed.

"That's your problem, isn't it? Always blaming people. Always so ugly. Ray was right about you."

"Ray's a hairy-arsed moron."

"Always the smartass, aren't you?" Octavia snatched up the heavy-duty trash bag filled with Gran's stuff and slung it over her shoulder. "I'll be back for more."

"You'd better not."

Without another word, Octavia turned and stomped through the kitchen and living room, threw open the front door, and slammed it behind her.

Quinn stood in the middle of the warm kitchen, alone but for the cats wrapping themselves around her ankles. She blinked back the sudden wetness in her eyes. "Merry freaking Christmas to you, too."

20

NOAH

DAY TWO

T he board room was plain and unadorned with beige walls, beige carpet, and a long rectangular table in the center. About ten people sat around the table.

Having lived in this town most of his life, Noah recognized everyone, including the police chief, several police officers, the rotary club president, and several local business owners.

Township superintendent Rosamond Sinclair sat at the head of the table. She was a short, slender woman with blonde hair styled into a sharp bob at her chin, accentuating her strong cheekbones and attractive features.

A good-looking woman in her early fifties, Rosamond was a careful, precise woman. Nothing was ever said carelessly. Every item of clothing, every gesture and mood calibrated, deliberately chosen.

Rosamond gestured to Noah with manicured fingers. "Come in, come in. Julian tells me you were at Bittersweet yesterday when the power went out. I'm sure it was quite the adventure getting back."

An image of Quinn's frozen grandfather flashed through

Noah's mind, followed immediately by Brock in agony and shock, dying right before their eyes.

Julian chose a chair near his mother and flopped into it. Stiffly, Noah took a seat beside him. "Something like that."

Rosamond flashed him a smile. "Glad you and Milo made it back safe."

Noah had spent much of his teens in and out of her house, spending the night on the floor of Julian's room, raiding the fridge at midnight, sneaking pot in her basement.

Of course, that was before he and Julian reformed themselves and became cops.

Though the Sinclair family came from money and small-town influence—Rosamond's father had served as a judge, and both of her uncles were township superintendents in the '90s and early 2000s—she'd never looked down on him or treated him as anything other than family.

Noah's mother had taken off to live with a boyfriend in Seattle when Noah was still in middle school. His accountant father had been convicted for money-laundering and tossed in prison when he was nineteen, but he'd been a crap father long before that. The Sinclair family had become his de facto family.

"Thank you all again for coming at such short notice. And Christmas Day at that." Rosamond motioned around the room. "I asked our trusted law enforcement officials to be present along with Chief Briggs. I'm sure you all understand why."

Heads nodded soberly around the table. People's faces were tense and drawn.

"We may have an enormous crisis on our hands," Rosamond said, "and I, for one, wish to be ready to meet it."

"It's just a power outage," Chief Briggs insisted. In his early sixties, he boasted a cantankerous personality and a wrinkled bulldog face to match. "A little different than usual, but nothing we can't handle."

The department had four full-time officers, two part-time officers, and ten reserve officers, who were usually only called in for extra security at parades, county fairs, and other community events.

The other officer in the room besides Noah, Julian, and Chief Briggs was Jose Reynoso, a burly former Marine in his forties. He was built like a tank and knew how to fight like one, too. He was quiet and kept to himself, but he was loyal as hell.

"I didn't say we couldn't handle it," Rosamond said evenly, "only that we need to be prepared. As you all are aware, a serious power outage has affected our town. And not only our town."

"How far-reaching is this thing?" asked Dave Farris.

"I was in Kalamazoo County yesterday," Noah said. "Sixty miles north. The same thing happened to us, and at the same time, too. A little after noon."

Jose Reynoso scratched his jaw. "The only radio stations coming through are the canned emergency responses from the governor's office. We're in the dark here, literally and figuratively."

"Which leads us to believe that this may be statewide," Rosamond said. "At least."

"What about the rest of Southwest Michigan?" Noah asked. "Grand Rapids? Detroit? Kalamazoo? Has anyone heard from the governor personally?"

Rosamond shook her head. "No. Nothing. We haven't been able to make contact via the regular channels with anyone. Two part-time officers, Samantha Perez and Oren Truitt, volunteered to take snowmobiles to Lansing to make physical contact with state government officials until we can get communications up and running."

Briggs grunted dismissively.

"This isn't normal, Briggs," Dave Farris said. In his early sixties, Dave was a generous, loud, boisterous Caucasian man who loved fishing, his ham radio, and sports cars. "Our vehicles aren't working. Our phones are dead. What kind of power outage ever affected any of that before?"

"Something's going on," said Annette King, principal of Fall Creek High school. She was in her late forties, an avid jogger with a compact, athletic physique and silver hair cut in a short pixie style. Annette was normally a confident, self-assured woman, but her face was drawn and tense. "My daughter is on vacation in Cancún. I can't reach her."

Chief Briggs crossed his arms over his burly chest. "They'll figure it out and get things up and running in a few days. No reason to get everyone's panties in a wad."

"I'm sorry, Annette." Rosamond intervened before Chief Briggs could respond. "Some of you know that my own son didn't make it back to town last night."

Noah looked around for Julian's half-brother, Gavin Pike. While not an official councilmember, he seemed to always be around, whispering in his mother's ear, skulking in the shadows, smiling that silky fake smile of his.

Noah had never liked the guy. Not since high school, when there were rumors that he'd sprained that girl's arm on a date gone wrong. Noah had never been able to pin anything on him, much as he'd wanted to.

Noah didn't want to worry about him right now. He was thinking about Quinn's theory. He needed to hear it from someone else to make it real. He spread out his hands. "What exactly happened? Does anyone know?"

A young black guy Noah had never seen before stood abruptly and cleared his throat. The guy looked barely twenty. Tall and skinny, he wore tight preppy jeans with a slim-fitting striped sweater.

"This is Mike Duncan's nephew, Jamal Duncan," Rosamond said. "He's studying electrical engineering at U of M. Luckily for us, he's visiting for Christmas. Since our communication systems are . . . lacking at the moment, Jamal has been kind enough to shed some valuable light on our situation. Jamal?"

"Yeah, sure." Jamal shifted awkwardly, his eyes darting around the room. "The United States has most likely been hit by an electromagnetic pulse from a nuclear bomb."

Several people gasped. Julian sat up straighter. Chief Briggs stiffened.

Even though he suspected what was coming, Noah's heart still sank into the pit of his stomach. He gripped the arms of his chair to steady himself.

"Are you saying we've just been nuked?" Darryl Wiggins asked incredulously. He was a stiff, sour-faced man in his fifties, Wiggins was the rotary club president and the manager of Community Trust Bank.

A slick small-town politician, he was always trying to endear himself to Rosamond and garner himself more influence. If he could come out ahead on someone else's dime, even better.

"Yes," Jamal said. "However—"

"Are we going to die of radiation, then?" Wiggins cut in. "What about fallout? Have we already been poisoned?"

"It's not how you think," Jamal said. "Because the nuke is detonated in the atmosphere, there's no danger of fallout or radiation. That's not the problem."

"Then what is?" Dave Farris asked.

"It's an EMP. Maybe a Super-EMP. An electromagnetic pulse is created during a nuclear detonation high above our atmosphere. If the pulse is strong enough—and this one appears to be—it fries most electronics, whether they're plugged in or not. Everything's made with computers these days. Everything in our cars. Our phones. Even our refrigerators are connected to the internet of things."

"What does a Super-EMP do?" Rosamond asked.

"It does way more damage than a regular nuclear weapon. It

doesn't take that much physics knowledge to create a high-altitude EMP that would generate dramatically more gamma radiation than 'normal' nukes, which could more efficiently turn that gamma radiation into an electromagnetic pulse. It'd be a sophisticated design, but it wouldn't be that difficult for any nuclear weapons state to build one that would produce more than 25,000 volts per square meter. I mean, with a two-stage thermonuclear weapon utilizing a shielded primary fission stage and—"

"Jamal, get to the point." Mike Duncan prodded his nephew not-so-gently. "How far reaching are we talking about here?"

"Yeah, sorry. Okay." Jamal cleared his throat. "A single Super-EMP hit could localize the damage to several states. Or it could be a coordinated attack of multiple EMPs spread out to do the most damage."

"What do you mean by the most damage?" Mike Duncan asked.

"Most of the continental United States could be dark right now."

For a long moment, no one said anything. They stared at each other, stunned, in shock, trying to take it all in.

Darryl Wiggins looked like he might pass out.

"How do you know it's not a solar flare?" Noah asked, trying to remember what Quinn had called it. "Or a coronal mass thing?"

"A coronal mass ejection," Jamal corrected. "A CME happens when plasma, which is a super-heated and ionized gas, is expelled from the surface of the Sun. It produces a magnetic shockwave that extends billions of miles into space. If Earth is in the path of that shockwave, our electrical systems become overloaded. It mainly affects the power grid by destroying transformers and long power lines. In this case, because most vehicles, computers, and phones aren't functional, we can surmise that this is a nuclear EMP event."

"That's rather farfetched," Briggs growled. "A whole lotta imagination and fear-mongering."

"Then how else do you explain all this?" Reynoso said. "It's the only thing that makes sense."

"The United States of America is under attack!" Wiggin's voice rose in alarm. "He just said—"

"Let's just say this is a reasonable possibility, given what we know," Rosamond said evenly. She turned to Jamal. "How long until the grid is operational again?"

Jamal dropped his gaze to the table. "Years."

"I'm sorry," Reynoso said, leaning forward. "Did you just say 'years?'"

"Yes." Jamal raked a hand through his wiry hair. "Each transformer is custom-made and takes something like twenty months to design, develop, and deliver. They're made in factories that require electricity. So if the whole country is out . . . we'll have to commission them one by one overseas—only our cargo ships are manufactured with electronic systems. How many were within range? What percentage of our aircraft are permanently grounded? How many lost control of their systems and crash-landed? You see where I'm going with this."

Several council members exchanged glances.

"Plane crashes?" Mike Duncan asked, alarmed.

"It gets worse. Without power, the gas stations shut down. No way to get the gas out. No easy way, anyway. No refineries working without power. Or very few. Not enough for all of us, not by a long shot. No gas; the delivery trucks don't work. They can't get through the snow now, anyway. So the stores don't get food. The hospitals don't get supplies. The water treatment plants don't get their chemicals."

The pharmacies don't get their medications. The realization struck Noah like a physical blow. His breath fled his lungs. He almost doubled over.

He hadn't even thought about the precarious supply chain. How critical each element was, each link in the sequence. How he would no longer be able to just stroll into Vinson Pharmacy and pick up his son's life-saving pills in a crinkly white bag.

What was he going to do? For a minute, the room buzzed with white noise. Everything went tinny and distant. He didn't hear a thing.

He'd have to find a way to get Milo's pills. To keep his son warm and safe and fed. There wasn't any other option. He'd find a way.

"Everything operates on just-in-time delivery these days," Mike said. "If the trucks stop, within twenty-four hours, hospitals and medical facilities will run out of basic supplies. Within three days, gas stations will be completely out of fuel. Store and restaurant shelves will be bare. ATMs and banks will run out of cash—though without power, we can't access our money anyway. Within four weeks, the nation's clean water supply will be completely exhausted."

"This is a catastrophe," Annette said quietly, her face stricken. "Far more serious even than dealing with a lack of heat and electricity."

Jamal cleared his throat. "The federal EMP commission predicted up to 90 percent of the population would die off within a year."

The room fell into a stunned silence. Noah's chest tightened. A moment ago, the room had been too cold. Now it was too hot, too small.

"In a nutshell," Jamal said, "we're screwed."

21

NOAH
DAY TWO

"Who the hell did this to us?" Julian snarled through clenched teeth. Gone was his congenial grin. A vein pulsed in the center of his forehead. His hands were balled into fists on the table.

Jamal sat back down, looking abject and miserable. Rosamond remained seated with her hands folded in front of her, her suit spotless, not a hair out of place, a neutral expression on her face. A tiny muscle twitching at the corner of her mouth was her only tell.

"Probably Russia," Mike said.

Annette nodded. "My odds are on China."

"Don't forget about Iran," Reynoso said. "They're a powder keg waiting to blow up."

Noah shook his head. He felt sick. "Yeah, but anyone who attacks us has to know we're going to respond with a scorched-earth policy. It'll hurt them way worse than they've hurt us."

"Maybe their leader is certifiably insane, like North Korea. Or maybe they're smart enough to lay the blame at another country's feet." Reynoso gave a tense shrug. "Who knows?"

The conference room filled with murmurs of concern that

quickly escalated to alarm, even barely restrained panic. If they gave in to their fear, things would go downhill fast.

They needed to regain control of the room, or they'd all lose it.

"Right this minute, it doesn't matter who did this to us," Noah said. "We need to figure out how to survive right here in Fall Creek. Seems like that's the biggest problem we're facing right now."

"He's right," Annette said. "We can figure out whether it's China or North Korea later when our houses are warm, and our kids have food in their bellies."

Somber nods around the room.

"Thank you, Noah and Annette." Rosamond dipped her chin at them. "We can waste our precious energy on panic and worry, or we can act to protect ourselves and shore up our resources. I, for one, prefer action."

"Where the hell is FEMA?" Wiggins whined. He had a nasally, high-pitched voice that grated on Noah's nerves. "The army and the National Guard? Other countries? They'll send aid. They have to. That's their job."

"FEMA can't handle a national crisis," Dave Farris said quietly. "The emergency response chain is only as strong as its weakest link. All you gotta do is visit the DMV to understand how incredibly inefficient the government is. Do we really want to put all our trust in that?"

Wiggins shook his head, disbelieving. "We pay taxes! The government has plans and procedures. They have stockpiles!"

"Not for Fall Creek, they don't," Julian scoffed. "Whatever they have is going to Detroit, Kalamazoo, or Grand Rapids first."

"Even when FEMA does come, it might take weeks for that help to filter to the small towns," Dave said. "The way I see it, we're going to have to take care of our own for a while."

"And we're already seeing a desperate need," Rosamond said. She turned from Briggs and settled her gaze on Reynoso. "Officer

Reynoso, if you could be so kind as to give us an updated report of the last twenty-four hours."

Reynoso cleared his throat and sat up straighter. "Someone broke into the McClintock's home last night and stole half their pantry. No one was hurt. Eighty-six-year-old Grover Massengill passed away sometime during the night. No one checked on him. He had a fireplace and firewood, but he never got out of bed."

Horrified murmurs filled the room.

"We have four deaths tallied so far," Reynoso said gravely. "All elderly citizens living alone. One, an apparent stroke, and three from hypothermia. They either didn't have a fireplace or were unable to get a fire started."

"Six deaths," Noah corrected. "I found Mrs. Norah Gomez dead in her bed this morning. And one of the men who died at Bittersweet last night was Dương Văn Dũng, a long-time resident of Fall Creek."

Noah thought of Quinn with a pang. He needed to make sure to check on her later. "We need to retrieve his body. I promised his granddaughter."

"We will, I assure you," Rosamond said. "We have a lot on our plate, and it will only get worse. Right now, the living are the priority. Food, heat, and shelter."

"And medical," Noah added. "Is Dr. Prentice in town?"

"He's in California visiting his daughter," Rosamond said. "We're without a doctor."

Noah's gut tightened. He fiddled nervously with his wedding ring. He needed to talk to Robert Vinson as soon as possible and get more of Milo's medication.

"Shen Lee is around," Annette said. "He's a pediatric nurse. I'm sure he'll be willing to help with any medical needs."

"Excellent." Rosamond leaned forward. "We need to be thinking about communications, food collection and distribution, transportation, sanitation. We need to figure out the number of people we're talking about, and how many are children, elderly, and special needs. We need to think about nutrition, healthcare, sanitation, and mobility. We need to switch to conservation mode and ration our supplies. We can't blow through our limited resources too quickly."

"And gas," said Mike. He was a short, heavy black man with a full beard and wire-framed glasses. He owned the only gas station in town. "Generators, snowmobiles, trucks. They'll all stop real quick if we don't get fuel out of the tanks. I've got the pumps working on a portable generator but that'll run out eventually. I'll try to figure out how to hook up a manual pump system to the underground tanks."

"Maybe we can start siphoning gas from all the stalled vehicles to increase our supplies," Noah suggested.

Chief Briggs glared at him like he'd grown three heads. "Are you serious?"

"Great ideas, Mike and Noah." Rosamond studiously ignored the chief. "Let's put a five-gallon limit on everyone but critical personnel, as well. Also, we have a few older generators that we can set up at the high school. That'll be our emergency shelter for those without a means of heating their homes. We'll need to gather food and water to make sure we have enough for everyone until FEMA or the National Guard arrive." She paused. "If they arrive."

"How are you planning on getting all these supplies?" Chief Briggs asked, glowering. "We sure aren't taking them from our citizens."

Rosamond steepled her fingers over the table. "Of course not. We're asking for our community to pitch in and help each other out. Everything is voluntary."

"I'm willing to open the Inn, if it comes to that," Dave said.

"Atticus Bishop runs that huge food pantry at Crossway Church," Julian said. "I'm sure they'd be happy to help."

Rosamond turned to Noah. "You're friends with him, aren't you? Why don't you stop by and see what they can do?"

"Of course," Noah said. "Anything I can do to help."

"Absolutely," Annette echoed. "Just tell us what we need to do."

"We can help with communication." Reynoso passed Noah an older model decommissioned radio. "We found seven of these in the basement this morning. They were tucked away in a metal locker. I took the liberty of fiddling around with them, switched out some parts with our new radios, and got them to work. We'll need to rummage around for batteries, but for now, this is how we communicate."

"We need to establish outside communication as well." Noah turned to Dave Farris. "Don't you have a ham radio set up? We may need it if we can't get information through official channels."

"I think a few circuits got fried," Dave said. "But Tina Gundy, James's daughter, said she'd take a look. She's just like her father—another mechanical genius, and pretty brilliant with anything electronic, too."

The Gundy family owned the mechanic shop in town. James had been in Detroit at a conference when the EMP hit and hadn't returned yet. His twenty-three-year-old daughter, Tina, a cute bubbly blonde who was also incredibly smart, was home on Christmas break from Michigan State.

"I can help," Jamal offered.

"Excellent," Rosamond said. "Dave, Jamal, and Tina are in charge of getting the radio up and running and providing the council with updates."

"I'll get some folks together," Mike offered. "We'll get some volunteers set up with a couple of snowmobiles and have them notify the residents of information updates. We can figure out a grid or quadrant system for communication."

"Give that to the teenagers," Annette said. "It'll give them something to do. I'll help you with names and addresses. And I'll start organizing the gym and get the high school open as an emergency shelter by tonight."

"I will, of course, pitch in in whatever way is needed," Wiggins said grandly. "You know you can depend on me, Rosamond."

Noah and Julian exchanged a look. Noah resisted rolling his eyes. Everyone knew Wiggins wouldn't actually do a thing unless it benefited himself most.

Rosamond smiled, but the corner of her mouth twitched ever so slightly. "As long as everyone understands that it's all-hands-on-deck. We'll all need to pull together to get through this."

22

NOAH
DAY TWO

"What about Winter Haven?" Annette asked.

"What about it?" Rosamond asked evenly.

"Do they have power?"

"We have a resource available to us that we must take extreme care to protect," Rosamond said carefully.

"So that's a yes," Mike said.

Winter Haven was the brainchild of a rich multimillionaire developer from Chicago who'd discovered Fall Creek in the early 2000s. He'd fallen in love with the gently rolling hills, the picturesque river, the welcoming small-town feel.

The developer had purchased fifty acres of a former Boy Scout camp on the opposite side of Fall Creek and built a self-sufficient community of upscale log cabins with their own water, sanitation, and solar power arrays. Even in winter, the solar setup provided enough off-grid electricity to fill most people's needs.

Rosamond Sinclair owned one of the homes in Winter Haven. No wonder she looked so refreshed. Noah tried not to feel a prick of envy. He didn't care about himself, only Milo.

"The Winter Haven community does have power," Rosamond

said. "The solar panels and battery banks are still working. I'll admit we all thought Arthur Bradford was a bit paranoid when he insisted on hardening the computerized systems and keeping the controls in some kind of protective contraption—"

"A Faraday cage," Jamal piped up. "A Faraday shield is an enclosure used to block electromagnetic fields, usually made with a continuous or mesh covering of conductive material."

"Yes. That. It's such a shame that Arthur passed a few years ago. I think he'd feel vindicated today. At any rate, Winter Haven does have heat, power, and running water."

"Good for them," Reynoso said, sounding more than a little jealous. "But what's that to the rest of us? How does that keep me warm at night?"

Rosamond ignored him. "The community includes fifty-one homes. Twenty-nine of them are empty."

Chief Briggs scowled. "You checked them already, did you?"

"Only to see who's home. We shouldn't let those resources go to waste. We're only doing our due diligence."

Chief Briggs shoved back his chair. "Absolutely not. We're not sanctioning taking over people's homes. Are you crazy? Two days, and we're already forging the Constitution?"

Tension crackled through the room. All eyes turned to Chief Briggs and the superintendent.

Wiggins grimaced. Noah was sure he had an opinion on the matter but hesitated to sound like he was crossing Rosamond. Instead, he stewed in silence.

Rosamond steepled her fingers beneath her chin. Her gaze remained clear, her eyes calm. "Don't be dramatic, Sam. It doesn't become you. In normal times, I would never consider such a thing. You know that. But I'm afraid we're no longer in normal times."

"There's absolutely no justification for this!" Chief Briggs bellowed. "You can't just—"

"That's enough," Rosamond cut in, her voice quiet but insistent. It commanded attention as much as if she'd shouted.

Chief Brigg's mouth tightened in a bloodless line, his eyes flashing.

"What about transportation?" Mike asked, changing the subject. "There's over two feet of fresh snowfall and it's still coming. I can't even get out of my driveway. I wouldn't even have made it if Dave hadn't picked me up."

"We requisitioned nine working snowmobiles, three ATVs, and two trucks with attached snowplows for the town's needs," Julian said. "And a few old clunkers we can jack up with snow chains. And we'll get more."

"Requisitioned?" Noah raised his brows. "From where?"

"The community, Julian said with a tight grin. "We already have reserve officers heading out to assess individual needs and tally resources. The snowmobile we rode in on this morning belonged to the Carter brothers."

Noah noted the past-tense verb *belonged*. "They just let you take it?"

Julian shrugged. "They were agreeable."

Noah had never known the Carter brothers to be agreeable about anything. The Fall Creek Police Department had arrested them multiple times for possession, theft, battery—a whole litany of crimes. Along with their passel of useless no-good cousins, they were well known throughout the county.

Rosamond gazed around the table, pausing at each face. "We have resources here. The river. Winter Haven. A lot of houses are on well and septic. We can take care of our own, but only if we work together. The task is monumental. Fall Creek needs each one of you."

The men and women around the table nodded slowly, all but Chief Briggs.

The chief slammed his fist on the table. "I'm not sanctioning this crap. Not in my town."

Rosamond turned toward him, a smile still fixed on her face, but Noah recognized the stiffness in her shoulders, the tightness in her mouth. "Sam. Don't you think you might be overreacting a bit here? We're simply taking a census of what we have and who needs help."

He shoved back his chair and stood gruffly. He jabbed his finger at the superintendent, then the council members. "You're the ones overreacting! Acting like a few months without the internet is the end of the world! We've all gone without creature comforts. We can do it again." His eyes narrowed as his gaze landed on Jamal. "Well, my generation at least. You coddled babies wouldn't know toughness if it bit you on the ass."

Jamal blanched. "I don't think you understand how completely technology has infiltrated every aspect of—"

The chief waved his arms in the air, his bulldog face purpling in anger. "I don't need a . . . a *millennial* to explain life to me!"

Frustration flared through Noah, but he tamped it down quickly. Chief Briggs was his boss; his personal feelings about Briggs didn't matter. Briggs liked rules and regulations. He had a hard time thinking outside the box about anything. He was also crotchety and set in his ways.

Noah was an easygoing, good-natured guy. He didn't want to cause more problems when tension was already vibrating through the room. He gritted his teeth and forced a smile. "I think we should all take a breath."

"I don't need to take a damn breath!" the chief nearly shouted. "No one in this town is going to 'pool' their resources while I'm in charge! We're not doing it."

He spun on his heels and stalked from the room. The door slammed behind him.

For a moment, no one spoke in the stunned silence.

"I'll talk to him," Noah said evenly. "We're all a little stressed right now. He'll come around. We're all just trying to help."

"Excellent start, everyone." Rosamond's gaze slanted toward the closed door with the slightest frown. "We're family here. We'll stick together like a family, too. And we will get through this. I promise you." She smiled. "And despite everything, Merry Christmas."

The room broke into tepid applause, but it quickly grew louder and more enthusiastic. Noah found himself clapping, too, despite the growing anxiety tangled in his gut.

People needed someone to take charge. They needed hope, a plan.

Rosamond Sinclair knew how to give it to them.

23

QUINN
DAY THREE

Q uinn had never seen Friendly's Grocery like this. It felt like there were more people crammed into the grocery store right now than existed in the entire town.

A cashier—a bubbly redheaded chick named Whitney that Quinn went to high school with but didn't particularly like—wandered up and down the aisles, announcing the credit card machines were down and only cash would be accepted.

The generators were running, but they were mostly on for the refrigerated and freezer sections of the store. Half the fluorescent lights were off, and the other half buzzed and flickered, the most bland and boring grocery store taking on an eerie, even sinister, vibe.

Not to mention the headache it was giving her.

Whoever thought it would take a while for people to figure out this EMP thing was a long-term crisis was an idiot. The masses had grown up glued to Instagram, Facebook, YouTube, and Netflix, but they weren't totally clueless.

Even though the government was still spewing their "temporary blackout" nonsense over the emergency broadcasts, people had figured out things were more serious than that.

Soccer moms and preppy dads were rushing through the aisles, their faces strained and tight-lipped, dragging their whiny kids behind them, nearly crashing their carts into other shoppers in their rush to grab everything they could.

Things hadn't devolved to full chaos, though. This wasn't a dense, high-crime city bristling with gangs, like Detroit or Benton Harbor.

Fall Creek was a small town. These people all knew each other, were always sticking their noses into each other's business. You sure knew who your enemies were.

Quinn gripped her cart with fresh determination, nearly accidentally sideswiping Annette King, the principal of the high school, who was busy piling bags of rice and dry beans into her cart.

She had a bunch of salt containers, jugs of bleach, jars of instant coffee, and oil, which could be used in lamps, not just for cooking. At least ten packages of toilet paper were stuffed in the rack underneath the cart.

For a principal, she was smart. Definitely too smart to go after the frozen meats or refrigerated perishables like the big crowd of idiots in the back.

The principal gave her a tight wave. Quinn nodded back, feeling just as tense.

The list Gran had given her didn't have any food on it, which was weird. Gran's pantry was stuffed with weeks' worth of goods, but it still didn't feel like enough to endure a long Michigan winter that promised snow well into March, even April.

Quinn glanced at the hastily scrawled list in her hand again. On a low fixed income, Gran only had a hundred and fifty dollars in cash. Quinn had tossed in her own savings of a whopping twenty-five dollars, which a distant aunt had sent her as an early birthday present.

"Just get as much as you can," Gran had told her.

So she did. She maneuvered away from the food aisles and headed for the health section. She'd already grabbed rechargeable batteries of different sizes. She toppled a row of ibuprofen and aspirin bottles and antibacterial ointment into her cart, followed by a bunch of bottles of hand soap, tubes of toothpaste, and feminine hygiene products. It would really suck to run out of that stuff.

She wished Friendly's sold her brand of blue hair dye so she could stock up, but she'd had to order it on Amazon. Prime shipping wasn't exactly happening anymore.

Thing was, she didn't care as much as she'd thought she would. Tragedy had a way of putting everything into sharp focus.

She brushed her bangs out of her eyes, took a weary breath, and kept going. As much as she tried to focus on the task at hand, her mind kept straying to thoughts of Gramps.

She kept seeing his frozen face. His wrinkled brown skin turning that weird, sickening bluish gray. The snowflakes collecting on his dead glassy eyeballs.

Her chest ached. Like a giant hand squeezing her heart. She'd never known grief was such a physical thing.

Staying busy helped a little. Gran had her running around like a chicken with her head cut off. She'd spent yesterday afternoon—Christmas Day, not like it mattered—helping Gran plaster every window with aluminum foil to help insulate the house and reflect the heat back into the room.

Stillness wasn't a part of Gran's makeup. She was always working on the house, the garden, attending prayer meetings, or volunteering at church. She needed to be moving, bustling around, making or building or cooking things. Even after the stroke and the cane, Gran didn't let anything stop her.

Quinn blinked against the sudden tears. She wouldn't cry. If she did, she'd fall apart right here in the store. And no way was she letting that happen. Besides, it'd wreck her eye makeup.

A tall, scowling Caucasian man in an expensive-looking wool coat rammed into her cart. He pushed past her on the way toward a display table in the center aisle stacked with packs of bottled water.

She recognized him as the father of Whitney, the bubbly redheaded cashier, but she didn't know his name. Didn't care, either.

"Hey!" she yelled after him. "You don't have to be rude!"

The man in the wool coat completely ignored her. He shouldered in and grabbed the last package of bottled waters right out of the hands of a young mom with two little kids crammed into the cart, along with boxes of breakfast cereal, pasta, and Pop-Tarts.

Quinn didn't hesitate. It didn't matter that she had a list, a task. Or that she didn't know that mother and her snotty-nosed kids. One thing she hated was a bully. And wool coat guy was a total jerkwad.

She was half-tempted to pull out the tactical slingshot she'd started carrying around for protection and use it on him, just to teach him a lesson.

Instead, she jerked her cart around, took two striding steps, and slammed her cart into his as hard as she could. It bucked backward and smashed into him, the handle striking him in the stomach.

He let out an *oof*. He turned toward her, his eyes widening in surprise. "What the—"

"Don't be a dick." She smiled. "It's store policy."

He scowled. His whole face turned beet red. "Get the hell out of this store before I call the store manager and have you arrested for assault!"

Quinn didn't flinch. Angry adults didn't scare her. She was

used to being screamed at. "Go ahead. And we'll just tell him how you were stealing from this poor woman."

Other customers were watching now. Some rubbernecking just to see what was happening, others looking perturbed.

"It's okay," the mom said tremulously. "I don't need it that bad. He can just have it."

Quinn lifted her chin. "He's a bully, and he should be called out for it."

Wool Coat dropped the precious pack of bottled waters into his already overstuffed cart and lurched toward her, hands balled into fists. "Look here, you little—"

"Leave her alone!" Principal King stood in the center aisle, pale but frowning. "Mr. Blair, what on Earth are you doing?"

Wool Coat—Mr. Blair—seemed to notice the growing crowd for the first time. Instead of embarrassment, he glared at them in self-righteous fury.

"Don't you get it?" Mr. Blair snarled. "This is it! World War III has started and you lot are still worried about being cordial with your neighbors? How are you gonna feel in two weeks when you've got empty cupboards and nothing to feed your kids? What are you going to tell them? That you waited in line nicely? There's no blue ribbon or sticker awards for being nice, people! That time is done and gone. War isn't coming. It's already here!"

Principal King blanched.

"You're on the town council," Mr. Blair hissed at her. "You probably already know, don't you? This is some sort of cyberattack by Iran or Russia or whoever. The government knows—you know —but you aren't telling the truth. What aren't you telling us, *Annette*?"

Flustered, Principal King raised both hands, a can of kidney beans still gripped in one hand. Her face had gone white. "Now, Mr. Blair. That's not how it is—"

"They're keeping things from us!" Mr. Blair said loudly, so

loud most of the store could hear him. "Superintendent Sinclair. The council. It goes all the way to the governor! Are you going to just let them control us—"

"Ladies and gentlemen!" a loud voice blared through a megaphone. "Please remain calm."

Startled, everyone in the store froze.

24

QUINN
DAY THREE

"This is Officer Daniel Hayes," the voice over the megaphone continued. "Officer Reynoso is with me, along with four reserve officers. For everyone's protection, we are closing down Friendly's early."

Groans and gasps followed his announcement. People looked at each other, confusion, stress, and frustration quickly transforming to actual fear.

Quinn disentangled her cart from Mr. Blair's and turned toward the front entrance of the grocery store. Several police officers in uniform stood in front of the checkout line. The heavy, middle-aged Caucasian guy in the middle—Officer Hayes—held the megaphone.

"Friendly's will reopen tomorrow," he said, "but purchase limits will be in place to prevent a run on food. A fifty-dollar limit per family per day is effective as of today, December 27th. Transactions will remain cash-only. Please make your way to the checkout line immediately. Items in excess of the limit will be removed. If you do not comply, you will be escorted from the store without your items."

"Fifty dollars?" someone shouted. "Are you kidding me?"

"We can't feed our families with that!"

"This can't be right."

"This is illegal!"

"Did the council approve this dreck?" Mr. Blair turned on Principal King, contempt in his gaze. "I told you they were against us!"

Voices grew louder, frustration and fear and anger rising. The tension was fast reaching a boiling point. Anxiety twisted in Quinn's belly. This wasn't good.

Officer Hayes cleared his throat nervously. "You may speak with Superintendent Sinclair about the town's policies. We're only doing our jobs."

"First time for everything, eh Hayes?" Mr. Blair spat.

Folks that had been tense but cordial five minutes ago quickly became agitated, almost frantic. Several customers who'd been headed for the checkout now turned and headed back for more supplies—Officer Hayes' decree be damned.

Carts banged against each other. No one apologized. Little kids started crying.

Officer Hayes gave further instructions to remain calm and orderly, but few people were listening to him. A few men and a woman angrily confronted the officers, waving and pointing their fingers in their faces, Mr. Blair included.

Officer Reynoso's expression grew strained. His hand lowered to his service weapon. "We will maintain order, no matter how much you don't like it, Mr. Blair. Please take a step back, right now."

Things were going to get ugly fast.

Quinn needed to get out of here. She glanced toward the two checkout counters. A dozen people at least in each, all with stuffed carts. Two reserve officers were stopping the carts and sorting through them.

It would take forever. And they wouldn't let her take even half the stuff in her cart.

"Hey, Quinn!" a small voice piped up.

Quinn whirled around.

Little Milo Sheridan peeked around the endcap of the pasta aisle and grinned at her, all black curly hair and big dark eyes.

She didn't like kids. They were all annoying little devil monkeys. This one wasn't horrible, though. "Hey, Small Fry."

Noah came around the corner and plopped a few oversized jars of Jif creamy peanut butter into his nearly empty cart. The shadows under his eyes were darker than the last time she'd seen him on Christmas Eve. Day one of whatever the hell this was.

"Hey, Noah the Cop."

He looked at her. "It's Officer Sheridan to you."

Quinn gave a flippant shrug, trying to hide her anxiety. "As I recall, my brilliant fence-as-trampoline idea may have saved your kid's life. Or at least a broken bone or two. You owe me."

He ran a hand over his stubbled jaw and sighed. He hadn't shaved, and he looked tired. "Fine. Should I call you Smurf then?"

"Like I haven't heard that one before." She rolled her eyes. "Why aren't you helping the law enact their draconian orders?"

"I'm off for the night. Milo and I were hoping to stock up on supplies before they went into effect." He gave a wry smile. "Looks like I'm too late to the party."

His cart was filled with stuff parents bought—boxes of Kraft macaroni and cheese, Jif peanut butter, all-natural fruit snacks, granola bars, Rice-a-Roni, electrolyte drinks, and a few packs of batteries, toilet paper, and other items.

Deeper in the store, someone shouted angrily. Another voice—this one female—yelled back, equally furious.

Quinn rolled her eyes. "I think the party's just starting, actually."

"Not one we want to attend, trust me." Noah motioned at her cart. "You got enough to cover that?"

"Yeah. But it's gonna be over the fifty-dollar limit."

"Give it to me. I'll hand it to the cashier on the way out."

"But you're a cop."

Noah smiled tightly. "You're still paying for it. It's not stealing. Hurry up before they get to us."

Quinn complied. Noah took her cash and they skirted the checkout counters on the entrance side. Noah surreptitiously placed her cash along with a wad of twenties from his pocket on the end counter while Milo grabbed several plastic grocery bags from the carousel rack.

Whitney glanced anxiously back at him, but he just smiled at her. "Everything's fine. I'm just checking out on my own. I've got to get back to work."

"Okay, Officer Sheridan," she said, and returned to her endless line of frustrated, amped-up customers.

They quickly dumped their things into the grocery bags and headed out of the store.

A grandfather with a little kid saw what they'd done and started for the entrance with his full cart, not even bothering to stop and pay a thing. Two women followed suit, one holding a crying toddler in one arm.

From across the store, Officer Reynoso caught sight of the leaving customers. "Hey!" he shouted, hurrying over. "Stop right there!"

Quinn, Milo, and Noah were already out of the store. They left the angry, shouting crowd behind.

It was cold inside Friendly's, but outside, it was brutal.

"Thanks!" Quinn said as Noah and Milo headed for their snowmobile. Milo waved at her.

"Have a good night, Smurf!" Noah called over the wind.

Quinn kept moving. She sucked in a sharp breath at the startling cold, the frigid air searing her lungs and burning her nostrils. The wind battered her and kicked up swirling gusts of snow. Dusk was fast approaching.

She could barely see across the parking lot. There were a few dozen snowmobiles, but only a handful of working cars or trucks parked in the store's parking lot. Most people had walked here from their homes.

Beyond the parking lot, she couldn't even see the road or the other buildings along Main Street through the swirling snow. The four miles back to Gran's house would be a dangerous drive. At least there wouldn't be many other vehicles on the road.

Twenty feet from the Orange Julius, she suddenly stopped. A chill trickled down her spine.

Two figures lurked along the perimeter of the parking lot. They were just dark blurred shapes against so much blinding whiteness.

There was something about them that gave her pause, that lifted the hairs on the back of her neck. The way they moved—low and skulking. Like predators creeping toward their prey.

Quinn Riley sure as hell wasn't prey.

"You there! I can see you!" She dropped her grocery bags to the snow and shoved her hand into her pocket, going for the slingshot. "Get away from my grandpa's truck, or I promise you're gonna regret it!"

25

QUINN
DAY THREE

"We were just admiring your F150, darling," the first, taller guy drawled.

"Get away from the truck," Quinn warned.

The taller figure stepped forward. He was maybe ten feet away. "Still a free country, far as I know. It still a free country, Billy?"

The shorter figure moved closer. He was short and compact, five-foot-four at most, the same height as Quinn. But that didn't make him any less dangerous.

Quinn stiffened. They were both bundled in heavy winter gear, but this close, she could make out the white exposed ovals of their faces. She knew them.

They were cousins of Ray Shultz, her mother's deadbeat, drug-dealing boyfriend. Billy and Tommy Carter, brothers and partners in crime. Scumbags she'd always hated.

"Hey, I know you." Billy Carter was watching her with his oily, beetle black eyes. He had a lazy eye that made him look particularly shifty. "You're Octavia Riley's little girl."

"Not so little anymore." Tommy sneered. He was tall and thin with a narrow, horsey face and a weird southern drawl he'd picked up somewhere. He spoke slow and languid, drawing out every word, every sentence. It was creepy as hell.

She noticed the hunting rifles slung over both their backs. The parking lot was eerily silent. And empty. It was almost dark now. Everyone else was still inside, getting held up by the mandatory inspections.

Billy smiled, showing his yellowed crooked teeth, damaged from all the meth he did.

Instinctively, she took a step back, her boots sinking into deep snow.

She wouldn't retreat any further. It took her away from the truck. The truck had belonged to Gramps. She wasn't losing it.

She whipped the slingshot out of her pocket, along with a three-eighth-inch steel pellet, and aimed it at them, drawing back to her right cheek underneath her dominant eye and sighting down the bands. Checking the angle of the fork was second nature.

She and Gramps loved shooting old cans in the backyard for target practice or catching Gran a rabbit or two for stew. It was great for small game—squirrels, rabbits, quail, doves. Not so much for people, but there was no time like the present to give it a go.

"Get lost, losers."

Neither of them moved back. They didn't look scared. If anything, they were amused. She hated them for that.

Tommy patted the hood of the Julius. "Not many cars working these days."

"Touch the truck again and I'll take out an eye, jerkface."

Tommy didn't remove his gloved hand. He stroked the hood, smiled at her. "We had some beautiful snowmobiles. They were stolen from us. We're just in need of a ride, darlin'. That's all."

"Not my problem."

"Oh, I think it is." Billy took a quick, darting step forward. In an instant, he was less than five feet away.

Quinn's heart jolted. She stretched the bands back as far as they would go, tightened her position, and aimed right for his lazy eye. "Get back, or I'll—"

His hands balled into fists. He leered at her. "Or you'll what?"

"Hey! What's going on here?"

Everyone started. They'd all been so intent on each other, on their tense exchange, that they hadn't heard Noah Sheridan's approach over the gusting wind.

Quinn didn't move.

Billy's shoulders relaxed, his fists loosening. A dark smile played across his thin lips. He turned to face Noah, but his lazy eye remained fixed on Quinn.

"Nothin' much, officer," Tommy drawled. He patted the hood again. "Just admiring this fine machine."

Noah's shoulders were tense. His right hand hovered just above the holster attached to the service belt at his hip. A warning. "It's not yours. And you'd best be on your way."

Billy Carter glanced across the parking lot to where Noah's snowmobile idled, headlights catching swirling snowflakes. Milo straddled the front seat wearing an oversized helmet, waiting obediently.

Billy's gaze moved slowly back to Noah, his lips thin as a knife blade. His lazy eye made it look like he was glaring at Noah and Quinn at the same time. "Nice Kawasaki. It looks particularly . . . familiar."

"I'm sure it does," Noah said evenly. "We needed to requisition a few machines to help us protect the town and keep the peace. They will be returned to you as soon as we find some additional resources."

Billy watched them with pure hatred and disgust glimmering in his black eyes.

"Where I come from, we call that stealing," Tommy said easily, his voice light but his eyes as hard as Billy's.

"I don't really care what you call it. I'm going to need you boys to leave this girl alone and move along. And if I hear that you've bothered her again, I'll have no choice but to arrest you."

Billy smirked. "We hear you loud and clear. *Officer*."

Noah didn't relax. His hand hovered just above his service pistol. "I said to leave."

The front doors of Friendly's opened and two families hurried out into the parking lot, ducking their faces against the wind, carrying only a few flimsy grocery bags each.

Tommy elbowed Billy. "Come on. Let's get outta here already. I need a nice warm body to keep me company." His gaze slid over Quinn. "You got any suggestions?"

"Tell your mom we said hi," Billy said, still smirking.

Quinn tightened her grip on the slingshot handle, anger firing through her. "Screw you!"

Tommy just laughed.

They turned and strode away, headed for Main Street, still laughing. They faded into the swirling darkness and disappeared.

She shoved the slingshot in her pocket and whirled on Noah, still shaking both from adrenaline and fury. She should've shot one of them. Maybe both. They sure as hell deserved it. "I can handle myself. Thank you very much."

"It wasn't a question of you, Quinn," Noah said quietly, lowering his voice as Milo scampered toward them through the snow. "Those two men are extremely dangerous. Criminals with long arrest records who've both done prison time."

"I know," she said, sharp and defiant. "I wasn't born yesterday. I know exactly who they are."

Noah nodded, understanding dawning. "Through your mom."

"I don't want to talk about her."

"That was awesome, Quinn!" Milo said excitedly. He mimed her slingshot. "You were like, 'don't mess with me!' BAM!"

Quinn couldn't keep a small grin off her face. "It would've been more awesome if I'd actually let loose and hit one of them."

"It'd probably go right through an eyeball into the brain, right?"

"A good shot with enough velocity? Sure it could—"

"Okay, well, let's not advocate for violence." Noah retrieved her shopping bags—already covered with a thin film of snow—and handed them to her. "Right?"

She took them grudgingly. Yeah, she had a slingshot. She could do some damage. But she wasn't stupid enough to think she could singlehandedly take on Billy and Tommy Carter if they really wanted to hurt her. "Whatever."

Noah the Cop might have just saved her from something awful.

Now, she owed him. She hated owing people things.

"Milo, you were supposed to stay with the snowmobile," Noah said. "It wasn't safe for you."

"I'm fine, Dad!" Milo huffed. "I'm not a baby. I'm eight whole years."

"Eight whole years?" Quinn winked at him. Milo grinned back.

"We'll talk about this later." Noah rolled his eyes and turned back to Quinn. "You okay at home? Staying warm enough?"

"I'm staying with my Gran. We're fine."

"It's freezing at our house!" Milo said, his teeth chattering. "Colder than an ice cube."

"That's not entirely true," Noah said. "We've got firewood for the fireplace."

Milo rolled his eyes. "That's just one place. I can't even play in my bedroom. Our beds are in the living room now."

She felt herself softening. "Do you have a kerosene or propane heater?"

Noah shook his head. "The hardware store is already sold out."

"Do you have a terracotta flowerpot and small candles, like tea lights? Steel washers and bolts? You can make a small heater with that."

"We've got that stuff at home. Can you tell me how to make one?"

She quickly explained. "So some people claim it can heat a small room, but it can't. It'll only give off as much heat as the candle gives off, but with the flowerpot, you catch the heat instead of letting it float up to the ceiling, where it won't do you any good. Basically, you use a set of nesting clay pots, separated by and attached to a central steel bolt, with steel washers spaced in between the pots to form a heat exchanger thing.

"Then you flip it over and support it on a few bricks to position the center bolt directly above a small candle or three. The flame heats the steel bolt directly, causing it to heat the clay pots and trap the hot air rising from the flame. The clay radiates heat. You'll have to huddle close to it or use it in a small space, though. You can also use a couple of Sterno cans and a larger pot to get even more heat."

He looked impressed. "That's genius. I should get this information to the townspeople. It could save lives."

She touched her eyebrow piercing absently. Gran didn't like visitors unannounced. But this was a special case. And it would make her and Noah even.

"Oh, fine." She sighed heavily, a cloud of crystalized air misting her face. "Come to my Gran's house. She taught me everything I know. She can teach you exactly how to make one and even more survival stuff. Maybe even feed you supper. But only if she likes you."

"What if she doesn't like you?" Milo asked in complete seriousness.

Quinn wriggled her half-frozen eyebrows at him. "Then she chops you up, puts you in a pot, and makes *you* for supper."

Noah frowned. "Please don't scare him."

But Milo didn't look scared at all. He grinned. "Mmm . . . tasty."

26

QUINN
DAY THREE

"We can just go in already," Quinn said when Noah paused on the front porch.

It was completely dark out. Without the ambient light of street and security lights or the warm yellow squares of their neighbors' windows, the night was pitch black.

The wind moaned around the corners of the house. Tree branches creaked and snow blew from all directions, whipping into her face.

"I'm a stranger," Noah said. "It's polite to knock."

"Oh! Can I do the knocking?" Milo asked, way too excited for such a small thing. Kids were so weird. "Please?"

"Hurry up already, Small Fry. I'm freezing my tail off out here."

The screen door of Gran's house sagged. The whole house was old and creaking, slowly falling into disrepair as Gramps and Gran got too old to properly care for it. It was the land that made it valuable—five rolling wooded acres abutting the river at the end of Tanglewood Drive, a long country road.

Quinn scowled. She hated feeling embarrassed in front of

anyone. She loved this house, even if it was looking a little faded and worse for wear.

Gran finally shuffled to the front door. She pushed open the front door and looked them over with a frown. "Took you long enough."

Her words were sharp, but Gran's face was blotchy. Her eyes were wet and red-rimmed. She'd been crying again, Quinn realized with a jolt. She'd just waited until Quinn had left the house.

"Everything you requested." Quinn handed Gran the grocery bags, and then pushed her way inside. It was too damn cold to remain on the porch a second longer. Noah and Milo quickly followed.

Quinn stomped her boots on the welcome mat and swallowed the rising lump in her throat. She resisted the urge to wrap Gran in a hug. She knew Gran would be embarrassed, especially in front of guests.

She gestured at her new friends instead. "Noah the Cop and Small Fry, this is my Gran, otherwise known as Molly. Gran, this is Noah the Cop and Small Fry."

Noah stuck out his hand. "It's nice to officially meet you, Molly. Your granddaughter is something special."

Quinn rolled her eyes. "Please."

So did Gran. "I already know that. You trying to butter us up, officer? You're gonna have to do better than that."

Noah looked a little taken aback for a moment, but then he snorted. "Yeah, I guess I will. I can see I'll have to stay on my toes with you two."

"See that you do." Gran wiped her face quickly before turning back to them. "Something we can help you with?"

"Yes, I hope so." Suddenly looking nervous, Noah glanced from Gran to Quinn and back again. "Quinn mentioned you had a lot of old-school knowledge that could help the town."

Gran's face brightened. Humility had never been one of her

strong suits. Quinn knew she loved helping and being useful, even if she'd never admit it. "Sure do. I grew up on a farm not twenty miles from here. We did everything ourselves. Grew our own crops. Made our own milk and butter. Butchered our own deer and cattle."

"Walked six miles to school every day, uphill both ways," Quinn muttered.

"Were you there?" Gran snapped. "Who says I didn't?"

Gran had worked the land her whole life, and she was proud of it. She still cooked everything from scratch on the woodstove, had a winter garden in her barn, raised chickens, and even chopped her own wood until the last two years after her stroke.

Quinn had occasionally taken over that job to give Gramps a break.

A pang struck her chest. Now it would be her job permanently.

Noah smiled. "I guess we're all going old-school for a while. Might as well get used to it."

Surprisingly, Gran smiled back at him. "Shoot, I guess I've got a few minutes before I have to get back to canning. People need to know how to take care of themselves. Come on in and ask your questions."

They removed their snow-covered boots and coats at the door and traipsed into the warm kitchen. Cats were everywhere.

One was curled up in Quinn's usual kitchen chair. Two more darted over, tails high, already preparing to rub all over their new visitors. A fourth one watched them from his perch on top of the cat tree in the corner, tail twitching.

It seemed like twenty but was only five.

"Oh!" Milo squealed, his dark eyes lighting up. "Can I pet them?"

"This is Odin, Loki, Thor, Valkyrie, and Hel, ruler of the underworld." Quinn pointed them out. "That orange one is Thor.

He's whiny and always begs to be petted. The fat lazy one who loves to climb on people's laps is Odin. He spends his life sleeping. The tabby with the cunning face is Loki—he's sneaky, mischievous, and always getting into trouble. That sleek black one over there is Valkyrie. She's the hunter who brings us mice and rats and leaves them on the back patio."

Quinn bent and petted the last one as he rubbed against her leg with a welcoming meow. "And this white fluffy hellion is Hel, ruler of the underworld. He's too stuck up for anyone and hates to be held. But sometimes, you can lure him out of hiding with a treat."

Milo plopped down on the rug on the floor and was instantly covered in furry creatures. They arched their backs and pressed against him, several tails in his face all at once. Loud, contented purring filled the room.

"They like you," Gran said kindly, a strange look on her face as she watched him, that deep sadness back in her eyes. "They don't like just anyone."

Milo's grin widened.

The table was spread with old newspaper and Gran's canning supplies—mason jars, lids, a funnel, tongs, and stirring sticks. A large stainless-steel pot and canning rack sat on top of the wood-stove. The room smelled of firewood, candle wax, and delicious, home-cooked meals.

Quinn moved aside a large wicker basket full of zucchinis and took a seat at the table. Gran was canning all the fresh food they'd gotten from the store and from her winter garden—carrots, onions, potatoes, and winter squash.

Fat, fluffy Odin leapt into her lap and spun in a circle, his claws kneading Quinn's thighs.

Gran sat in her customary chair and patted her thigh. Thor disentangled himself from Milo's arms and settled himself in Gran's lap. He'd been particularly attentive to Gran ever since

Gramps hadn't come home. Almost as if he knew something had happened, and Gran needed extra love.

Gran scratched him absently behind the ears. "How's the world holding up out there?"

Noah pulled a pencil and a small notepad out of his pocket as he sat down beside Quinn. "Friendly's is no longer so friendly. And they're completely out of bottled water already. Some people were smart and filled up their bathtubs and sinks, but that's running out, too."

"On my way to the store, I saw some people collecting snow," Quinn said. "And a few dragging buckets from the river."

"Snow is fine." Gran clucked her tongue. "If those folks drink dirty or contaminated water, they could get diarrhea, dysentery, cholera, typhoid. Water-related diseases still kill over three million people a year around the world."

"I think we're about to drastically increase those numbers," Quinn said.

"I hope not." Noah glanced down at his notebook. "So we should tell people that if they need to get water from the river, they should boil it first."

Gran shook her head. "It's a waste of precious fuel to boil so much water. All you need is ordinary Clorox bleach. A three-quart bottle of six-percent sodium hypochlorite costs about two dollars, and will treat nearly forty-eight hundred gallons of clear water. A drop per pint is the recipe."

Noah scribbled in his notebook. "Okay, we'll add this to the list to disseminate to the neighborhoods."

"Remember, that's clear water. For cloudy river water, tell 'em to filter it through a clean cloth like a T-shirt first and double the bleach. Then let it sit for an hour or so. But why are they going to the river? Sixty to seventy percent of the homes in Fall Creek are on well water, aren't they?"

"Most people don't have hand or solar pumps, so they can't access that water."

Gran shook her head. "Bullocks! You sure as heck can."

"We have a hand pump," Quinn said. "I know because I pumped five gallons this morning in negative five-degree temperatures. It was practically child abuse."

"Which you can now use to wash the dishes for that snark," Gran snapped, but not harshly.

This was a good thing—Gran was acting half-normal again. Quinn would gladly do dishes for the rest of her life if it brought Gran back to herself.

"As I was saying." Gran cleared her throat and turned back to Noah. "They can build an Amish bucket—a manual, hand-operated well bucket—out of four-foot-long by four- or five-inch wide PVC piping with a check valve cap on the bottom. Use a rope to drop it down and haul it up, and it'll bring up about a gallon each haul."

Noah bent his head and scribbled it down. Milo put down all three cats he was holding simultaneously, rose to his feet, and leaned over Noah's shoulder. "Your handwriting looks like scribbles, Dad."

"Yeah, I know. I grew up typing on the computer like everybody else. Guess you'll have to teach me cursive all over again."

"Sheesh. I hope not." Quinn made a face. The only good thing about this whole EMP fiasco was the no school part. Of course, they were still technically on break and didn't have school anyway, but Quinn couldn't imagine classes starting up again on Monday.

No lights. No computers. And all her textbooks were online anyway. Who knew what was happening with the internet?

"Great ideas." Noah chewed on his pencil. "What about food? We've got the emergency shelter at the high school and the pantry at Crossway church. Friendly's Grocery will reopen once they get things under control. But if FEMA doesn't show up soon, we'll run out within a few weeks. Should we start hunting and trapping?"

"I can hunt," Quinn said. Both Gramps and Gran had taught her how.

"Really?" Milo asked.

"It's true," Gran said proudly. "Quinn can hold her own. We made sure she knew how. But not everyone can. Still, I suppose people willing to learn can be taught. It's those folks who have never shot a rifle and aren't willing to do so that'll be in the worst shape."

"I have a Remington 700 in .30-06, but not nearly enough ammo," Noah said. "I admit I haven't gone deer hunting in a few years. Julian's always bugging me to go with him, but . . ."

"Well, I'd say it's damn time to get started, wouldn't you?" Gran reached out a gnarled hand and patted Noah's belly. "Though some people seem to have ample stores to last at least a few weeks, at any rate."

Quinn snorted.

Noah blushed but recovered quickly. He gave a good-natured shrug. "Guilty as charged."

Milo snickered. Gran snickered right along with him. Quinn smiled. And then she laughed out loud for the first time since Gramps had died right next to her.

It felt good. It felt right, like here in this warm, cozy room was where all the good memories of Gramps lived, not the bad scary ones. And for this one moment in time, the ache in her heart lessened a little bit.

27

QUINN
DAY FOUR

Quinn hadn't expected Octavia to return so quickly. She shouldn't have been surprised at anything her mother did—and yet, she still was.

This time, Octavia brought Ray Shultz with her.

Quinn was in the kitchen stirring the stew she and Gran were making together. She'd hunted a rabbit with her .22 that morning. The rabbit provided the protein, and Gran was harvesting some kale, garlic, and onions from her garden for added flavor.

The fire crackled and popped in the woodstove. Steam from the almost boiling liquid heated Quinn's face. Outside, it was freezing, but inside was warm and toasty.

Octavia barged in unannounced, demanding food. Quinn refused. She wasn't allowing Octavia to steal from Gran right under her nose again. No way.

"Octavia!" The front door slammed open. "What the hell's taking so long? Octavia!"

Ray Shultz stalked into the kitchen, his boots trailing clots of dirty snow and mud across the floor. He didn't bother to wipe them off.

"Where the hell's the food? We gotta get to Tommy's. He's got the H, but we've gotta bring him something, or he'll keep all the good crap for himself. Nickel says it's 'bout dried up. No saying when or where we can get more after this."

Odin and Thor, who'd been curled comfortably in front of the woodstove, leapt to their feet and raced toward the living room, fur raised and ears laid back. Loki stayed under the table, hissing.

They could sense the threat that had entered the house and wanted to get as far away as possible. So did Quinn.

Odin and Thor darted around Ray's legs to reach the safety of the living room. With a savage grin, Ray kicked at them.

Thor was fast enough to escape unscathed, but Odin was fat and slow. Ray's boot connected with his fluffy backside. Odin let out a yowl, scrambled up, and fled after Thor. Under the table, Loki hissed louder.

"Leave them alone!" Quinn said.

"Just having a little fun." Ray was a thin, wiry white guy in his early forties, his salt-and-pepper hair already balding. He wasn't big and bulky, but he was mean and vicious, and that counted more.

It was his eyes that gave him away—deep-set, bulging like a frog's, and shiny with whatever high he was riding and barely contained malevolence.

Anger slashed through Quinn. A raw, helpless fury she could barely control. She hated him. Hated his gross, bulgy frog-eyes, his thick blackened fingers, and the stink of grease that hung on him.

He was occasionally a mechanic, but mostly just a junkie, always drinking and playing card games with his high school dropout cousins and friends in Octavia's filthy trailer at the Fall Creek Estates mobile home park across the bridge.

"No one said you could come in," Quinn snapped. "Get lost."

Ray whirled on her, amusement quickly flashing to anger.

"Get the hell out."

Ray jabbed his finger at her chest. "Don't you dare come home after this, you little slut."

"I wouldn't set foot in that hovel if you paid me." She couldn't help herself. She never could. The ugly words were out even before she thought them. "Oh, that's right. You can't pay me, since you're too stupid and lazy to get a real job."

Ray surged forward and grabbed a hunk of her hair, dragging her away from the stove. Her scalp stung. It would've been better to hold still and endure it, but Quinn had never been the weak, submissive type.

That was her mother.

She spun, wrenching away while simultaneously punching at Ray's chest and face. Her fingers raked the skin of his right cheek. Her scalp burned as several strands of blue hair ripped away.

"Stop it!" Octavia shrieked. "Ray! Leave her alone!"

But her mother didn't do anything, only cowered against the fridge like she always did. Behind the table, Loki hissed and yowled.

Ray shoved Quinn hard against the wall. Her head bounced dully and knocked the calendar to the linoleum floor.

Pain spiked through her skull. Fear blossomed in her chest.

She should shut the hell up. She shouldn't antagonize him further. But it wasn't in her to submit to anyone, let alone assholes.

Her scalp smarting, hot tears in her eyes, Quinn straightened, forced herself to meet his gaze. Gave him her best condescending smile.

Ray went for Quinn again, his hand raised to backhand her. Scorn and hatred radiated off him. His rage was a palpable thing, a menacing threat that filled the entire kitchen.

Heart slamming against her ribs, Quinn ducked, scrabbled sideways, and reached the counter. She pressed her back against the drawer with the kitchen knives.

Her gaze darted frantically around the room. Her slingshot

was tucked in her coat pocket hanging on the back of the dining room chair on the opposite side of the kitchen. Her .22 rifle was loaded but stored in the coat closet in the living room. Gran's Mossberg 500 was leaning against her nightstand in her bedroom.

The stew was boiling on the woodstove. Quinn could throw the boiling liquid at him if it came to that. But the pot was heavy and unwieldy, and she might miss.

She jerked open the drawer and pulled out a butcher knife. "I'm warning you."

He leered at her. "Just what do you think you're going to do with that?"

She kept it low, didn't point it at him. Didn't want to poke the bear, just let him know she wasn't his prey. Wouldn't be prey. "Touch me or Gran and I'll gut you. Don't think I won't."

"Ray!" Octavia shifted, nervous and twitchy. "Leave her alone. Let's just get something to eat and go. Come on."

Ray's gaze stayed on her, his deep-set eyes slitted and gleaming with malice. He touched the scratch on his cheek Quinn had left with her aqua-painted nails. A smear of blood streaked his fingers.

He spat on the floor. "Not until I teach this little slut a lesson."

Quinn adjusted her grip on the knife handle. Her palms were damp with sweat. "No, you sure as hell won't."

The back door swung open. Cold air blasted the kitchen.

Gran stood in her winter work gear, the Mossberg 500 pump-action shotgun stock pressed against her shoulder, one hand on the slide, the other on the grip, finger on the trigger. She aimed the barrel at Ray's chest. "Don't you dare touch my granddaughter!"

28

QUINN
DAY FOUR

S tartled, Ray faltered.

"Get away from her!" Gran ordered.

"I'll do whatever the hell I want, you old hag."

"Not in my house, you won't. Get out. The both of you. I can't stand to look at your pathetic faces."

"Mom—" Octavia whined. "You don't gotta be like this. We just wanted—"

"That's the problem, isn't it? You just want and want and are never satisfied, not even when you suck everyone around you dry. Get out of my house so I can mourn my husband in peace."

"You don't get to tell me what to do, woman!" Ray flexed his fists, his face purpling. His hand moved toward the Smith & Wesson tucked into his belt. "You won't really—"

CH-CHUNK! The distinctive sound of the pump-action shotgun being racked split the air. Gran took two shuffling steps into the center of the kitchen. "I will."

Ray's expression froze in surprise. His eyes bulged.

"You are going to leave," she ordered. "And if you come back, you won't particularly like how you'll be greeted."

Something changed in his expression. A hint of wariness. Of hesitation. Like maybe he was starting to realize that Gran was fully capable of shooting him.

Hands raised, he took a step back, away from Quinn, toward the doorway into the living room. "You don't want to do that."

"Don't tell me what I want to do."

Octavia pulled anxiously on Ray's arm. "Come on. You said we had to get to Tommy's. We gotta go before it's gone."

Ray smiled, revealing his crooked, yellowed teeth. As charming as a crocodile. "No need to be inhospitable. To your own family, too."

"Get out of this house, Ray Shultz," Gran said. "Right now."

"We've got better things to do, trust me." Ray glared at Quinn. "And you. I mean what I said. Don't you even think about coming crawling home to beg for mercy. It won't be mercy I give you. I can promise you that."

Octavia just stared at the floor, said nothing at all.

Quinn opened her mouth to snap something ugly and sarcastic but managed to swallow it back. For once, she was smart enough not to egg him on.

He was finally leaving.

Quinn and Gran watched in tense silence as Ray turned and stomped out of the house. Octavia scurried after him, her head down like a shamed puppy.

A moment later, the Fourtrax 300 coughed and hacked to life. Octavia and Ray roared out of the driveway. Gran didn't lower the Mossberg until the sound of the ATV had faded.

Quinn set the knife on the counter with a clatter. Her hands were trembling. She sagged against the cabinets, breathing hard.

She wanted to ask Gran if she was okay. She felt far from okay herself. They were both shaken. She could see it written all over Gran's face.

There were some things too hard to talk about. She chose the safety of sarcasm instead. "Well, that was a treat. Ray can shove his mercy right up his rancid arse."

Gran flashed her a weary smile, a hint of her old vitality returning. "I couldn't have said it better myself, my dear."

Quinn tried to return the smile, but it froze on her face. "They won't stop. They're going to cause trouble."

Gran didn't say anything for a long moment. She leaned the shotgun against one of the kitchen chairs, closed the kitchen door she'd left open when she barged in, and retrieved her cane.

The cats reappeared from their hiding spots, meowing plaintively. Valkyrie and Odin rubbed against Quinn's shins, while Thor limped to Gran, begging to be picked up.

Loki darted out from beneath the table and jumped onto a kitchen chair. Even Hel made an appearance, peeking out from behind the fridge, his white tail twitching indignantly.

Gran scratched Loki behind the ears. When she spoke, her voice was rough. "Octavia's caused trouble since the moment she left the womb. Ain't nothing new under the sun, as your grandfather always loved to say."

"I thought the shotgun was in your bedroom."

Gran shrugged. "I decided I should keep it with me."

"You should. Ray and Octavia aren't the only ones hungry. We need to stay armed at all times."

"Yes, we do."

"We should hide the rest of the supplies."

"Most of them already are."

Quinn shot her a look. "What?"

"I've got a few things squirreled away."

"Like what?"

Gran just clucked her tongue. "That's on a need-to-know basis."

Quinn rolled her eyes. "But you know I'm right."

Gran nodded, abruptly serious. "If it's not Ray, it'll be someone else. We need to be very, very careful. They get hungry enough, even our neighbors will turn on us."

Gran leaned down and picked up Odin, checking him for injuries. He purred in contentment. Gran sighed. "Take the afternoon, Quinn. You have those new paint cans Gramps got for you for Christmas. Use them."

Quinn turned back toward the stove. The soup was bubbling. "But the stew—"

"I'll finish it. I wanted to try some new herbs to spice up rabbit meat anyway."

"The firewood—"

"Will still be here tomorrow."

Quinn couldn't argue. Her emotions were a tangled mess of fury and heartbreak. She wanted nothing more than to retreat to the bedroom Gran and Gramps had given her to paint some of the hurt away.

She fiddled hesitantly with her eyebrow piercing. She wanted to say more but didn't know how. She and Gran had never been great about talking about their feelings. Gramps had been the one to do it for them. Now they'd have to figure it out themselves.

A sudden surge of emotion thickened her throat. "I . . . I love you, Gran."

"Don't get all soft on me." Gran made a face, a network of wrinkles spanning the skin around her eyes like a spider's web, but her eyes were wet.

She leaned in and squeezed Quinn's shoulder affectionately before letting go. "Get out of here before I paddle you, girl. This cane ain't just for walking, you know."

Quinn got the .22 out of the closet and kept it with her. She'd sleep with it from now on. She touched her still smarting scalp.

She couldn't get Ray's face out of her mind. His eyes. How they'd gleamed with hostility, a thirst for mayhem and violence.

There was something malignant inside him. A dark, poisonous cancer. He wasn't hungry enough yet. Wasn't desperate or enraged enough. But he would get there.

Maybe tomorrow or next week, but it was coming. Quinn was sure of it.

29

NOAH
DAY FOUR

D espite his promise to Rosamond Sinclair, it was two days before Noah managed to visit Atticus Bishop at Crossway Church on Main Street.

He'd spent the morning helping volunteers move snow-covered vehicles that had stalled in the middle of the street and needed to be towed to the shoulder or moved to less-used side streets to keep Main Street clear and plowed.

The ancient plow still worked after Tina Gundy, the mechanic's daughter, tinkered with it a bit. Thank goodness for small blessings. Fall Creek's tight budget had kept them from upgrading to a newer machine for over a decade.

The gray stone church with its towering steeple and stained-glass windows perched on the corner of Main and Riverside Road, the Asian Bistro on one side and Fuller's Hardware store on the other. The Fireside Tavern was located right across the street.

Drunk patrons often stumbled to Bishop's doorstep for late-night confessions. Bishop always accepted them with open arms.

The Crossway food pantry was served out of a side door on the left side of the church. Well over a hundred people stood in a line three-to-four people across, snaking across the empty parking lot all the way into the street.

Noah's first instinct was to steer people out of the road, but he overrode it. The streets were empty. Vehicles and snowmobiles could be heard from a mile away in this eerie stillness.

People in line turned to stare at him as he roared up in the clunky requisitioned Kawasaki. The old engine coughed, spewing choking clouds of fumes.

Nestled between his arms, Milo shivered on the seat in front of him. Noah still didn't have a sitter, so Milo had come to work with him for the third day in a row.

He was hoping to talk to Bishop about that problem. Bishop's wife, Daphne, was a vet tech, but she currently stayed home with their two little girls.

Maybe she could watch Milo too, just until things got settled.

Noah removed his helmet and hopped off the Kawasaki, stuck the key fob in his pocket, and helped Milo down. The boy sunk well past his knees into the thick snow.

Milo tugged off the oversized helmet Noah had found for him. His black curls flew around his face in a mass of static. His cheeks were flushed, dark eyes bright.

"You okay, buddy?"

Milo wrinkled his nose. "Dad. I'm fine. You don't have to ask so much."

"Sorry. Just making sure."

The day was heavily overcast, the gunmetal sky promising even more snow. The temps were barely above freezing. Crystal-ized clouds misted his face with every breath.

It was too cold to be outside for more than a few minutes without arctic-quality gear, and yet the crowd looked like they'd been stuck outside waiting for a while.

Families huddled together. Fathers held toddlers in their

arms. Older couples wrapped their arms around each other's waists, pressing close for any bit of extra warmth they could get.

Everyone's coats were zipped to their throats, their scarves and neck gaiters wrapped around their necks and the lower half of their faces.

They stamped their feet and shivered and tightened their hold on their baskets, shopping bags, and cardboard boxes—all empty. As empty as their pantries and fridges, as empty as their growling bellies and the bellies of their children.

Only four days after the event, people were already running out of food. Just like Molly Dương, Quinn's grandmother, had said they would.

After his shopping trip at Friendly's, Noah had a couple of weeks of food left. He'd used the rest of the cash to buy as much firewood as he could from Mike Duncan. With the fire burning all night, he was going through it fast.

Molly had helped him rig an Amish bucket for the well on his property. A bucket of water next to the toilet took care of their sanitation needs. Thank goodness for the septic system.

It wasn't fun, easy, or comfortable, but they were making do so far.

Noah bent down to Milo. "Walk right behind me in my foot-prints. Stay close."

"I can do it."

"Right. I know you can."

"Officer Sheridan!" someone cried. "What's going on?"

"Why can't we buy food at the store?"

"You people are guarding the pharmacy!"

"I can't even get my mother's medication!"

After the near-riot at Friendly's the night before, Rosamond and Chief Briggs had both agreed to close Friendly's, the gas station, and Vinson Pharmacy for a day or two until a guard rotation could be worked out.

"It's for everyone's protection," Noah said calmly. "Once order is restored, we'll open everything to the public again, within reason. We're doing everything we can, I promise."

An old Hispanic man spat on the snow. "Doesn't that snowmobile belong to Billy Carter? I recognize that spidery design on the sides."

Noah recognized him as a part-time teller at Community Trust Bank. Daniel Rodriquez was usually friendly and pleasant, not ornery like this. People were starting to change, and he didn't like it.

He forced a smile he didn't feel. "This snowmobile was donated to law enforcement for a short time so we can do our jobs and make sure you folks get the help you need and stay safe."

"Donated, my ass," the man grumbled.

Noah chose to ignore him. The old man was tired and stressed and hungry, just like everyone else. No reason to get him more upset by engaging in an argument.

Noah's issued overcoat had zippers on the side to access his service weapon. He unzipped it, willing to trade some warmth for speed. Just in case.

Making sure Milo was still close behind him, Noah slogged through the snow along the outer perimeter of the line. His nostrils were raw, the cold hurting his lungs. The tips of his fingers still burned and stung from his bout of frostnip.

"How long's the blackout gonna last?" Maxine Hammond yelled. "I got no food left to feed my kids. No firewood neither. Last night, I thought we might actually freeze to death."

"We're not sure, Mrs. Hammond," Noah said carefully. "But we have plans already in place. The high school is available as an emergency shelter if you need it. Someone should've come around and notified you."

Over the last two days, three officers, five reserve officers, and about thirty volunteers had gone door to door—some on ATVs and snowmobiles, others on skis and snowshoes—passing along the clean water information he'd learned from Molly and checking which homes were occupied and which were empty.

They'd also asked a few questions about resources and supplies. Some citizens were more open to answering them than others. The more resources they had as a community, the more they could help everyone.

"Yeah, so?" Mrs. Hammond shook her head, frowning. "Heard they packed in almost two hundred people last night. Barely fed them soup, let alone a decent dinner. Not enough cots, and most people were stuck sleeping on the gym floor, stuffed together like sardines in a can."

"We're working on that," Noah said. "Please, just be patient a little longer. We're doing the best we can."

Mrs. Hammond turned away with a disdainful snort. "That's not good enough."

More people called out to him. He couldn't answer their questions, not to their satisfaction. He kept walking.

Three people had died in the last two days: a woman sick with kidney failure, a wheelchair-bound man in his eighties, and a three-year-old boy who'd kicked off his blankets in the middle of the night.

The little boy's family didn't have a fireplace, woodstove, or generator. They hadn't come to the shelter, either.

The nightly temperatures were dropping into the negatives, even without wind chill factored in. And with the lake-effect storms from Lake Michigan, there was always wind chill.

Without a means of heat, houses were simply too cold.

Even with a crackling fire, he and Milo slept fully clothed in several pairs of pajamas, thick socks, and sweaters. Last night, he'd built the flowerpot heater as Quinn had suggested.

It provided a surprising amount of warmth. In fact, the pots had gotten too hot to touch with bare hands.

Even with the added heat, he still couldn't sleep. He had tossed and turned all night, constantly worrying about everything —the dangerous cold, the near-riots, the dwindling food, but mostly, Milo's medication.

After visiting Quinn and her grandmother yesterday, he'd stopped by Vinson's pharmacy. Robert Vinson was a slim, precise Caucasian man in his early sixties, his thinning white hair receding sharply from his forehead.

"I checked every single box in the back," the pharmacist had said grimly. "Another shipment was supposed to arrive on the twenty-fourth, but it never came in. And with the holidays and that snowstorm that hit right before Christmas Eve that delayed a lot of deliveries, some of our prescriptions are out or on backorder. I'm sorry, Noah, but I'm all out of hydrocortisone."

Noah had swallowed hard. Because he'd been giving Milo a double dosage for the last few days, he only had a week's supply left. And the one stress dose injection in case of an emergency. That was it. "That can't be right."

Dr. Vinson rubbed his eyes. "Look. Milo can take prednisone as a last resort, but doctors don't want to prescribe it to children because there are long-term side effects, including delayed growth. But in an emergency . . ."

He thrust a small bottle into Noah's hand. It was less than half full. "You're supposed to have an RX for this, but I know that's near impossible right now. I'm sorry. I wish it was more. I've got patients with Hodgkin's lymphoma, Crohn's disease, autoimmune disorders. I'd love to give it all to your boy, but I just can't."

Noah nodded dully. The prednisone would give Milo another two weeks or so.

Then what? The words kept echoing in his mind over and over, haunting him. *Then what?* He didn't have an answer.

"Noah Sheridan!" a booming voice shouted, bringing him sharply back to the present. "I didn't know it would take this much to get you to a church, but I suppose the good Lord does what He must!"

A big burly black man slammed open the side door, side-stepped past a volunteer filling someone's shopping bag with canned beans, and propelled himself at Noah.

He enveloped Noah in a massive bear hug, nearly crushing his ribs.

"Bishop," Noah said, his voice muffled against his friend's chest. "Nice to see you, too."

Atticus Bishop pulled back and peered into his face. "Can't even see you under all that crap. It's freezing out here. Come inside!"

He motioned to Milo and offered a high five. "Hey, Milo. What's up?"

Milo jumped to reach his hand, nearly falling in the snow but grinning wide. "I get to ride a snowmobile now. Dad says I can even drive it! Dad doesn't go fast enough, but I'll definitely go eighty miles an hour, like warp speed."

"Maybe, I said maybe," Noah qualified. "And no, you definitely won't."

"Why does he get to skip the line?" someone shouted.

"We've been waiting two hours!"

"That's not fair!"

"All will be fed," Bishop said to the crowd with a friendly wave. "Don't you worry."

Several people still grumbled. Bishop just grinned and ignored them.

"Patience is a virtue," he said in a lowered voice, winking at Milo, "but somehow, I don't think they'd appreciate a sermon just now."

30

NOAH
DAY FOUR

Noah and Milo followed Bishop inside into a large room. Hundreds of bags, boxes, and cans of food stuffed the floor-to-ceiling metal shelving. Every inch of available space was packed with supplies.

Next to the side door was a half-wall with a window-like opening through which two volunteers were distributing the supplies—a few meals' worth to each person, including kids.

"Wow," Noah said. "I'm officially impressed."

Bishop grinned. "We've got three more rooms even more packed than this."

Noah knew Crossway Church provided the largest food bank in the county, but he hadn't realized just how big. "How did you—?"

Bishop shrugged, but he was beaming with pride. "Don't give me the credit. It's Daphne's passion. She's the one who's worked so hard all these years—rabbiting things away, organizing the volunteers, forcing me to allocate a larger and larger portion of the budget for community needs. She always said the government wouldn't be worth much if anything went wrong for real. Well, you don't need to hear me say it. She's right here."

Daphne didn't turn from her position at the half-window. She stuffed a can each of SpaghettiOs, tuna, green beans, and two boxes of spiral pasta into a Meijer's plastic shopping bag. "Good to see you again, Noah. You too, Milo."

"Hi, Miss Daphne," Milo said.

"And you, Daphne. Keeping Bishop on his toes, I see."

"Always." Daphne handed a full bag across the counter to a retired Middle Eastern couple in their early seventies. "Here you go, Mr. and Mrs. Amari. Make sure to stay warm now. And remember, you're welcome to come to the sanctuary tonight if you need to."

Noah raised his brows. "Another prayer meeting?"

Bishop did that wry grin of his. He was dressed in his usual Hawaiian shirt, worn leather jacket, and jeans. His only acquiescence to the brutal weather was a gray Detroit Lions scarf wrapped around his thick neck.

He always said he didn't need a hat, that his afro kept his head warm enough. Even in high school, he'd often come to school in shorts and a T-shirt in the dead of winter. The man had a different metabolism than the rest of humanity.

They'd been good friends since freshman year, when they both made varsity, along with Julian Sinclair. Julian and Bishop had never liked each other, but they'd tolerated each other for Noah's sake.

Atticus Bishop was built like the "nose tackle" middle lineman that he had been. He'd been a monster on the field, but off it, he was one of the kindest, gentlest men Noah had ever known.

He'd served as a chaplain in the military for several years before returning home to serve his church and community with the same dedication and ceaseless energy he'd applied to football and his country.

"We have that big generator we bought off Craigslist several years ago after that Snowmaggedon storm took out power for five days," Bishop said. "Anyway, Daphne says it'd be a crime to heat an empty church. And you know I can't ever disagree with her."

"That's the truth!" Daphne called back, a grin in her voice. "Don't let him ever tell you otherwise."

Daphne was plump and curvy, with a wide beaming smile, a generous laugh, and warm brown skin that seemed to glow. Like her husband, she radiated a contagious energy and was graced with a natural ability to bring out the best in others.

"That fuel would last you and your family a long time."

"*This* is my family." Bishop gestured at the volunteers gathering the food, then at the line of people outside. "We're opening the sanctuary at sundown each night and letting in anyone who needs a safe, warm place to sleep. We had almost thirty people last night. We've taken in a few families with very young children indefinitely."

"How long until you run out?"

"Three or four weeks, at least. We were smart—Daphne was, anyway—and we stored diesel as well. Thank goodness the generator is old. I heard some of the newer models aren't working, either."

"They aren't. All the newer model generators have computer chips in them. They're just as fried as everything else. The Myers' and Rick Reynold's solar panels won't work, either. I guess because they were connected to the grid when it went down." Noah wiped melting snow from his forehead. "Most of Winter Haven still has solar power, though."

"Good for them," Bishop said, and sounded like he meant it, unlike the rest of the town. "Have you heard any other news? Like what happened and who did this to us?"

"No news yet," Noah said. "Tina Gundy tinkered with Dave's ham radio and got it working yesterday. The government's not revealing anything at this point. It's mostly rumors and hearsay. Most people on the radio seem to agree that it was an EMP attack, and it's affected most of the country.

"We did find out that the National Guard is guarding the state borders. They're working to clear the roads and re-establish supply lines. They've set up checkpoints along major highway arteries into and out of the bigger cities."

"Well, that's something, at least. What about FEMA? The governor?"

Chief Briggs had given them the report that morning. "We made contact with the governor's office. But we couldn't establish radio contact, we had to send our guys there physically. FEMA is working to distribute aid, but logistics are difficult. They're focusing on the dense population centers first, then making their way out to the rural towns and villages. The governor wouldn't tell us how long it will be before aid arrives. I doubt he even knows.

"The governor said there are reports of muggings and hijackings along all the major highways. And lots of looting, muggings, and gang violence in the cities. Our officers were ambushed on the way back along I-94. They were held at gunpoint while their weapons and snowmobiles were taken. That's why it took so long for them to return."

"Thank God they're okay," Bishop said soberly. "How are things here in town? Did you finish the census?"

Noah raised his eyebrows.

Bishop waved his hand. "People talk. It's all I've heard about the last few days."

"We just want to know who's here so we can check up on them and make sure everyone is doing okay." He hesitated. "Rosamond thinks that if we consolidate some of our resources, we can help more people."

"Huh," Bishop said, his voice not betraying his feelings on the matter.

Milo tugged on Noah's coat. "Dad, what about Juniper and Chloe?"

Noah glanced at Daphne. "I meant to ask you if you'd be willing to watch Milo during the day when I'm on duty. I know it's a lot to ask, but—"

Daphne didn't hesitate. "Of course! The girls will be thrilled."

"I have a fanny pack of salty snacks, Pedialyte, and Milo's medication."

"We have some more electrolyte drinks here, too," Daphne said. "I'll dig them out for you."

Noah smiled gratefully. "You don't know how much that means to me."

"I'll take you to the girls." Bishop grinned down at Milo. "You've been very patient, young man. Come on."

Noah and Milo followed him down a narrow hallway into a second room where a handful of volunteers in coats and boots were sorting supplies on tables. Three battery-operated lanterns spread across the room provided lighting.

They were using the generator for heat only, with the thermostat set to the mid-sixties. The single window was blocked off by a blanket secured on all sides with duct tape to keep the warm air in and the cold out.

"The girls are here somewhere . . . They're counting and separating canned veggies and fruits. Exciting, I know. But I'm pretty sure they're also building castles out of soup cans over there in the corner when they think no one is looking."

A little girl of about six jumped up from behind a three-foot-tall wall of green beans, corn, and olive cans. Chloe had her mother's medium-brown skin tone and wide smile. The plastic butterfly clips in her braids clacked as she did a goofy little dance.

"Milo!" she shouted gleefully.

Bishop's nine-year-old daughter, Juniper, poked her head around the corner of one of the shelves. She was the tomboy with dirt always under her nails, dressed in jean overalls beneath a blue-striped jacket, her wiry black hair tugged into two buns.

"Come play!" Juniper glanced at her father. "I mean, work really hard with no breaks!"

Bishop and Noah chuckled. Bishop shoved his hand in his jacket pocket and pulled out an opened bag of marshmallows. He tossed them at the girls, and they shrieked with laughter and ducked behind the wall of cans.

Milo looked questioningly up at Noah, his dark eyes beseeching. "Can I?"

Noah squatted in front of him. "You feel good?"

"Dad." Milo wrinkled his nose. "I feel great!"

"Then go for it, buddy."

Juniper and Chloe were both sweet, energetic little girls, full of bubbling laughter and squeals of delight. They pulled solemn, serious Milo into their orbit and danced and chattered at him until he, too, was smiling and giggling.

Warmth filled Noah's heart. With a pang, he thought of their cold, silent, too-empty house. It had been empty and silent long before the grid went down.

Milo needed more of this. More chances to just be a kid without the weight of their combined grief always weighing on his small shoulders.

Noah and Bishop left the kids to play happily and retreated down a series of hallways, through the foyer, and entered the sanctuary.

It was large but simply furnished, with two rows of wooden pews and a wide center aisle leading to the dais. The plain wooden pulpit stood in front of a life-sized cross that hung on the back wall.

Solar lanterns scattered about lit the room. Several propane heaters warmed the large space. The stained-glass windows were all covered with blankets nailed or taped to the walls.

A half-dozen families were huddled in the pews. A mother paced with a stroller, lulling her baby to sleep. In the opposite corner, a father stood, a tiny bundled lump on his chest, trying to quiet the infant's scratchy wails.

"How could I turn them away?" Bishop said quietly. "This is our ministry. Our calling. Like Joseph and his storehouses in Egypt, we were preparing for such a time as this."

"Somehow, that doesn't surprise me." Noah cleared his throat, adjusted his coat over his uniform. This was the part of the visit he dreaded. "So . . . you know that Rosamond opened an emergency shelter at the high school. They're asking local folks who have a bit more than others to donate some supplies. Just until FEMA arrives and we can figure out what to do next."

Bishop crossed his huge arms over his chest. He said nothing, just waited.

Noah's face heated. "We were hoping you would be willing to consolidate with us."

"We?"

Noah shifted uncomfortably. "We've got to be in this together, Bishop. All of us."

Bishop remained skeptical. "This is our ministry. Can't say I like the idea of someone else deciding who gets what."

Noah sighed. This was exactly what he'd worried about. Bishop had always been a stubborn, do-it-himself kind of guy. He liked to run things his way.

So did Rosamond.

"What does it matter who gives as long as the people don't starve or freeze to death?"

Bishop laid his dark, steady gaze on Noah. "I could ask the same of her."

Noah opened his mouth, said nothing. He had no answer to that. Not a good one anyway.

"It's simple." Bishop set his jaw. "Let the superintendent do her thing, and we'll do ours."

Noah said, "I hope it's that simple."

He wasn't sure why, but a feeling of unease niggled deep in his gut.

Nothing seemed simple anymore.

31

QUINN
DAY FIVE

Quinn stared in dismay at the red four-wheeler parked at the side of the drive leading to the Crossway Church. Apprehension torqued through her.

Ray and Octavia were here. After she and Gran had kicked them out of Gran's house yesterday, they must have decided a church was easier pickings.

This was not good. Not at all.

Gran had asked her to bring over a few bags of canned and boxed goods. According to Gran, you had to be careful and not let your neighbors know how much food you had, but that didn't mean you didn't give back to your community.

Giving through the Crossway food pantry allowed them to do good while still keeping their supplies on the down-low.

Quinn parked the Orange Julius right in the middle of the road before the church. Who was going to stop her?

She left the bags on the passenger seat. She was too worried about what Ray and Octavia might do to concern herself with canned peas.

She locked the Julius, pocketed the keys, and hurried toward the building. Quinn had been here before. Gran and Gramps had dragged her to a few services. She didn't exactly do church.

The hard crust of snow crackled beneath her boots. The iron-gray sky hung low and ominous above the trees. The cold air stung her cheeks and ears.

The stink of exhaust still hung in the air. They must have just arrived.

A long, ragged line of about a hundred people spilled across the snow-covered parking lot. Families with kids, older couples, single folks all holding empty shopping bags or cardboard boxes waiting to be filled.

Ahead of her, she glimpsed Octavia's tangle of dark hair and dirty yellow parka. Ray stalked beside her. They were elbowing through the crowd to get to the front of the line.

"Hey! You need to wait in line like everyone else!" a man yelled as Octavia pushed past him.

Octavia didn't even bother to turn around. "Piss off. We're hungry."

"And you think we aren't?"

Octavia ignored the man and the rumblings of complaints behind her. She reached the front of the line, reached across the counter, and ripped the bag from the volunteer's hands.

Ray shouldered in next to her and seized his own bag. He loomed over the second volunteer—a middle-aged Korean woman —who visibly shrank back from him.

Quinn picked up her pace. She strode forward to the front of the line. "Octavia! What are you doing?"

Octavia ignored her. She glanced into the bag and sneered. "This is nothing. It'll be gone in less than a day. Where's the rest?"

"Only one bag per person," the Korean lady said. She glanced nervously from Octavia to Ray. "You can come back tomorrow for more—"

"It took almost an hour just to get here!" Octavia lied. "And we're practically out of gas. We're not making this trek tomorrow. Hell, no. Give us more supplies."

"I'm sorry, ma'am—"

"Get out of line!" a man yelled.

"Move on!"

"Come on! Let the next person go!"

"We're not leaving," Ray said through gritted teeth, "until we get what we're due."

He wiped shakily at his mouth with the back of his arm. His hands were trembling. His whole body was twitchy and thrumming. He was strung out on something—meth or crack.

Hot shame flooded Quinn's cheeks. She grabbed her mother's arm. "You're not owed any of this. Just go already!"

Octavia shook her off. "Stay out of this, baby girl!"

"What is the problem here?" The pastor's wife—a plump black woman—moved to the pantry window and put her arm on the volunteer's shoulder, gently pushing her back out of the line of fire. Quinn recognized her but didn't remember her name.

The woman smiled kindly at Ray and Octavia. "We're giving away a little each day to make our supplies last so we can help as many of you for as long as possible. Hopefully, you are also figuring out how to barter what you have to get what you need, hunt for it, or are using your fifty-dollar allotment at the grocery store. This is only a supplement to help you get by. We do expect that you are working on finding a long-term solution."

"You heard her," Quinn said more forcefully. "Go. Now."

Octavia turned and gave Quinn a vicious shove. "I said, leave me alone!"

Quinn lost her balance and fell hard on her butt in the snow. It didn't hurt as much as it mortified her. Her ears rang with the pitying murmurs of the crowd. Her cheeks burned.

She hated their pity. Despised it. Didn't want an ounce of it.

Poor little Quinn, the troubled girl with no father and the horrid junkie for a mother.

Well, screw them. Screw them all.

Quinn pulled herself unceremoniously to her feet, turned to the waiting crowd, and raised both hands. She gave them the finger—times two.

She expected the judgmental expressions and offended glares. The self-righteous tongue-clucks and shaking heads.

She didn't expect the gasps of surprise and shock, the faces contorted in sudden fear. Something was wrong.

Quinn whipped around.

Ray had pulled his pistol. She'd seen it a hundred times before —the Smith and Wesson 9 mm M&P Shield. Ray aimed it at the pastor's wife.

"Nobody move, or I shoot," he growled.

Terrified, the two volunteers shrieked and ducked.

Half the crowd scattered with shouts and screams. The other half froze in place. Shocked into stillness. Mothers and fathers pushed their children behind them, but they were afraid to defy Ray, to run and draw Ray's attention—and a bullet —themselves.

The pastor's wife shrank back, but she didn't duck or cower. "This is wrong," she said shakily. "You don't have to do this."

Fear lanced through Quinn. Her heart stuttered in her chest. She wanted to turn and flee, or duck like everyone else.

She didn't. Her legs felt like cooked spaghetti noodles, but she managed to stand her ground. "Octavia! Stop him!"

Octavia pretended her daughter didn't exist. Her gaunt face hardened. She thrust her free hand at Daphne.

"Give me the damn food!" Octavia snarled. "Or I'll tell him to shoot you myself."

The pastor's wife quickly obliged. She offered three filled

plastic shopping bags. Octavia seized them and squeezed them greedily to her chest.

Ray gestured with the gun. "We're taking what we want. Ain't nobody gonna stop us."

"I'm stopping you," a familiar voice said.

32

QUINN
DAY FIVE

Quinn shifted her gaze slightly to the right, unwilling to take her eyes off Ray and the gun. The side door had opened silently without anyone's notice.

Noah Sheridan stood in the doorway, legs spread, service pistol unholstered and held in a two-handed grip, muzzle pointed at Ray.

She didn't know whether to feel relieved or more terrified. Heart hammering in her chest, Quinn looked from Noah to Ray back to Noah. They were about twenty-five feet apart, Quinn perpendicular to them both.

Ray's crazed, bulging eyes darted wildly. "Don't move! Don't move, or I shoot!"

No one moved a muscle. Tension crackled through the air.

A memory shot through her—her and Noah clinging precariously to the cable thirty feet above the ground. The fear, the cold, the snow and endless darkness. How they'd gotten down together.

Noah was smart and capable. He talked to her like she was a real person, like he valued her opinions, not like most adults—most cops—treated sullen, churlish teenagers.

She was glad he was here.

Noah stepped out of the doorway. He kept his gaze locked on Ray. "Put your weapon down, Ray Shultz. Everyone else, please walk slowly and calmly to the rear of the parking lot and safely around the church building. Ray, I'm going to need you to put that away."

Quinn didn't know if the crowd obeyed. For all she knew, they could've vanished into thin air or spontaneously combusted.

Her pulse pounded in her ears. Her mouth was bone-dry. Tunnel vision had taken over. Her focus had narrowed to a fine point.

She saw only Ray and the gun, and Octavia beside him. And Noah, his own weapon pointed at Ray. And by proxy, her mother.

It didn't matter how much she despised her mother, Quinn didn't want her dead. Her ears filled with a dull buzzing. Time seemed to slow down, everything going blurry and slow motion.

Ray refused to put the weapon down. He backed away deeper into the parking lot, never taking the gun off the pastor's wife. "Nah, I don't think so. Octavia, get the four-by-four. We're leaving."

Octavia shuffled backward at his side, her face taut with a strange mix of fear, glee, greed, and doubt. She clutched the bags to her bony chest. Her lank black hair stuck to her chapped and reddened cheeks. Her eyes were glassy and bloodshot.

"Mom!" Quinn cried, stricken.

Octavia acted like she couldn't even hear her. Maybe she couldn't. Maybe she was too far gone. Or maybe she really didn't care about Quinn at all.

It didn't surprise her. It still hurt, though. Like a sucker punch to the gut.

"Don't move, Octavia," Noah warned. "This isn't going to end the way you think it will."

"It's going to end exactly how I want it to," Ray snarled. "You gonna fire with all these civilians present? You can't do jack squat, *Officer*."

"There's no need for violence," the pastor's wife said, loud and clear and firm. "We've given you everything you need."

Ray snorted. "Isn't that a joke."

"Believe it or not, we want to help you. Why don't you put the weapon away? You don't need it. We can talk."

"Your cop friend is the one with his gun pointed at my head. Why don't you tell him to lower his first!"

"You know I can't do that," Noah said evenly. "But Daphne is right. You haven't gone too far yet. Just put the damn gun away, and we can figure this out. Everyone's scared. Everyone's hungry. We understand you're afraid."

Ray's eyes bulged, crazed with hatred and malice. The scratch she'd left on his cheek was the same shade of pulsing red as the rest of his face. "I ain't afraid of you, *Sheridan*."

Ray shifted toward Daphne. "You think you're better than me, that it? You and your self-righteous bunch of stupid sheep!"

"No!" Daphne said. "We're here to help you—"

Ray lifted the gun.

People screamed. Sound went tinny and distant.

Movement out of the corner of her eye.

It happened in an instant. A huge dark streak rushed in from the side and barreled into Ray. Ray grunted and went down hard, collapsing sideways.

The gun went flying from his hands. It landed in the snow a couple of yards away.

The man tackled Ray, flipped him onto his belly, and kneed him in the back, effectively subduing him in less than a second. He was a big burly black guy with an afro and a leather jacket. The pastor of Crossway Church.

"Get off me!" Ray screamed.

"Can't do that," Bishop said, breathing hard.

Noah rushed forward, holstered his pistol, and pulled out a pair of handcuffs. He knelt beside Ray and wrestled his hands behind his back. "Ray Shultz, you are under arrest. You have the right to remain silent—"

Two yards behind him, Octavia bent for the Smith and Wesson. She picked it up, turning toward Noah and Bishop, a look of pure hatred contorting her face.

"Noah!" Quinn cried.

Noah leapt to his feet and spun around. Swiftly, he pulled a small, strange weapon—a Taser—from his utility belt, aimed it at Octavia, and squeezed the trigger.

Octavia jerked. She twitched and jittered and fell sideways into the snow. She writhed and moaned. The weapon slipped from her fingers.

Noah picked it up and stuffed it into his coat pocket.

Quinn just stared at her mother thrashing in the snow, a sour-sick taste in the back of her throat. Her stomach plummeted with humiliation, a vile, wriggling shame.

She didn't want to believe this was happening. Didn't want to believe her mother would do something so incredibly stupid. And yet, she had. Quinn was the stupid one.

Bishop finished securing Ray with the handcuffs—Ray cursing and hurling insults—while Noah pulled out a second set and slapped them on Octavia's limp wrists.

"You're a dead man, Bishop!" Ray screamed. "You hear me? I'll kill you!"

Bishop ignored him. He stood and brushed the snow off his jeans and Hawaiian shirt. How he wasn't freezing to death, Quinn had no idea.

The volunteers huddled behind the counter, crying and hugging each other. The dispersed crowd slowly returned in clumps of threes and fours, reluctantly, still stunned and cautious. They stared and pointed at Ray, trussed up in the snow like a stuck pig.

He cursed and swore at them, hurling insults and threats, spitting out the dirty snow that kept spilling into his mouth. Octavia just moaned.

Sickened, Quinn turned away from them both.

"You're safe now, folks," Noah said. "The danger is over."

Somehow, that didn't make her feel any better.

33

NOAH
DAY FIVE

His heart still racing, Noah keyed his radio. There were three other officers currently on duty and within range. "I need assistance at Crossway Church on the corner of Main and Riverside Road. Suspects are Ray Shultz and Octavia Riley. Both subdued and handcuffed."

Julian answered. "I'm on Apple Blossom, only three blocks away. I'm coming."

The radio crackled again. "Reynoso here. I'm at the shelter with Hayes. Heading over now."

Noah clipped the radio to his belt. His hands were trembling. The adrenaline dump left him light-headed and shaky.

Sounds slowly returned—hushed voices, a kid whimpering, chickadees and blue jays chattering in the trees across the parking lot. Ray's rabid ranting.

Noah clamped his teeth together to keep them from chattering. It wasn't snowing or windy today, but that didn't make the cold any less brutal. His nose and fingers ached, and he couldn't feel his ears anymore.

He turned to Quinn, Bishop, and Daphne. Quinn stood with

her hands at her sides, looking lost and forlorn. Bishop had his arm around Daphne and held her close. Only after the danger was over had Daphne allowed herself to cry.

"Thank God you're okay," she said to Bishop, her voice quavering. "You could've been shot. You could've been killed."

"But I wasn't," Bishop soothed her. "God chose to keep us safe. We're fine. We're all fine."

"The kids—" Noah said.

"The kids are still inside," Daphne said. "Playing just as happily as they were five minutes ago, when you saw them. Don't worry."

Noah's muscles felt like they were all tied in knots, his shoulders tense. He'd dropped by the church that afternoon just to check on Milo for a minute. It was blind luck that he was even here.

Bishop would call it providence, or a miracle, but Noah wasn't sure where he stood on that kind of stuff. It couldn't hurt to have God on their side. Especially when the pastor was former military.

He'd been on the verge of pulling the trigger when he glimpsed Bishop sneaking across the road. Then it was a matter of distracting Ray long enough to allow Bishop to do his thing. Which he'd done spectacularly.

Bishop ran a hand over his afro, straightened his leather jacket, and flashed a sheepish grin. "I was across the street, inviting the bar's patrons to our Bible study tonight, tempting them with a warm, cooked meal. I heard the shouting and headed right back. Guess my military training kicked in, and I just did what I had to do. Didn't really think about it."

"I thought I was going to have to shoot him in front of dozens of witnesses, including kids."

"Thank God you didn't," Daphne said, shaking her head.

A young mother stepped forward. She hoisted a toddler on her hip, a cute little thing with big blue eyes who held an empty bottle in his chubby hands. "I—I hope I don't sound insensitive, Pastor Bishop . . ." She glanced self-consciously from Bishop to Daphne. "But we don't have anything left at home. Just a can of bean sprouts I was meaning to make in a stir-fry. I'll eat that for supper, but little Jason won't."

Daphne's face softened. She extricated herself from her husband's embrace and gave the worried mother a hug. "Don't worry, honey."

"We're not sending anyone home without food," Bishop said to the crowd. "Get back in line, and we'll keep going."

The growl of snowmobile engines split the air as Julian and Reynoso drove up, their department-issued Remington 870 shotguns slung over their shoulders. Daniel Hayes, one of the part-time officers, followed them in a white 1977 Ford F250 outfitted with snow tires and "Police" painted along the sides in black spray paint.

They parked in the parking lot and hurried over. Noah moved to meet them so they could speak without civilians overhearing.

Julian scowled at Ray, who was still shouting threats at every person he laid eyes on. "You haven't put him out of his misery yet?"

"We've got to figure out where to put them," Noah said.

"Lock him up and throw away the key," Julian muttered.

"What did he do this time?" Hayes asked.

Noah quickly explained. He'd known Ray Shultz and his kind would be trouble. He just hadn't expected it to happen quite like this.

Shultz was a local junkie and dealer who lived in the Fall Creek Estates trailer park just past the bridge. He'd been busted for trafficking narcotics, assault and battery, and breaking and entering. He'd done several years of hard time at Lakeland Correctional Facility in Coldwater, only to return to the same lifestyle as soon as he got out.

He and his cousins—the four worthless Carter brothers, along with a bunch of second cousins and like-minded losers—were spread out in the surrounding communities of Bridgman, Niles, Baroda, St. Joe, and Benton Harbor.

As soon as law enforcement put one away, another just popped up to take his relative's place. They were blights on the entire county.

"We've got to take them to the courthouse for arraignment," Hayes said.

"What arraignment?" Reynoso asked. "No judges and certainly no lawyers are showing up for court."

There were no holding cells in Fall Creek. Their township was too small for a legit precinct. They usually took their suspects to the larger neighboring township. "What about Van Buren and Cass county jails?"

"I topped off the Yamaha yesterday and drove all over creation," Reynoso said. "Every county within seventy miles. It's a no-go for anyone. They can't even handle their own county, let alone take on our problems. Berrien County Jail can't process anyone electronically, obviously, but the cells all have a manual override. They're still accepting inmates, but only the worst offenders. Less than a week since the event, and they're already overflowing with rapists and murderers. All the crazies are coming out of the woodwork. The opportunists who thought they could get away with crap in the middle of a national disaster."

"So you're saying not even Berrien will take our guys?" Noah asked.

"Not a chance," Julian spat, furious. "They've all abandoned us."

"There's the old prison cell in the basement of town hall," Noah said. "In the museum section of the old courthouse. Milo's class just did a tour there. It still works. We could use it as a holding cell until we figure out what to do."

"Oh hell, no," Julian said.

"We've got to think outside the box," Noah said.

"It's a good idea," Hayes said. "What else are we going to do?"

Julian grimaced. "You ask me, criminals should all be lined up against the wall and shot in the head, Gestapo-style. Why the hell are we watching kids go hungry when they're still getting three square meals a day courtesy of the government? FEMA's there. Did Reynoso tell you? Those low-life animals are getting fed and we're not."

There was a tense beat of silence.

Noah huffed a cold, steaming breath. Julian was getting himself all worked up. He wasn't wrong. It wasn't fair. He felt his own frustration rising, but moaning about it didn't solve any problems.

When Julian spoke again, his voice was artificially pleasant. "Well, if that's the plan, then we should pick up the Carter brothers at the same time."

Noah raised his brows. "What?"

"We all know they're a serious problem. Why aren't we rounding them up now? Taking out the bad guys *before* they wreak havoc."

"That's not how the law works," Noah said.

"That's how it *should* work." Julian shrugged. "Especially now. You're the one who said we need to think outside the box."

"You know Chief Briggs will never agree to that," Hayes said hesitantly.

"He doesn't need to know everything," Reynoso said with an apologetic glance at Noah. He usually sided with Julian on things.

"That's right," Julian said. "We'll just pay them a visit, okay? See how things go. No harm in that, is there, Sheridan?"

"I'll go with you—"

"Stay at the church with your son," Julian said, his words clipped. "We've got this."

Noah nodded, wishing he felt relieved, but he didn't.

Julian didn't say anything more. He turned and headed for the cuffed suspects. Hayes flashed him a sympathetic smile before turning to follow him, Reynoso on his heels.

Hayes went to Octavia, helped her to her feet, and herded her stumbling and groaning toward the snowplow. As Julian and Reynoso hauled Ray up, Ray twisted around.

"I'm coming for you!" Ray shouted at Bishop. "You better be afraid of me. You better be afraid!"

34

NOAH
DAY FIVE

Noah crossed the parking lot and returned to the food pantry. Bishop, Daphne, and Quinn were waiting for him.

Quinn crossed her arms over her chest and fixed him with an even stare. "Are you gonna lock him up?"

"Absolutely."

"And Octavia?"

"Your mother is an accomplice. But I'll see what I can do to cut her a break."

"She doesn't deserve a break." A shadow passed over her face. "She went after that gun, too."

"You're right. But because of you, she didn't get a chance to hurt anyone. Nice work, by the way. Maybe we should make you a volunteer officer."

She glared at him. Her bright blue hair was tucked beneath an equally vibrant teal beanie. Her eyebrow and lip rings were silver and studded with tiny sapphire-like jewels.

"You're Molly Dương's granddaughter, right?" Daphne asked her. "You came for our Christmas program last year."

Quinn frowned. "Only because Gran made me."

"Blunt and honest." Bishop gave a deep belly laugh. "I'll always know where I stand with you, that's for sure. I'm Atticus Bishop and this is my wife, Daphne. My friends just call me Bishop. They think it's amusing that I'm a pastor, not a priest."

Quinn just stared at him.

"Are you okay?" Noah asked her.

She scowled. "Fine and dandy. I can practically feel the sprinkles and rainbows bursting out of my ass."

Noah managed a tight smile. "I daresay we keep meeting under less than ideal circumstances."

"Yeah, it's a real series of unfortunate events around here." Her heavily made-up eyes narrowed. "Maybe you're bad luck."

"Maybe you are," he retorted.

She rolled her eyes. Just as quickly, her expression shifted. The sarcasm and snark dropped away. She kicked at a chunk of snow. "Any update on Gramps?"

A shard of guilt speared him. Quinn's grandfather was probably still up there on the chairlift. Ski resorts were the last thing on anyone's priority list.

He still had a mile-long list of tasks himself that included dealing with sanitation for those families without septic systems, not to mention the piles of trash piling up along the curb of every street.

He'd spent hours taking statements after four more break-ins occurred last night. Several fights between neighbors had broken out over the last few days, one accusing the other of stealing their kerosene heater, last jerrycan of gasoline, or a stash of canned goods.

And two more people had died overnight from hypothermia. They were currently storing bodies in the cemetery vault at Mercy Funeral Home a few miles up the road on Old 31. It was already almost full.

"I haven't forgotten, Quinn."

"And?"

"I will do it, I promise. We're in crisis, here. Right now, I'm working as hard as I can to protect the living. People are scared. And when they're scared, they do stupid things. Exhibit A: Raymond Terrance Shultz."

"Speaking of doing stupid things." Quinn's jaw clenched. She turned to Bishop and Daphne. "Octavia stole from you. Let me pay for it. I don't have any money, but I'm not afraid of work."

Daphne waved her hand. "Oh, don't worry about it. We still have plenty."

"I'm not a thief. I'm not my mother."

Noah's heart swelled with compassion for this tough kid. It couldn't be easy to be Octavia Riley's daughter. In a small town like this, everyone knew everyone else's business. People were quick to judge.

"We know you're not," he said quietly.

"I said I would work it off, and I will."

"Okay." Daphne gave her a warm smile. "We'd be happy to put you to work, Quinn."

"And you might want to think about exchanging a day of food for a few hours of work. It's not asking too much of people to cut some wood, wash blankets, prepare soup, or whatever else you do here." She angled her chin at the church. "You've got the space in the fellowship hall to start growing food indoors with hydroponics. And I'm sure at least a few of your parishioners know how to hunt proficiently."

"I imagine Molly would say the exact same thing if she were here," Daphne said, sounding impressed. "That's a great idea."

"She'd rap you on the head with her cane for your stupidity, is what she'd do. But I don't have a cane."

Bishop snorted. "Yep. Definitely Molly's granddaughter."

Bright peals of laughter echoed from inside the church. Three small blurs burst out of the side door. They dashed through the snow and catapulted themselves at Daphne and Bishop.

Juniper and Chloe wrapped their arms around their parents' legs. "We're so bored! Come play with us! Please, please, please!"

Milo came more hesitantly, checking out the scene first. To Noah's surprise, Milo made straight for Quinn. He stopped in front of her and stuck out his hand. "Hi, Quinn," he said shyly.

Quinn took Milo's hand and gave it a firm shake. "Hey, Small Fry. How's it hanging? Jumped off any giant chairlifts lately?"

Milo's serious face broke into a grin. "Not in a few days. Should we go look for another one?"

"Nah. I like to vary my flavors of deadly peril. Let's try something different this time. Maybe a little more thrilling rather than terrifying."

Milo's smile widened. "Deal."

Noah watched Milo and Quinn, an idea percolating in his mind. "You want to work, Quinn? I've got a proposal for you. Daphne has agreed to watch Milo during the week until supper, but I need someone for the weekends, occasional weeknights, and emergencies. I can pay you with a few cans of food."

Quinn pulled a face. "I don't do babysitting."

Milo squeezed her hand. "Please?"

Quinn's eyes darkened. She huffed her bangs out of her eyes. "Fine. Whatever. Food is food. I'll do it."

Milo pumped his mittened fist in the air. "BAM! Yes!"

"Keeping the food pantry running takes a lot of our focus," Daphne said. "Even though Juniper, Chloe, and Milo are here during the day, we can't give them the time and attention that they deserve. If you could come keep an eye on them sometimes, maybe play some games with them—that would be a huge help."

Quinn looked slightly terrified, but she didn't refuse.

"I want a babysitter too!" Juniper shrieked. "I want to have fun!"

"I'm not fun," Quinn said sternly. "I tie up my charges with shoelaces and lock them in dark bathrooms."

Chloe's hand shot up. "Me first! Me first!"

"No, me!" Juniper squealed.

"And I make them scrub toilets. With toothbrushes."

"Can we use Juniper's?" Chloe asked with glee.

"Don't say I didn't warn you," Quinn said darkly.

Daphne patted Chloe's head and smiled at Quinn. "I think you'll do just fine."

"It's too cold out here!" Juniper declared. "Come on! Let's plan a babysitting *party!*" She gestured at Milo and her little sister, who both followed obediently and darted back inside.

"Another thing. Milo has Addison's disease. He has to take pills at specific times and can't miss a dose. It's very important."

"I saw his medical bracelet. I knew it was something." She frowned at him. "I can handle it."

Noah didn't doubt that she could handle pretty much anything thrown her way. It was a character trait needed now more than ever.

"Thanks for meeting with me," Rosamond said.

"Of course," Noah said.

Rosamond had asked to speak to Noah outside her office. The dim fluorescent lights flickered overhead, and the building was chilly. Everyone still wore their coats inside.

They were trying to conserve as much fuel for the generator as they could.

It was late afternoon, and he'd just come from the courthouse basement after checking on Ray and Octavia in their cell. The four Carter brothers were locked up as well.

When Julian, Reynoso, and Hayes had approached their compound, Tommy Carter had opened fire on them. The half-drunk brothers weren't expecting the visit and were quickly subdued.

Julian had gotten his way, after all. Noah wasn't sure how he felt about that, yet.

"I wanted to commend you for everything you're doing," Rosamond said. "Not just for your bravery today, but your commitment to the community and excellent ideas."

At the council meeting yesterday morning, Noah had brought in a can of red spray paint and suggested they mark the empty homes so law enforcement and other approved volunteers could carefully and respectfully scavenge their supplies to share with the townsfolk who needed it.

People had started breaking into the empty homes anyway; it was better to have the supplies distributed fairly.

At least 20 percent of the houses were unoccupied due to people being trapped elsewhere for the holidays. Nineteen houses had also become empty after their owners succumbed to hypothermia or preexisting conditions.

When people finally made it home, they would have to understand that Fall Creek did what it had to do to keep their neighbors and friends alive. They would get it.

Chief Briggs had resisted at first but had eventually come around. Certain council members had seemed a little too thrilled with the idea of breaking into their neighbor's homes, namely Darryl Wiggins.

Rosamond rested her manicured fingers on Noah's forearm. "Thank you, from the bottom of my heart."

"You're welcome. We're all doing the best that we can. We'll pull together."

Abruptly, the careful calm gave way, and a few cracks in her composure appeared. For the first time, he saw the worry in her eyes.

"Are you okay?" he asked her.

She sniffed. "I can't tell you how grateful I am that you're here, Noah. I love Julian, but he's not . . . reliable like you are. I know I can always depend on you. Always. At least I have you. My Gavin hasn't returned yet."

Noah would forever be grateful to her for the way she'd always included him as one of the boys. As if he was really one of her sons and not just some stray tagalong.

He'd tried to like Gavin Pike for her sake. There was just something about him that rubbed Noah the wrong way. He'd never really been able to put a finger on it, or articulate why. Hannah hadn't cared for him either.

Gavin was easy to ignore. He was just this quiet guy in the background. He was Rosamond's favorite, which Julian had always resented, but it hadn't bothered Noah.

Rosamond's first husband, a musician, had taken off when Gavin was little. Rosamond had remarried a lawyer and had Julian a few years later. The lawyer had cheated, and Rosamond had booted him and raised both boys by herself.

Maybe Rosamond had leaned on Gavin more, since he was the oldest. Noah had never really understood their dynamics. He just knew that he had Julian, who was as close as a brother, and Rosamond, a surrogate mother and grandmother rolled into one.

"He was supposed to come home for Christmas Eve dinner. Five p.m. sharp, like clockwork every single year." Her eyes took on a distant look, like she was reliving good memories. "He always brings me lilies, did you know that?"

"Maybe he's helping corral the inmates at the prison and can't get word back to you. It's horrible with the lack of communication. I'm sure he'll be fine."

"I'm sure he will. Still, it's a mother's prerogative to worry, isn't it?" She smoothed the front of her navy suit jacket, composing herself. When she looked at Noah again, her eyes were clear and filled with purpose. "Speaking of worry. I'm worried about you and Milo in that freezing house of yours."

"We're fine," he said automatically, even though they weren't, not by a long shot.

He was shocked at how quickly they went through firewood. He'd already set aside two end tables, an old bookshelf, and a credenza to be chopped up first for added fuel. Even if he burned all his furniture, he'd still run out sooner rather than later.

At least he didn't have to worry about keeping the house warm during the day with Milo at the church with Quinn and the Bishop girls.

"And food?"

"We're getting low, but we're making do."

He fiddled with his wedding ring, embarrassed they didn't have more. Hannah had always tried to have a month's worth of food in winter, if not more. Their pantry had always been fully stocked—as much as their budget would allow.

With work and parenting responsibilities, Noah had let things slip. His face warmed with shame.

How wrong he had been, about so many things.

Rosamond shook her head. "It won't do, Noah. I won't have Milo freezing cold in that drafty house. Not with his condition. It's not right." She leaned in and lowered her voice. "I have a surprise. I've set aside a house in Winter Haven."

Noah balked. "I can't take someone's house—"

"The Garcias are in Aruba. When do you think they're coming home? Not for a while. If and when they return, we'll gladly give them their home back, in the same condition that we found it. But I will not stand by and let that boy freeze to death when there is a perfectly good home for him with lights and heat and hot water."

Noah shook his head. It still felt wrong, like stealing. Like invading someone else's personal space. Taking something that belonged to someone else, that wasn't his, shouldn't be his.

"We must utilize unused resources." Rosamond squeezed his arm. "I know you're too humble to accept this for yourself. But you *do* deserve it. After all you've been through? That boy needs a hot bath and homemade macaroni and cheese baking in the oven. And electricity to power his PlayStation. Milo deserves it. Do it for him, for my adopted grandson."

"But—" Noah sputtered.

"It's already done. I'm sending some people by your place around six. Have your bags packed."

Everything Rosamond said was true. Milo was medically fragile. His vulnerability was something Noah never forgot, not for one second.

Noah remembered the terror and helplessness he'd felt trapped on the chairlift. That sense of powerlessness. He'd do nearly anything to keep from feeling that way again.

He was Milo's father. It was his job to keep his son safe. At any cost.

If that meant accepting a monumental gift that he didn't deserve or earn, then so be it.

A tightness released inside his chest. Wetness filled Noah's eyes against his will. He blinked hard, gratitude filling him. "I can't repay you—"

Rosamond waved her hand. "Forget it. You've always been a son to me, since that first time you came over, a shy skinny kid who could barely look me in the eye. What I remember is how you nearly ate me out of house and home."

Noah blushed.

"I need you, Noah. I need to know I can depend on you. Tempers are getting short. Reality is starting to sink in. You've always been the peacemaker. That's what we need now more than ever."

"Of course. Whatever I can do."

A genuine smile spread across her face. "We're family, Noah. This is what family does."

He started to say something else, but she was already turning away as two of her office staff approached, strained expressions on their faces. One of them whispered something urgently in her ear, and she turned on her heel and strode after them without a backward glance.

Noah was left standing alone in the beige hallway, his mouth hanging open, still not entirely sure what had just happened. That was the way things went with Rosamond Sinclair.

She got her way, whether you liked it or not.

She was a brisk, tough, no-nonsense woman. Not everyone liked her. But in Noah's experience, she had always done right by him.

And for that, she had his gratitude. And his loyalty.

36

NOAH
DAY SIX

"What's the superintendent up to now?" Reynoso murmured.

Noah shrugged and scratched at the grizzle of new beard growing along his jawline. He liked to keep his face smooth-shaven, but he'd had little time or inclination over the last week.

More important things had taken precedence—like keeping Fall Creek from falling apart.

"Who cares?" Hayes shot back. He stuffed another roll of oven-warmed artisan bread smothered with melted cheese into his mouth. Crumbs spilled down his chest. "If all committee meetings are like this from here on out, I'll die a happy man."

Rosamond Sinclair had called another morning council meeting, this one at her house in Winter Haven. There were more important buildings than town hall that needed electricity. In one fell swoop, she'd moved headquarters to her place.

Her home was a self-sufficient mini-mansion with a log-hewn exterior, the interior boasting Brazilian wood floors, vaulted ceilings, crystal chandeliers, and marble counters and bathroom tiles.

Everything was oversized, ornate, and lavish. Not Noah's style at all, but he still admired every elegant detail.

Everyone else was far more jealous of the lights and heat, the working stove, and the delicious hum of the stainless-steel refrigerator.

The council members gathered in the elaborate formal living room, sprawling on the velvet sofas and chairs. Stools and brocade dining room chairs had been dragged into the room for additional seating.

Two of the superintendent's assistants were passing around platters of finger foods—pigs in a blanket, quiches, and tiny burritos. All hot and steaming. All delicious.

For a second, you could almost forget the country had just been plunged into chaos. That their small town was cut off from the world, trapped in cold and darkness, utterly alone. That no help from the government had come and might not be coming for weeks or months. Almost.

Guilt pricked him. Noah and Milo had moved into their own beautiful log cabin in the Winter Haven community last night. It wasn't nearly as fancy as Rosamond's, but that didn't matter.

The solar panels were working, along with a generator for the days without enough sunlight. The pantry still had a good two weeks' worth of food.

After only a few days without electricity, it already felt like a precious luxury. Noah and Milo had wallowed in it. Took hot showers. Baked a frozen pan of gooey mac and cheese, just like Rosamond had suggested, and ate the whole thing between them.

It was the first night Noah had slept soundly since the EMP.

Still, it was a solution to only one of the many insurmountable problems facing him. His worry over Milo's meds was growing every day.

Rosamond clapped her hands, drawing everyone's attention. The room grew respectfully silent. Stiff-backed, she sat on a stool beneath the arched entrance between the living room and dining room, the bright shiny kitchen behind her.

"Thank you all for coming. I hope you enjoyed dinner. There's more where that came from, I assure you. I promised I would take care of you, and I will. But first, a few important items.

"As we've discussed, we simply do not have enough trained law enforcement professionals to keep the peace. We've already recruited as many former military townspeople as we could find as reserve officers. It's not enough.

"We need trained, specialized individuals to provide security and ensure that what's ours remains ours, and that our families— our children—are safe here. No one wants to see a tragedy like what nearly happened yesterday. Thanks to Officer Sheridan's quick thinking, no one was killed. As optimistic as I am, I don't believe we will be that lucky again."

Low murmurs around the room. The news of the altercation at the Crossway food pantry had spread quickly. People were relieved that the culprits were locked up in the courthouse basement, but they weren't the town's only problems.

"Some of you know my second cousin, Mattias Sutter, commander of the Volunteer Militia Brigade of Southwest Michigan up near Allegan. Dave Farris has successfully contacted him over the ham radio. He is willing to assist us in providing security—"

"You want to invite the Michigan Militia into Fall Creek?" Chief Briggs interrupted, incredulous.

"Technically, they broke off from the Michigan Militia last year and formed their own brigade." Rosamond pressed her lips together. "I'm merely offering some resources for discussion. I do think they could offer significant security benefits."

"We can use all the help we can get," Julian said. "It's only a matter of time before the chaos in the cities makes its way here. We need to put up barricades with abandoned vehicles and a few guards on Old 31 coming into and going out of town."

"We're already stretched too thin to set up roadblocks," Reynoso said, glancing at Julian for affirmation. "Not effective ones, anyway. There aren't enough of us."

Dave Farris stood and pushed back his stool. "I'm not against security and safety. But we better think mighty hard before we let a bunch of strangers into our town. Fall Creek isn't as hard-off as a lot of other places. We have several freshwater sources nearby for drinking and fishing. Fall Creek, not to mention the St. Joe River, Lake Chapin, and of course, Lake Michigan. Once spring and summer hits, we have orchards and farms everywhere. Michigan has almost ten million acres of farmland."

Dave had a point. The counties along the southwestern border of Michigan were known as the fruit belt. The softly rolling hills, sandy and fertile soil, and proximity to Lake Michigan created a favorable climate for fruit production. Grapes, peaches, apples, pears, plums, and strawberries all flourished here.

Michigan farmland also produced corn, soybeans, wheat, potatoes, onions, tomatoes, asparagus, blueberries, and raspberries —the list went on. Not to mention the thousands of acres reserved for dairy cows and egg production. U-pick farms and orchards were scattered across Berrien and neighboring counties.

"The way I see it, if we can just make it through this winter, we'll be alright," Dave said. "We've also got Winter Haven—a whole neighborhood with power. Seems these folks might come in and decide they like it enough to just take over and push us out. And what's to stop them if they're bigger and stronger than we are?"

Low murmurs of agreement rippled through the living room.

"We aren't inviting in an unknown element," Chief Briggs growled. "The Fall Creek Police Force oversees enforcing law and order in Fall Creek. Period. No discussion."

"The militia isn't the law," Dave said. "They don't exactly have the best reputation."

"That's not all of 'em, Dave," Mike said. "The Michigan Militia numbers in the thousands. Lots of good folks ready to defend themselves and their loved ones from threats foreign and domestic. My brother and nephews are in a brigade up near Holland."

"It's no different than a company hiring private security," Wiggins said loudly. Deep circles ringed his eyes. He looked exhausted. "It's the smart thing to do. We need to be safe, period. The world is going to hell out there and we need protection."

"Not sure if we want men we don't know with guns and the run of the town," Annette King said. "Sounds like a recipe for trouble, you ask me."

Several council members nodded adamantly. Most looked confused and unsure.

Noah fiddled anxiously with his wedding ring. He didn't want armed strangers in their town any more than anyone else did, but he also knew how shorthanded they were, how vulnerable.

"If Rosamond is for it, then we should acquiesce to her expertise," Wiggins said. He glanced around at the council. "Come on."

"This isn't a dictatorship, Rosamond," Chief Briggs snapped. "You can't just take over and ram this through—"

"I would never push my agenda on any of you. It must be a group vote." Rosamond's expression was as serene as always, but the corner of her eye twitched. "Let's have a raise of hands, shall we?"

The vote was cast quickly. Most were against, but Rosamond, Julian, and Wiggins voted for it.

Rosamond's face didn't change. She removed a nonexistent piece of lint from her skirt and folded her hands in her lap. "If you think Fall Creek is better off on our own, then so be it."

Julian glanced at his mother, frowning. "That's it then? We

just table it because of a few old boomers who can't get with the times?"

Rosamond pursed her lips. "That's what the council is for."

"They're wrong!"

"That's enough." Rosamond shot Julian a tense look of disapproval but kept her own voice even and steady. "The decision has already been made."

"But—"

"Enough. You're embarrassing yourself, Julian. Was that your intention?"

She didn't have to raise her voice. It had a way of transforming from sweet and melodious to sharp in an instant.

Chastised, Julian leaned back with an indignant huff and crossed his arms over his chest, face reddening with embarrassment.

Noah placed a hand on his shoulder. "It's okay, brother," he said quietly.

Bristling, Julian shrugged him off.

Noah tried not to take it personally. Julian never could think clearly when he was mad. He'd always been a hothead, letting his emotions get the best of him. A day or two and he'd be back to his old self—Noah's best friend again.

At least, he hoped so.

37

OCTAVIA RILEY

DAY SIX

Octavia Riley was too damn exhausted to move. She slumped against the concrete wall and groaned. The wooden bench was uncomfortable as hell and made her butt ache, especially after being stuck in this craphole for the last twenty-four hours.

Maybe it had been longer. They had no clocks in here. No way to tell time but the slop their guard fed them every once in a while. Three meals—nasty canned beans and beets and water.

She couldn't care less about the soggy, tasteless food. It was something else she craved.

Her nerves were raw and thrummed with need. Cold sweat prickled her forehead. She flashed hot and cold and hot again despite the near-freezing temps.

A shivery fever wracked her entire body. She'd hurled twice already in the piss bucket. The entire cell reeked of sour sweat, body odor, and vomit.

All she wanted was more. More and more and more. She needed it. Craved it. It was the only thing that took away the darkness, that made her pathetic miserable life seem different, brighter, better.

"I'll kill you, Atticus Bishop, you hear me!" Ray shouted. "I'll cut off your teeny-tiny dipstick and feed it to you and that rat-faced cop Sheridan!"

Octavia moaned, shifting again to try to get comfortable but failing. She was so damn exhausted, but sleep wouldn't come. "Stop it already, would you? I've got a killer headache."

Ray just continued his pacing. "I'll make him pay for this! I'll make them all pay!"

He'd been stalking the narrow cell for hours, spitting and cursing, screaming and howling and banging his fists on the ancient iron bars like that might make a difference.

They were in the basement of the historic courthouse. She'd never been inside but had driven by it on Main Street a thousand times. It was tucked between the Asian Bistro and the laundromat and across from the town's only stoplight.

The courthouse had been preserved, though it was used now as a museum for school kids, occasional fancy fundraising dinners, and boring township council meetings.

The single holding cell in the basement was a hundred and thirty years old and still in pristine working condition, in case anyone cared. Iron bars. Concrete walls. A single kerosene lantern hanging on a hook by the stairs.

One of the cops had smashed a glass case that housed the antique key ring and used it to lock them in here. They'd probably throw away the key.

"Let me out!" Ray screamed. "I'm coming for you!"

Octavia barely cracked her eyes open. Less than ten feet across from her, Ray's four cousins were stacked in a row along a second wooden bench. Tommy was sleeping, mouth open and snoring loudly, his head flung back against the bars.

Randy, nicknamed "Nickel" for some asinine reason she couldn't recall, and the youngest brother, Bucky, were sitting still, heads down and hunched over, their forearms resting on their knees. They'd been muttering quietly to each other, cursing and fantasizing about what they'd do to these mothers once they got out of this damn cell.

Billy was the scariest. He sat ramrod straight, skinny shoulders pulled back, his eyes shiny and black as a beetle shell. He had a lazy eye that made him seem like he was looking through you rather than *at* you.

She didn't think he'd slept since they'd been hauled in a few hours after Ray and Octavia. Octavia couldn't remember ever seeing him sleeping.

He'd killed people, Ray had told her. Pulled one guy out of his trailer and strangled him with his bare hands. Cut up his body with a chainsaw and threw the pieces into Lake Michigan. She believed it.

Billy and his brothers hadn't even done anything this time. Stupid small-town cops thought they could do anything, were above the law. Right after they'd arrested Ray and Octavia, they'd gone after the Carters. Arrested them right on their own property.

Ray's cousins had been hungover, drowsy, unprepared. Without cell phones, Octavia and Ray had had no way to warn them.

The automatic weapons were stored in the cellar behind a false wall. Due to their numerous prison records, the Carters hid the arsenal they'd collected over the years: AR-15s, AK-47s, M4 carbines, and all the shiny ammo to go with them.

Tommy only had time to grab a hunting rifle and storm onto the porch. He'd opened fire, but more cops arrived before the fireworks could really start.

They'd been arrested and handcuffed before they'd even gotten a chance to fight.

Octavia seethed with fury. She knew Ray and the others felt

the same. They'd been scorned and humiliated. Treated like utter garbage.

They weren't beasts to be caged in a dank, damp underground. They deserved better, so much better.

All this—the way they were being so unfairly treated—it had to be against the law or something. No lawyers. No damn phone call.

She'd been arrested plenty of times before. She knew how it was supposed to go.

They hadn't let any visitors down to see them. Wouldn't even let her own daughter in to see her. If she would even come.

Why would you think she'd ever want to visit you? She hates you. And you deserve it.

Octavia tried to push that nasty, sniveling voice right out of her head. That was what the dope was for. To get rid of all the ugly thoughts. All the dark and nasty things she didn't like thinking about, would rather pretend out of existence.

Billy was still watching her. So still, except for that bizarre wandering eye. It gave her the creeps. Everything about him gave her the creeps.

She had worse things to think about than Ray's maniacal cousin. Her anxious, fractured brain could hardly settle on any single thought. Only the *need,* that desperate craving clawing through her veins.

She had to get out of here, had to get her next fix, no matter what. She felt like she'd die without it. She'd die right here, shivering in a miserable pool of her own piss and vomit.

38

NOAH

DAY SIX

"We're making a pit stop," Julian yelled back at Noah. He'd parked his snowmobile in front of Crossway Church and removed his helmet.

Noah eased up beside him and switched off the coughing, rattling engine. He pulled off his helmet and driving snow struck him full in the face. "What? Why? It's time to go home. The storm's coming. Hell, it feels like it's already here."

It was nearly dusk. Low black clouds roiled across the sky just above the tree line.

The winter shadows grew long and dark. The bone-chilling wind howled around the buildings, rattling and creaking through the trees. The wind swept crystals off the snow in great clouds and sent debris skittering along the sidewalks.

Fall Creek was a ghost town, but instead of tumbleweeds, cold and ice and snow swirled like tiny tornadoes.

"It'll just take a minute." Julian slid off his machine and rewrapped his scarf over the lower half of his face. His voice was muffled through the fabric. "Relax, Sheridan."

Julian kicked through the snow, strode up the concrete steps, and rapped his gloved knuckles against Crossway Church's solid wood double front doors.

Reluctantly, Noah followed. He ducked his head against the stinging snow and pulled his hood tighter around his face. His cheeks, lips, and nose were raw and chapped. He could feel the little hairs in his nose freezing.

It had to be below zero at least. The lethal, unrelenting cold was deadly. The low temperatures were breaking Michigan records day after day after day.

They'd probably get a foot or more in the next few hours, which would put them over three feet just in the last week. It felt like they were trapped here, cut off almost entirely from the outside world.

It was making everyone short-tempered and antsy. They were all under an incredible amount of stress.

"I still don't understand what we're doing here," Noah said. "I already told you, Bishop wants to do his own thing. I don't see why he shouldn't be able to. He's giving away everything he has."

Four more snowmobiles pulled up behind them, snow swirling and diving in the yellow cones of their headlights. Two men were officers—Hayes and Reynoso—and two more were ex-military volunteers from the community that Chief Briggs grudgingly deputized as reserve officers a few days ago.

The townspeople were getting more and more disgruntled with each passing day. Rosamond was starting to lose her hold on the town. Chief Briggs, too. Everyone wanted someone to blame, especially when no one knew who had really done this to them, or why.

Everyone was cold and hungry and tired of scrambling for every single thing they needed. Water no longer came from the tap. Food didn't just appear on grocery store shelves. Heat wasn't a simple adjustment to the thermostat.

Guilt pricked him. He and Milo were the lucky ones.

Several break-ins had been attempted in the last three days, the majority in the community of Winter Haven. Someone had defaced and vandalized Daniel Barber's house with crude images.

And last night, a couple of teenagers had climbed onto the roof of Mary Jones's home and dismantled two of the solar panels before she'd caught them and threatened to shoot off their balls.

Noah had had to let them go with a stern warning. They had nowhere to keep them, since the single holding cell in the basement of the historic courthouse was currently being utilized by Ray Shultz, Octavia Riley, and the Carter brothers until they figured out what to do with them.

Julian shot him a look. His nose and cheeks were reddened, his eyes bloodshot. "The superintendent's orders."

"But the chief—"

"Briggs needs to get with the times. And so do you, Sheridan." There was an edge in Julian's voice. He sounded tense. Angry.

Much like Noah felt now, standing here half-freezing, his legs like lead, his ears and nose numb, snow freezing in his eyebrows and eyelashes.

The door swung open and Atticus Bishop stood there, all burly arms, broad shoulders, and big afro, dressed in his quintessential black leather jacket and a new Hawaiian shirt—this one blue with palm trees.

Bishop didn't look at Noah. He stared at Julian for several seconds before slowly sweeping his gaze to the bundled men standing at the foot of the steps, bracing themselves against the wind and snow.

Everyone was armed, though weapons were holstered.

Bishop's mouth pressed into a thin line. "Sinclair. What are you doing here?"

Julian pushed down his scarf so he could speak clearly. "We're just making rounds and requesting help from the community.

We've got almost a hundred hungry kids at the emergency shelter and only a few days left of food. I'm sure you understand how it is."

"I understand that I'm helping the people who come to me. I understand that me and my congregation bought and paid for the cans and boxes of food and bottles of water inside this building. I get to decide what to do with it."

"Wow, dude. Slow your roll." Julian raised both hands in a placating gesture and gave a wide, guileless smile. "We're not forcing anything, Bishop. You misunderstand us. We're offering our aid. Our help. We're just asking you for a little something in return. Not for us, but for those hungry kids. Think about them."

Bishop didn't break Julian's gaze. "I am thinking about them. And everyone else. Seems to me you'll start here, and when you get what you want, you'll keep going. Seems like your 'innocent' asking might quickly turn into demanding."

Julian stiffened. "That's ridiculous."

"Is it?" Bishop said evenly.

"You always were too paranoid for your own good, Bishop."

"The government oversteps. It's what they do."

Noah's stomach knotted with apprehension. Julian and Bishop together never ended well. He didn't know whether Julian was jealous of his friendship with Bishop or if it was something else, but they'd always been tense and edgy around each other.

Noah was always the peacemaker between them, always walking a tightrope of neutrality. He didn't feel like walking it tonight.

He just wanted to get home to Milo. After helping serve dinner at the church, Quinn had taken him back to the new house in Winter Haven to build Lego spaceships.

He longed for a warm, relaxing evening in front of the fireplace reading 20,000 *Leagues Under the Sea* or *Treasure Island* to

Milo until he fell asleep. After Hannah had gone, Milo had asked Noah to sing over and over, but Noah was no good at singing. Reading, though, he could do.

"We just want to help," Noah said.

Bishop's expression shuttered. "Be careful, Noah. Make sure you know whose side you're on."

"Oh, we're taking sides already?" Julian looked hurt. Or he went for a hurt expression. But Noah knew him well enough to see the anger flashing behind his eyes. "We're just trying to keep the peace here. You get to be home with your family, all nice and warm and cozy, while we're out here freezing, trying to save the town. Seems mighty selfish to refuse to help even a little, doesn't it?"

Bishop shrugged. "What you think isn't my problem. It's time for you to go now."

Julian lurched forward, his hands balling into fists. "Now wait just a minute—"

Noah stepped quickly between them. He held out a placating hand, forcing Julian back. "Hey! Remember where we are and what we're doing. No one is the enemy here. We're all friends."

"Are we?" Julian said darkly. "Because it looks to me like some folks are just in this for themselves, everyone else be damned."

The men behind him murmured in disgruntled agreement. Frowning, Reynoso moved to the bottom step, ready to back Julian up.

Noah's stomach sank. He hated the tension thrumming through the air, the anger and resentment bristling just below the surface. He'd do just about anything to make it go away.

"You're entitled to your opinion," Bishop said evenly. "But I know I'm doing the right thing. And that's not going to change."

"Atticus?" Daphne came up behind her husband and inched beside him in the doorway. She held a blond-haired toddler wrapped in a blanket on her hip—the same little boy from yesterday. Candlelight flickered across her pretty features. "Is everything okay?"

Behind them past the foyer, Noah could see people moving around inside the sanctuary, most of them lying on the pews and the floor with blankets and pillows. They looked warm and comfortable, if not happy.

"Everything is fine, Daphne," Noah said. "We were just stopping by to check on you. That's all."

"We're offering protection," Julian said, "for you and the families here. Just like we're doing at Friendly's, the gas station, and Vinson Pharmacy. We're dealing with looting and break-ins every night."

Daphne looked at Bishop uncertainly.

Bishop shook his head. "No thanks."

"Why not?"

"One, I already have protection. Two, I don't accept help that comes with a price."

"What does that mean?" Noah asked.

Bishop folded his arms across his chest, unmoved. "It's not the 'help' that's the problem. It's the cost."

Julian's lip curled in scorn. "That's a bunch of bull—"

"God will protect us," Daphne said softly. She patted the back of the child, who curled his tiny body against hers. Inside the sanctuary, a baby started crying. "Like my husband just said. God and our armed deacons, our faithful parishioners who've volunteered to keep an eye on the church."

"But—"

"Thank you for your offer, gentlemen. Sincerely. We do appreciate you thinking of us. But we'll be fine. Please come by the pantry tomorrow. We'll be handing out the last of the packaged pies before they go bad. We have a few pecan ones leftover from Christmas."

"That's not what I—" Julian sputtered.

"Thank you for your generosity," Noah said over Julian's protests. "We'll be sure to stop by."

Daphne's smile broadened, a hint of relief in her eyes. She dipped her chin at Noah. They were both working to diffuse the tension. "I'll save you one, Officer Sinclair. God bless you and keep you safe."

The heavy double doors closed. Just like that, they were dismissed.

Noah and Julian stood for a moment on the steps in the cold and the dark. The men returned to their snowmobiles and waited for them. The only light came from the beams of the snowmobiles' headlights.

Heavy snow fell in thick spiraling gusts. Frozen branches creaked as the wind howled and moaned around the church.

Julian whirled on Noah. "He's being selfish for no reason. How do you not see that? It won't help anyone if those meth heads get ahold of their supplies. Then everyone will go hungry."

"The meth heads are in a holding cell, remember?" Noah gave a helpless shrug. "Bishop is stubborn. He always has been."

Julian gave a derisive snort. "They aren't the only danger. You know that."

Noah couldn't see his friend's expression in the dark, but he knew Julian was upset. Not just with Bishop, but with him. "Julian—"

Julian turned away from him, stomped down the snow-covered steps, nearly slipping, and headed for his Ski-Doo. His hands were still balled into fists at his sides, his shoulders stiff.

He paused at his machine. "He's your friend. Get him to wise up to reality."

Or what? But Noah didn't want to ask that question. It hung suspended in the frigid air, unanswered.

A chill of unease spread through his chest as he looked out

past the darkened road, at the empty streets and buildings he knew were there but couldn't see—all of Fall Creek deserted, frozen, desolate.

39

OCTAVIA RILEY
DAY SEVEN

"Someone's coming," Octavia said.

She sat up quickly. A wave of sour nausea flushed through her. Her skin itched with cold, prickly sweat. She scratched fiercely at her arms. She'd been half-asleep, half-hallucinating. Spiders crawling under her skin. Cockroaches and maggots.

"So what?" Ray hadn't slept since they'd been in here. He'd sat and rested for a while, but now he was up and pacing again like a caged lion, tail twitching in suppressed rage. "Let them come!"

They'd eaten five meals now, but it had been hours since anyone had come down to feed them. It felt like an entire day. Their piss pot hadn't been emptied either, and it stank something foul.

She shivered. "I can hear him. It's real."

"Shut the hell up," Tommy snarled blearily. "We're trying to sleep."

They had no idea whether it was day or night. Not a single

damn window down here. The world could be ending, and they wouldn't even know it.

She let out a raspy snicker at that thought. Who was she kidding? The world had already ended. And here they were, missing out on all the fun.

Footsteps echoed dully in the stairwell. Everything down here was constructed with big old slabs of stone. Every noise was amplified.

"It's real," she whispered.

The footsteps grew louder. Someone stomped down the courthouse staircase into the basement. A figure appeared.

A man, by the height and girth of him, the broad shoulders. He wore a heavy black coat to his knees, the hood drawn over his face, the thick fur obscuring his features in the dim light from the single kerosene lantern.

"What the hell do you want?" Ray asked. "You here to spring us out of this hellhole?"

"You can't keep us here this long without a lawyer and a phone call!" Nickel said. "I know my rights!"

"You haven't fed us all day!" Bucky staggered to his feet. His massive scarred hands curled into fists at his sides. "We're gonna sue your asses to kingdom come."

"Nah," Tommy drawled. "We're gonna do better than that. We're gonna find your families. And then we're gonna carve them up into itty bitty pieces right in front of you."

Billy said nothing. He sat on the bench straight-backed, his black gaze roaming slowly over the man standing outside the bars, his wandering eye seeming to stare right at Octavia.

"You want to get out of here?" the man asked. His voice was deep and raspy, like he was trying to disguise it. "Then shut the hell up. Otherwise, I turn around right now and head back up those stairs. And I promise you, these people will let you rot in here. They're already discussing whether to feed you your next meal or not."

The Carter brothers swore and cursed at him. Tommy spat a loogie that landed on the man's boots.

"Shut up already!" Octavia managed to pull herself to her feet. Ignoring the sickening lurch in her belly, she teetered over to Ray and gripped the bars. The men were all blustering idiots. They needed a woman to handle this. "We're listening."

The man held up the rusty iron key. "This will get you out. Your guard is upstairs, snoring logs. But first, I need a favor out of you."

Ray's eyes bulged. He was seething. She'd seen that gleam of malice in his gaze before. He was furious enough to kill something. Or someone. "Why the hell would we do a thing for you?"

Octavia gazed greedily at the key. "We'll do it."

Billy and Nickel rose to their feet.

"We decide that," Nickel said, scowling. "Not you."

All of them had moved to the bars, even Billy. Five dangerous men tense and bristling, restless and hungry as wild dogs.

Octavia still couldn't make out his face. The kerosene lantern was hung on the wall behind him, so he remained in shadow. All she could tell was that he was Caucasian and not old. He seemed familiar, though. Like she should know him, if her rattled brain didn't feel like Swiss Cheese.

"A job, if you would," the man said calmly. "At Crossway Church."

"I'll kill Atticus Bishop! He's a dead man!" Ray cussed a blue streak. "Those pious asswipes are stealing food from good, upstanding regular folks like ourselves, then doling it out like they're gods! Like they have a right to it over us!"

"They have more than food," the man said quietly. "They have gold."

Ray glared at him like he was blabbering nonsense. "Gold."

"Yes, gold. Gold currency will remain even after paper money becomes worthless, like what's happening right now. They have at least twenty gold bars worth thirty to forty thousand dollars. Can you imagine what you could do with that right now? What necessities you could purchase when everyone else is stuck with worthless paper and pieces of plastic?"

Octavia's mouth watered. Her blood surged hungrily in her veins. She could imagine it. Oh yes, she could. She and Ray could store up a stash like they'd never had before, enough to last them months. Even years.

"Where?" Billy asked.

"Somewhere in the church. In a safe. That's all the information I have. But I've gotten word they're going to move it to a safer location. Now's the time to strike."

The man spread his gloved hands. "As you can imagine, I cannot form a team and strike myself. The way I see it, we can help each other. If you were to . . . break out . . . of this antique relic of a cell with its rusting, unreliable lock, and if you were to retrieve that safe and its contents, I would think you would be entitled to 60 percent of the bounty to split amongst yourselves."

"Ninety percent," Billy said. "Ten percent finders' fee for you."

"Seventy percent," the man said.

"Eighty," Ray said, "and you have a deal."

"Done," the man said.

"Hell, I'd almost do it for free." Ray laughed, an ugly, malicious sound echoing off the damp stone walls. "That pastor has it coming. A reckoning like you've never seen."

Octavia felt giddy. Not only were they getting out of here, they'd just struck a deal with the devil himself. They'd get rich. They'd live like lords and ladies.

She could buy a house for her and Quinn. She could buy her baby girl a freaking mansion.

That would get Quinn over her anger and resentment real fast. They could go back to being a family. They could be happy again, just like they used to be.

This was a brave new world. A world in which they could rule.

Who cared if the power was out for good? Law and order were crumbling. The way things had always been—that was all gone now.

Maybe the government would lose its hold completely. Maybe everyone would be free of stupid laws forever. It didn't really matter.

Octavia thought only in the moment. For today, this week, this month, the whole town of Fall Creek was cut off from the world. It might as well not exist.

There were no consequences. No lawyers and judges, no courthouses and prisons.

They could do whatever they wanted. And they would.

Just as soon as she got her next fix.

The man put the key in the lock. He hesitated.

Octavia stopped breathing. Her body thrummed with electric energy. She wanted nothing more than to get smashed and take revenge on those self-righteous losers who'd humiliated her and Ray, who'd dared to withhold what was rightfully theirs, and then mocked them for it.

They would pay. They deserved to pay. Like Ray had said, the gold was just a bonus.

The man hesitated, as if unsure for a moment. "They won't be forthcoming," the man said. "They won't just give it to you."

Billy smiled for the first time. His lips spread over crooked yellow teeth. His black eyes glinted with anticipation. "Don't you worry. We know just what to do."

40

QUINN
DAY SEVEN

"Show us again, Quinn! Please, please, please!"

Chloe grabbed Quinn's arm, bouncing on her toes, her dark eyes wide, the plastic barrettes on the ends of her braids clacking.

Quinn rolled her eyes. "It's too cold out here. I'm tired."

"Just once more? Puh-lease?" Juniper begged.

Quinn glanced at Milo. He stood on top of a snow hill they'd built that day near the rear exit of the church, bundled in snow gear to within an inch of his life. He didn't say anything, but he nodded with a shy grin, his eyes shining.

He was so much quieter than the girls. Almost like he was swallowed up by their energy and enthusiasm, their aura of bright spinning chaos.

But that wasn't quite right. He didn't disappear into their energy—he basked in it, like just being close to them made him brighter, too.

The four of them were hanging out in the overflow parking lot behind the church. The asphalt abutted a thick section of woods, the trees all bare and scraggly and heavy with wet snow.

A pair of angrily chattering squirrels chased each other across the branches, knocking chunks of snow to the ground with soft thuds.

The blustering storm yesterday had dumped another foot of snow overnight. Huge drifts several feet deep were everywhere. The vicious wind had finally died down sometime that morning.

Quinn had tried to make it a fun day. They'd built snowmen and crafted the most perfect snow angels, pulled each other around in an old-fashioned toboggan the Bishops brought from their house, and the kids had joyously and savagely attacked Quinn with snowballs.

In the afternoon, after several games of hide and seek, the girls had drawn her a pink and purple target on a huge piece of construction paper they'd scavenged from one of the Sunday school room's supply closets.

Milo had found some tacks and suggested they pin it to a tree so Quinn could teach them her slingshot skills. The girls had brought some assorted marbles from home, and the rest was history.

The kids were utterly fascinated and loved it when she hit the bull's eye from fifteen feet, twenty-five feet, and forty feet again and again.

They did *not* want to see her kill a squirrel, though. All three kids were adamant on that one.

Babysitting wasn't as bad as Quinn had expected. Milo and even the rambunctious girls were sweet and funny and obedient. They followed her around like annoying little ducklings.

All her life, she'd thought she hated kids. Turned out, it was only the entitled, bratty, snot-nosed ones. Some of them were actually decent human beings.

"Please, Quinn!" Juniper begged again.

"One more, but that's it," Quinn said sternly, shaking the

slingshot at Juniper. "Then we're going in to help your parents prepare and distribute dinner."

She shut out the sounds of the squealing girls, shut out every distraction. She fitted her wrist guard, loaded a marble in the pouch, and drew the tapered bands back to her cheek. She canted the frame horizontally, lined up her sight, exhaled, and released.

The marble struck the tree trunk with a *thunk*. Twilight was falling, but she knew she'd hit her mark. She usually did. "Well?"

Chloe, Juniper, and Milo all ran to the tree.

"I see it!" Milo squealed. "BAM! It ripped a hole right through the center! That bad guy is deader than dead!"

"Told ya." Quinn shrugged and grinned. She shoved the slingshot in her pocket. "Now get your little a—I mean butts, inside!"

The next few hours were a bustle of activity—cooking huge pots of tomato soup and assembling a few hundred grilled cheese sandwiches, dishing everything out onto the last of the paper bowls and plates, supervising the kids as they eagerly—and sloppily—served the families staying overnight in the sanctuary.

There were anywhere from fifty to seventy people staying at the church. Daphne had taken Quinn's suggestion to heart, and each family now helped hand wash the blankets and pillows, collect firewood, and other daily chores.

"Let's play hide and seek again!" Milo said after dinner was finally cleaned up and Quinn had given Milo his meds.

Noah had given her a mechanical watch to keep track of the times Milo needed his meds. It wasn't easy to remember without a timer on her phone, but she knew how important it was.

Noah was supposed to have picked up Quinn and Milo an hour ago. The man was working himself to the bone, deepening shadows beneath his eyes with each passing day. She couldn't fault him for being late, even though she wanted to.

She just wanted to go home and hang out with Gran by candlelight, maybe curl up in front of the woodstove with a pile of cats purring in her lap and her dog-eared copy of Robert A. Heinlein's *Friday*.

Quinn led them wearily back to the sanctuary. "I'm way too pooped for that, Small Fry. How about a story instead? Either that, or I whip you with cooked spaghetti noodles."

Juniper made a face. "Eww, gross!"

"Like I said, your choice."

"Story! I pick story! I know the perfect one!" Chloe ran off to get the book from one of the Sunday school rooms. Juniper hurried after her to "oversee" the process.

Quinn sank into one of the empty pews near the front of the sanctuary. The muscles in her legs ached and her eyes burned. She was exhausted.

Milo snuggled next to her, curling his small body against hers like a kitten. She leaned her head back and closed her eyes as she stroked his hair.

She felt different. Almost like a completely different person than a week ago.

Gramps had died. She'd survived a blizzard trapped on a chairlift. The whole state—maybe the whole country—had gone dark, but she was still here; she was making do.

All the things she'd let bother her before—mean girls, snobby former friends, bad grades, her tweaker mother, the horrible state of pretty much everything—none of it mattered as much anymore.

Her go-to defensive mode—sarcasm and snark, moody silences —had taken a back seat to actually *doing* something. She felt useful here. Wanted and appreciated.

Noah Sheridan was the first adult other than Gran and Gramps who'd treated her like a real person, with thoughts and feelings and ideas as valid as his own. Daphne and Atticus Bishop treated her the same way. Despite her natural cynicism, she liked them for that.

A distant scream echoed through the sanctuary.

Quinn opened her eyes.

She'd been subjected to screams and shrieks and squeals all day. Kids screamed all the time. But this was different.

This was an adult scream. High and desperate. It curdled her blood.

It came again, from somewhere outside. Or maybe the food pantry or fellowship hall on the other side of the church.

The back of her neck prickled. The hairs on her arms stood on end.

Quinn sat up straight. Milo murmured sleepily as she pushed him aside a little too hard. But she didn't have time to worry about his comfort.

Around her, men and women were glancing at each other, puzzled and confused, unsettled. Another cry—a high, hysterical shout.

A toddler started crying. His mother shushed him, pulling him close and rocking him on her hip. "What was that?" she asked the room.

No one had a chance to answer her.

The doors to the sanctuary burst open. Several figures dressed in black rushed in. Black ski masks covered their faces. Gripped in their hands were gleaming, wicked-looking automatic weapons.

For a terrible second, no one moved. Everyone in the pews stared at the figures in shock. Their brains couldn't compute this bizarre new information. It made no sense.

These people didn't belong here. The guns didn't belong here.

They were here anyway.

41

QUINN
DAY SEVEN

Quinn's heart leapt into her throat. Her lungs constricted. Everything turned slow and jerky, so vivid and bright, the images seared the backs of her eyelids.

Milo started to sit up. Instinctively, she pushed him back down.

It all happened so unbelievably fast. Her brain didn't have time to compute the stimuli firing through her synapses, to make sense of the scene unfolding right in front of her.

The figures with guns didn't say anything. They didn't make demands, didn't scream insults or threats.

They simply raised their weapons and opened fire.

The sanctuary exploded into noise and chaos. The *crack* and *boom* of gunshots. Panicked screams and shouts split the air.

Rounds slammed into the stone walls. Shattered the stained-glass windows. Punched through wooden pews, spraying stuffing into the air. The cacophonous *rat-a-tat* blasted her eardrums. So loud, impossibly loud.

And the bodies. Bodies jittering like puppets on a string. Bodies jerking, falling, collapsing.

She could barely hear through the ringing in her ears, the panic overtaking her. For a horrible frozen moment, Quinn couldn't move. She sat there, one hand on Milo, mouth open in shock, in silent horror as death announced itself all around her.

People fled, leaping over pews, falling and crawling on hands and knees toward the side exit. A dark-haired man running down the center aisle pitched suddenly forward, shot in the back. A woman's neck snapped to the side. She was already dead before she hit the carpet.

A man scrambled up the dais toward the big wooden cross as if that alone could save him. His legs weren't working right. He was using his arms to army-crawl, a spreading stain of red leaving a trail in his wake.

The figures in black spread out from the back of the sanctuary. Two were striding down the middle aisle. Two more each took the far aisles. The last two guarded the doors.

The masked men advanced, aiming and firing at anything that moved.

A Hispanic woman five pews in front of her spun to face Quinn. Their terrified eyes locked.

Quinn recognized her as the dental hygienist who worked at Brite Smiles Dental, who cleaned Quinn's teeth like clockwork twice a year and always complimented her blue hair.

The woman opened her mouth like she was going to say something to Quinn, to offer a warning or a crucial piece of advice—maybe the secret to surviving what was coming, a way to escape this monstrous horror that had snatched them up in its jaws.

Whatever she was going to say, Quinn never heard it.

The woman's body juddered as rounds ripped across her torso. Bright red blood sprayed from the side of her head as she toppled sideways.

The awful sight ripped Quinn from her shock. She ducked

low in the pew and pressed herself on top of Milo. As if a thin wedge of polished wood could save them from a spray of bullets.

She rolled off the pew and lowered herself to the carpet. She reached up, seized Milo's arm, and yanked him down. He fell on top of her, his bony elbow digging into her stomach, his foot kicking her shins.

She squeezed to the side, half under the next pew, and pulled him close to her. The space between the pews wasn't large, but Quinn was small enough and so was Milo. The stale air smelled like unwashed feet and dust.

A sneeze surged up her nose. She clamped one hand over her mouth and nose and fought it back.

Her heart thrashed in her chest, her pulse a roar in her ears. They had to get out of here.

Milo's face was inches from hers. His pupils were huge, his little chest heaving.

"Don't look," she whispered into his ear. "Be absolutely quiet. This is like a game. A terrible game. But we're going to win it. And the way you win is by *not looking*."

Milo nodded, eyes wide and frantic.

She rolled onto her stomach and inched forward a foot until she could see between the pews directly in front of her. She turned her head and craned her neck to see beneath the pews on either side.

The exit door was on the front left side of the sanctuary. She was on the right side. She couldn't see it from here, but her last image of it was fresh in her mind—dead, bloodied bodies slumped in front of the still-closed door. No one had gotten out. Not that way.

Her body flushed ice-cold as adrenaline pumped through her system. Her mouth was bone-dry. Her thoughts came in panicky, frenetic jerks and starts. *Think, damn it, think!*

If they ran for it, the attackers would see them and gun them down. There were too many of them. No way would they miss a girl and a little boy sprinting for safety.

They couldn't just sit here waiting to be slaughtered either.

Her heart in her throat, Quinn twisted her neck, cheek pressed to the carpet, and turned her head to look the other way, toward the back of the sanctuary—the foyer, the double door entrance.

She could see their feet. Black clomping boots. The attackers were moving slowly, systematically, checking each row before moving on.

They were still fifteen or so pews back. The barrage of gunfire had slowed to an occasional burst.

Because everyone else is already dead.

She didn't push the thought down or try to ignore it. She used the sour-sick fear churning in her belly to spur herself to *move.*

She tapped Milo's shoulder. When he looked at her, his little face stricken with terror, she pressed her finger to her lips.

Absolute silence. No talking.

Milo nodded. He understood.

Two of the attackers yelled something at each other, but her rattled brain couldn't focus on their words. Every ounce of her attention was on *getting out.*

She pushed Milo beneath the pew in front of them. She wriggled up to crawl beside him. Milo was tiny and squeezed easily beneath the pews.

Quinn was strong but scrawny for sixteen, and it saved her now as she squirmed after Milo, her head turned sideways, her cheek scraping the rough carpet, her body pressed flat. She clawed at the floor, using only her hands and arms to pull herself forward.

One pew. Then two. Three.

Someone moaned. A burst of gunfire and it went quiet.

Footsteps behind them, drawing closer. How far away were they now? Twelve rows? Ten?

They were moving faster than she and Milo could crawl.

The scent of coppery blood filled her nostrils. Blood soaked the carpet. It leached into her pants, her sweatshirt, slick and wet beneath her bare hands.

She pushed ahead of Milo, turning slightly so she blocked his view of what lay ahead. They reached the body of the hygienist. Appalled, Quinn forced herself to reach out and press two fingers to the woman's throat.

She was dead. They were all dead.

Another body lay next to the woman. And another and another. Glassy, staring eyes. Ravaged, bloodied torsos and limbs. Blood-spattered faces frozen in a rictus of horror.

The bodies blocked their path forward. She and Milo were stuck between two pews, their heads and torsos exposed between the rows, their legs hidden by the pew behind them.

Her mind recoiled. But she couldn't stop. She couldn't dwell on the heinous images searing her brain.

She and Milo had to live. That was all there was to it. She would do what she had to do.

She was still partially blocking Milo's view with her own body. She reached for the woman's body again, then tapped his shoulder.

When he turned to look at her, she spread blood across his cheeks and forehead. His eyes widened, alarmed and repulsed. His mouth opened, but no sound escaped his lips.

Someone cried out. Another gunshot.

Closer now.

They were running out of time. Panicked, she stretched her hand beneath the pew and touched the dead woman's head. Slick wetness, shards of bone and bits of brain tissue, only slippery goop where skull and skin and hair should be.

Her stomach convulsed, sour acid burning the back of her throat. She wiped the blood across her own face. She lowered her hand, turned with difficulty onto her side, and lathered her slick wet hands across her chest and belly. She did the same to Milo.

She hoped he understood, hating that she couldn't explain it to him. If he could understand, if he could listen to her and do what she needed him to do, maybe they would live through the next five minutes.

Quinn had no plan beyond that.

42

QUINN
DAY SEVEN

ootsteps and voices drew closer.

Her breath caught in her throat. They were out of time.

Quinn pressed her cheek to the carpet, made her body go limp and loose. She bent her head so Milo could see her face and closed her eyes, desperately sending whatever thoughts or prayers or vibes would get him to fathom what she needed him to do.

She peeked through her lids. Milo's eyes were closed. He lay unmoving. A shiver of dread went through her. Covered in blood and gore, he looked dead himself.

That, of course, was the plan.

Quinn forced herself to shut her eyes and willed the life from her arms and legs, the color from her cheeks. She'd matted her hair and plastered her face and neck with someone else's lifeblood. She hoped she looked as dead as Milo. It was their only chance.

A few pews behind them, someone cried out. Two gunshots. The cries went silent.

Quinn waited, her mind screaming inside her skull, her heart about to pound right outside of her chest. The fetid stench of guts and human excrement assailed her nostrils, nearly choking her. Her closed eyes watered and burned.

The footsteps stopped. They were close, so close. At their row or right behind them. Was he watching the bodies, studying them for movement, for any signs of life?

Quinn didn't breathe. She felt every muscle, every twitching nerve, and willed herself utterly still. Her pulse had never sounded so loud.

"You got anything?" a deep male voice shouted only feet away.

"Nothing here," another voice answered, this one from across the sanctuary. "They're all dead. All of them."

The attacker closest to them snorted. "Got what they deserved, didn't they?"

"We've got the wife!" a third attacker yelled from out in the foyer.

Her heart pounded in her ears, her held breath burning in her lungs. The voices sounded familiar. She couldn't think clearly. Frantic, fluttering panic muddled every thought but *stay alive.*

"Bring her in here," the first attacker said. "Bet she's ready to talk now."

Footsteps. The sound of something heavy dragging on the ground. Someone screamed—high and sharp and desperate.

"Let me go! You can't do this! You have no—" the voice cut off into a keening wail of anguish. "No! No, no, no!"

Quinn almost flinched. That voice she knew without a doubt —Daphne Bishop.

"My daughters!" Daphne cried. "What have you done with them? If you've hurt them, if they're hurt . . ." her voice dissolved into frantic, hiccupping sobs.

Daphne was losing it. She'd just laid eyes on unimaginable carnage. She probably thought her daughters were dead. And maybe they were.

Or maybe they were still in the Sunday school rooms, hiding. Still alive. Still able to be saved.

The boots finally moved away, footsteps thudding back toward the foyer.

She was too terrified to feel relief. She sucked in a desperate shallow breath but kept her head down, her body limp.

A sharp crack sounded. Daphne moaned.

"Tell us where the safe is, and maybe we'll let you live," said the twitchy one.

"What? I don't know—where's my husband? Where are my girls? Please, please don't hurt them. We'll do anything. Please . . ."

"The safe. Where is it?"

"What safe? I don't—"

"The gold, you stupid whore!"

Another sharp crack. As if one of them had struck her in the face or head with the butt of his rifle.

Daphne only moaned.

"We need to find those pretty girls of yours?" drawled the third voice, slow and sleepy and laced with menace. "Will that get you to open that pretty mouth of yours and tell us what we need to know?"

Quinn's heart raced. A cold chill skittered up her spine.

She recognized these voices from somewhere. She knew she did. The fractured, jumbled shards of her thoughts were coming together again. Shaping the pieces to a gruesome and terrible puzzle.

"No! Please! I'll tell you anything." Daphne's words were garbled and wet sounding, like her mouth was full of blood. "I don't—know—what you're talking about—"

"Look around you, lady. What do you see? You think we're patient men? Do you think we won't do it? You need another demonstration?"

"Please God." Daphne was weeping now, desperate, frantic, utterly helpless. "Protect my babies. Though I walk through the valley of the shadow of death, I will fear no evil. Thy rod and thy staff, they comfort me—"

"Shut up!" the twitchy one shouted. "Shut the hell up!"

More footsteps marched across the foyer tile floor.

"We found the preacher," a fourth voice said.

The ragged, growling timbre of that voice—it was unforgettable. How many times had she heard it hurling insults and curses through her flimsy bedroom door? Dozens. Hundreds.

Ray Shultz.

And now she knew the others. The slow drawl of Tommy Carter. The twitchy, high-pitched whine of his brother, Bucky. The deeper voice of Nickel.

Billy must be around somewhere.

And her mother? Was she here, too? Was she a part of this horror?

Something splintered inside her, something deep and dark and ugly.

"We've got the preacher in one of the supply rooms," Ray said. "Bring the wife. He's not talking, but he will once he sees her."

Something wet and slimy touched her hand.

Her heart kicked. Adrenaline iced her veins. She almost screamed out loud.

Milo. It was Milo. He slid his fingers through hers and squeezed. She squeezed back.

Quinn struggled to think clearly through the panic. She couldn't concern herself with Octavia now. Milo was right. They couldn't lay here and hope these scumbags would just leave. They wouldn't.

She'd seen enough movies to know that soldiers and trained combatants combed the battlefield post-attack and put a round in each victim's head, whether they appeared dead or not.

These monsters could still come back.

She had to get out of here, get Milo out of here, while they were still distracted with Daphne. She couldn't do anything to help Daphne.

Desperation congealing in her belly, she tried frantically to reconstruct the sanctuary in her mind. She'd only been in here a few times, but she'd explored while playing hide and seek with Milo and the girls.

Besides the double doors at the rear of the sanctuary that led to the foyer and the front entrance, there were two other doors: the exit door along the front left side and the door behind the dais on the front right side.

She didn't know their official titles, but there were several back rooms and a long hallway that led to the Sunday school classrooms. At the end of the hallway was an exit door leading to the overflow parking lot where she and the kids had set up the paper target only hours ago.

She strained her ears again. The voices and footsteps had drifted through the rear set of doors. The sanctuary was silent.

Her muscles aching from the tension, she wriggled her legs sideways, rolling her lower half out from beneath the pew behind her. Using her arms, she shuffled backward until she'd extricated herself from beneath both pews.

She rose onto her hands and knees, keeping her head down.

Milo turned his head toward her. All she could see of his face beneath the streaks of red were the frantic whites of his eyes. His chest was heaving, rapid, shallow breaths exhaling through his opened mouth.

He couldn't get too stressed, or his body would turn on itself. She knew that. But she didn't know what to do about it. All she could focus on was getting them out of here alive.

She held her finger to her lips again. He needed to be still and quiet just a little longer.

Cautiously, as silently as she possibly could, she crawled along the floor parallel with the pews. She moved gingerly over a man's legs and brushed aside a limp hand, a gold wedding band glinting beneath the vibrant red coating his skin like paint.

Once she reached the end of the pew, she peered around the edge. Three of the four attackers were gone. So was Daphne.

One attacker remained. He was leaning against the back of the first pew, turned away from the sanctuary and facing the opened double doors that led to the foyer and the front entrance of the church, smoking a cigarette.

She didn't see the rifle, but she was sure it was close by.

She looked the other way. The pews partially obscured her vision. Bodies lay everywhere, their limbs in grotesque contortions. Men and women. Children.

Her gaze skipped over the faces. She couldn't bear it.

All they needed to do was make it to the nearest exit. Open the door. Run out.

How easy it sounded. How difficult it would be.

43

QUINN
DAY SEVEN

With no room to turn in the narrow space between pews, Quinn crawled backward to Milo. Once she reached him, she managed to squirm around to face him. He looked at her, tense and scared, waiting for her to tell him what to do, where to go.

The exit door was located on the far left side, all the way across the sanctuary. The door leading to the Sunday school rooms and another exit was on their side, but it required exposing themselves as they crawled up the dais.

If the guard at the back turned around . . . If anyone entered at the exact moment they moved . . .

Too many ifs.

Maybe they could keep playing dead until these madmen finally left and someone came to rescue them. Maybe Ray and his crew wouldn't come through the sanctuary again and put a bullet in the head of every victim, just to make sure.

Too many maybes.

Either way, they could die. Either way might be the wrong choice. A decision had to be made.

Indecision was a decision.

She hesitated, conflicted, urgency and desperation crowding her chest, suffocating her breath.

You should leave him behind, a voice whispered in her mind. *He'll only hold you back. He'll probably get you killed.*

It wasn't her voice. It was Octavia's voice. A voice she despised. Ugly and selfish. But not always wrong either.

A small hand clasped hers. She looked down. Milo was staring back up at her, fear radiating from his entire body. But it was more than fear—trust shone in his eyes.

Milo Sheridan trusted Quinn to get him out of here alive. She was just a teenage girl, basically weaponless, without a plan or backup or anything but the slingshot in her pocket and her own frantic mind.

She was all he had. She was responsible for him.

She didn't want to be. A huge part of her just wanted to turn and run and find the nearest exit as quickly as possible, Milo and responsibility be damned. Take care of herself. Save herself.

It wasn't selfishness. It was self-preservation. The oldest instinct known to man.

Octavia would run. Octavia would've already abandoned the boy. Hell, she would've offered him up as a sacrifice if she thought it might save her own skin.

And not just Milo. Quinn knew she'd betray her own daughter for far less than a life. She'd already done it. For a shiny new boyfriend. For her next hit.

Her mother fled from responsibility, from obligation, from family, every chance she got. If Quinn did this—if she left this child behind—she would be as bad as Octavia.

And that, she could not, would not, do.

Quinn would stay with Milo. And she would find the Bishop girls and rescue them too if she could.

She squeezed Milo's hand, leaned in, and pressed her mouth

to his ear. She risked the faintest whisper. "If they come, drop and play dead. I'll distract them. Remember, Small Fry, don't look at anything but me. Just me."

He nodded.

She moved ahead of him. They crawled single-file, hardly breathing, blood rushing in their ears, the carpet scraping their palms and kneecaps.

Move, move, move. The mantra blared through her mind in garish lights the color of the blood spilled everywhere in this room, the blood staining her hands and face and clothes and soul.

Her left shoulder scuffed the shelf of hymnals lining the back of the pew.

Quinn and Milo froze. She strained her ears, expecting a grunt of surprise, waiting for the burst of automatic fire that would end them, then and there.

Nothing. No sound from the back of the sanctuary.

They kept going. They reached the aisle against the wall at the end of the row of pews and followed the wall down toward the front. Every hand or knee placed with extreme care and precision.

What if one of those monsters was sneaking up on them right now, muzzle aimed at their exposed backs? She twisted around, craning her neck to glance behind her.

Nothing. Just the bare wall. Stained-glass windows covered in blankets shredded with holes.

They reached the end of the pews at the front. Directly ahead, the raised dais with the organ, the pulpit, and the giant wooden cross.

She paused. Milo came up beside her. Behind the cover of the front pew, they rested for a moment on their hands and knees, breathing hard and listening.

Her pulse was a thunderous roar in her head. Every breath loud as an explosion. Dread coiling in her chest, her guts like water.

They had to cross several exposed feet to reach the dais steps. Climb the steps, run across the dais, swing around the organ and the potted plant to the hall hidden beyond it.

Just a few seconds.

One glance back and the masked man would see them, sound the alarm. That's all it would take. One sound. One misstep.

Don't overthink it. Just MOVE.

Their eyes met. She held up a finger. *One, two, three.*

Pushing Milo in front of her, her sweaty blood-slick hand gripping his, they rose to a crouch and darted across the wide aisle and up the steps of the dais. Bent double and keeping low, they crossed the dais, dodging the potted plant, the mangled bodies— don't look, don't *see.*

They skirted the organ and hugged the wall until they reached the back, then fled down the short hallway and halted in front of the closed door.

Her mind screamed at her to slam into it and keep running, but sound would betray them. She forced herself to turn the handle and opened it excruciatingly slowly.

She held her breath. *Don't squeak, stupid hinges. Don't squeak.*

They didn't.

Milo slipped ahead of her like a bloodied ghost. She followed and closed the door silently behind her, wincing at the faint *click.*

Her legs sagged. She leaned against the door for a moment, struggling to compose herself, to breathe.

They were out of the sanctuary, but they were still trapped inside the church with at least five masked madmen armed with automatic weapons. One of them was Ray Shultz. One of them might be her own mother.

She wiped her bloody hand on her coat and slipped her free hand into her pocket. She wanted to hold the slingshot. Needed the comforting feel of it.

If it came to it, she could use it to defend them.

She wasn't afraid of killing a man. Not if he deserved it.

She adjusted her grip on Milo's hand. "Run!"

44

NOAH

DAY SEVEN

"How's it going?" Noah asked. "Or shouldn't I ask?"

"We're making do, Noah," Shen Lee said without smiling.

Lee was a slightly overweight Chinese American guy in his mid-thirties with short, gel-spiked black hair, a gap-toothed smile, and an open, friendly face. He was usually insufferably positive, but today, he looked stressed.

Lee worked as a pediatric nurse at Lakeland Hospital in Niles, but he had volunteered to run the high school emergency shelter with Annette King. With Dr. Prentice stuck somewhere in California, Lee was their primary medical expert.

Noah glanced around the high school gym. There were almost two hundred townspeople spread out on cots, blankets, and gym mats inside the gymnasium. The generator kept the heat running along with several propane heaters and battery-operated and kerosene lanterns several people had scrounged up from their basement and garage camping supplies.

The adults hunched in groups and clusters while kids ran around shouting and screaming. A bunch of little kids were crying. Most people looked stressed and tense, their hair unwashed, clothing rumpled.

More than a few were coughing and sneezing. Several looked glassy-eyed and feverish.

"Are people getting sick?"

"We're dealing with several pneumonia and hypothermia cases," Lee explained. "And the flu is going around. Medical supplies are getting scarce, but we're handling it so far. As long as there's no outbreaks of anything."

Noah nodded, relieved.

"Mr. Vinson said the pharmacy is running low on antibiotics. Maybe we can organize a trip to Lakeland to request some aid?"

Noah knew all about the pharmacy's low supplies. Milo had five days of pills left. Noah didn't have the energy to explain that the other towns were already overwhelmed with their own needs and weren't interested in sharing. "We'll see what we can do."

The high school shelter was the last item on his checklist before he could clock out. He'd had a long night. He was more than ready to get Milo and go home.

He was supposed to pick up Milo and Quinn two hours ago. Time had slipped away from him. There was simply too much to do and not enough qualified manpower to do it.

He missed cell phones, when communication was instantaneous, only a quick text message away. Of all the conveniences of modern life they'd just lost, phones were one of the worst.

Annette King strode over, looking frazzled. "We're low on food. We only have another days' worth, maybe two if we really stretch it out. We had to cut rations the last few days, and people are still hungry. A lot of people got upset. The Johnsons started yelling, knocked over some trashcans. They pushed one of my volunteers. For a minute, I thought they might actually barge into the cafeteria and start stealing the remaining supplies. Once one person starts, everything will go downhill fast."

"Do you want me to ask them to leave?"

Annette lowered her voice. "They've got two kids. No fireplace and no well water. What are they going to do? We might reach that point, but not yet. I was hoping you could just warn them."

"Of course."

"What we need, besides more food—and toilet paper—is a security guard. Someone to keep things in check."

Noah twisted his wedding ring, his anxiety growing. Only one week in, the shelter was clearly struggling. People were getting more and more stressed. Rosamond's "everyone chips in" only went so far when folks had their own dwindling resources and children to feed.

"I can't promise you anything, other than we'll try to stop in more."

Annette sighed. "Yeah, I get it."

"Sorry, Annette," he said. "Okay, point me to the Johnsons—"

"Sheridan, you there?" The radio crackled. "We have a problem."

Noah unhooked the radio from his belt and moved away from Annette and Lee for privacy. "I'm here, Julian. What problem? What now?"

"Our suspects in the courthouse jail seem to have . . . disappeared."

Noah went very still. "What do you mean?"

"One of our new recruits—Channing Harris—he was in the courthouse pulling guard duty. He admitted to dozing off upstairs sometime around five p.m. He woke around seven, but didn't check on them to change the piss bucket until eight. They were gone."

Noah went rigid. "What?"

"The door was open. He says the key was on the table, but

now it's gone. He thinks they jimmied the antique lock somehow. The thing's a hundred and thirty years old."

"Then why would they take the key?"

"How the hell should I know, Sheridan?"

"How do we know Harris didn't let them out himself?"

"We don't. That's why Reynoso has him in custody until we figure out what the hell just happened."

Noah's gut tightened. "Could be one of the Carter lackeys just walked right past his sorry snoring ass, snatched the key, and let them out right under his nose."

"You're probably right. That's what you get when you're forced to trust civilians with crap like this, isn't it?"

He glanced at his watch. It was already eight-thirty. They'd been out for three hours, maybe more, depending on how honest Harris was regarding his nap. "Damn it!"

"We're going after them. No holds barred this time. To hell with Chief Briggs. I assume you're okay with that."

Noah strode toward the gymnasium's front doors. "I'm coming with you."

"We're gearing up and headed to the Carter's compound. Of course, they could be holed up with that second cousin of theirs, Frank Lambert, on Sanders Road near Baroda—"

"No!"

It was wrong. All wrong. Ray Shultz wouldn't "hole up." Not after what happened at the pantry yesterday. They'd had three hours. Plenty of time to hit their place, gather weapons, and head out.

His blood ran cold.

"Julian," he said in a shaking voice, breaking into a run, "I know where they are."

45

QUINN
DAY SEVEN

Quinn gripped Milo's hand with all her might and pulled him along behind her. They moved silently but quickly down the darkened hallway.

The Sunday school rooms were located on the right side. Along the left wall, a bank of high, narrow windows provided the faintest light. The generator was only used to power the sanctuary. Thick shadows clung to everything. She blinked to adjust her eyes.

They kept moving. This part of the church wasn't heated. The cold sank into their bones. They were both shivering.

They passed a Bible study room, a janitor's supply closet, a small bathroom—all empty. Quinn pushed open each door, crept inside, and waited, straining for sound or movement, every muscle in her body tensed.

She called for the girls in a raw, desperate whisper. "Chloe? Juniper?"

They never answered.

The church building was vaguely L-shaped with the sanctuary in the corner of the L. They were in the long wing of the L.

The food pantry and supply rooms were located on the opposite side of the sanctuary, in the shorter wing.

She figured Ray and his cronies were all in the shorter wing, but she didn't know for sure. They needed to be careful.

Quinn and Milo crept through the darkness. Their footsteps were soft on the carpet, but they still sounded too loud in her ears. She kept craning her neck, looking in every direction, searching for danger, half-expecting a masked attacker to lunge out of the shadows and seize her by the throat.

She paused outside the secretary's office, listening. No sound. No hint of movement. She placed her left hand on the door handle and turned it.

The *click* was deafening. The door slid open.

She stepped inside, taking in the shadowy shapes of book-cases, a big wooden desk, a large copier machine in the corner.

"Juniper? Chloe? It's me. Come out."

With Milo glued to her side, she searched the deeper shadows in the corners, around the sides of the copier, behind the desk. She shuffled forward, hand outstretched to feel her way.

Her fingers smeared something slick and wet on the desk. She touched a soft, squishy thing that should've been warm but was already cooling, already waxy.

A body.

She recoiled, stepping back so abruptly that she bumped into Milo.

He stumbled and smacked his head against the copier. The *thud* echoed in the unnatural stillness.

Adrenaline spiking, Quinn ducked into a crouch and pulled Milo down with her. She put her finger to her lips and froze.

They'd be discovered now. One of the attackers would have heard, surely. They'd come in with their guns and their crazed, hate-filled eyes behind their ski masks and they'd do to her and Milo what they'd done in the sanctuary.

They waited, their own heartbeats and ragged breaths the only sound.

Nothing.

No one came for them. No guns blazed.

Not yet.

She rose to her feet, trembling all over, and pulled Milo up beside her. They left the body splayed across the desk and moved back to the hallway, searching for the next door.

Run, her brain screamed at her. *Just run.*

But those girls. Lost and scared and hiding. She was them. She'd been them. Not exactly. But close enough.

Cowering and frightened in the closet, tiny hands clasped over her ears to drown out the shouting. So scared to come out, she'd peed her pants at age seven. Or other times, waking up to the dead silence of the trailer, knowing with absolute certainty that she was all alone, that her mother had abandoned her to party somewhere far away.

Quinn wouldn't be Octavia. She wouldn't leave them behind.

The next door opened to the pastor's office. It was empty.

The room after that was some sort of storage closet. Ten by ten. Shelves of large plastic totes. Dark lumps and shapes she didn't recognize. Her fingers found racks of clothing on hangers.

At first her brain wouldn't compute, but then she understood. Mesh strung tight over wire shaped like wings. Bathrobes and long cotton dresses. Pipe cleaners twisted around a circular wire. Kids' costumes. Angels and Bible characters for Christmas and Easter programs.

She pushed through the clothes, expecting to touch the wall. Her hand found something warm and soft instead.

It wriggled away from her with a cry.

"Shhh! It's me. It's Quinn," she whispered fiercely. "Shh."

The little girl went still. Quinn dropped Milo's hand and helped her out of the clothing rack. Chloe Bishop flung herself at

Quinn and buried her tear-streaked face in Quinn's stomach. Her tiny body shook violently.

Fabric rustled in the next rack, and Juniper clambered out. She was trembling, but her eyes were dry. "We heard loud bangs and scary sounds and we hid."

"Good thinking," Quinn whispered.

Milo hugged Juniper. "You're safe with us."

"What's going on?" Juniper's little voice was tremulous, like she was barely holding on, trying desperately to be the brave big sister.

"The bad guys are hurting people," Milo said.

Juniper and Chloe looked to Quinn for confirmation.

Most adults lied to kids. They thought they couldn't take it or that they were protecting them by withholding the truth. Quinn hated being lied to and patronized. She wouldn't do it to them.

She could barely make out the shapes of them, let alone read their faces or expressions. "There are bad guys. They're hurting people. Killing them."

"What about Mama and Papa?" Juniper asked.

"They're grown-ups. We can't worry about them. We have to worry about ourselves."

"What's that smell?" Chloe asked, her nose wrinkling.

Quinn had nearly forgotten the blood and gore she'd smeared over Milo and herself. "Blood," she answered truthfully. "We're okay, but other people aren't."

"We're escaping the bad guys," Milo whispered. "Quinn says we're getting the hell out of here."

"Don't leave us," Juniper said, tears in her voice. "I'm so scared."

"I won't," Quinn said, and she meant it. "We have to be as quiet as possible so we can get out of here and get to safety, okay?"

The girls nodded.

Beside her, Milo went rigid. He squeezed her arm.

She glanced down at him. He pointed in silence at something behind her.

Quinn whirled, her heart in her throat.

A flashlight beam played across the wall opposite the costume storage room. Someone was coming.

46

QUINN

DAY SEVEN

Q uinn pressed herself against the wall in the narrow space behind the opened door, sucking in her stomach, her head turned sideways, making herself as small as possible. She gripped the slingshot down at her side, her ammo ball already loaded.

Juniper and Chloe hid behind the clothing racks again. Milo crouched behind a stack of three plastic totes in the far corner. She urgently admonished the kids in her mind: *Stay quiet. Stay invisible.*

The light flashed brighter. Footsteps grew louder. Two pairs of footsteps? Or only one?

With her heart jackhammering in her ears, it was hard to tell. She willed herself not to breathe. The handle of the slingshot stuck to her palm, the blood drying tacky on her skin. Other people's blood. Dead people's blood.

The figure paused in the opened doorway. The flashlight beam swept the room. "Here, little piggy. Come out, come out. Wherever you are."

Quinn stiffened. Anxiety torqued through her. She knew that bored, simpering voice.

Billy Carter entered the room. She sensed rather than saw him, judging his movements by the way the flashlight shifted and grew exponentially brighter. He was somewhere to her left. The door blocked her view other than a narrow wedge directly in front of her.

The clothes on the racks. A couple of the hangers were still moving. Trembling ever so slightly.

Her veins went slick with terror. She tightened her grip on the slingshot.

Maybe he would miss it. Maybe he would just walk right out and—

Billy focused the flashlight on the costume rack. "There you are."

Before she could do anything, he lunged forward—into her line of sight—plunged one hand into the costumes, and yanked Chloe out.

He dropped her, shrieking and squealing, and lunged in again for Juniper.

In a heartbeat, both girls had been plucked from their hiding spots. They huddled on the floor, crying and sniffling, whimpering in terror, their small arms wrapped around each other.

Billy had dropped his semi-automatic rifle onto a sling to grab the girls, but he already had it in his hands again—ready to fire, to do horrible things.

She didn't remember seeing him put the flashlight down, but it was lying on the carpet next to the stacked plastic totes in the corner, the room alight in an eerie mix of harsh brightness and deep shadows.

Quinn's lungs contracted. She had to do something. What was a slingshot against a gun? Nothing. But she sure as hell wasn't going to stand by and watch him hurt little kids.

She needed a few seconds to calm her frantically beating heart, to think.

Stay down, she whispered to Milo in her mind. *Stay hidden, Small Fry. No matter what.*

He didn't.

Milo popped up from behind the plastic totes, his hands balled into tiny fists, his brave little face bone-white. "Don't hurt them! I won't let you hurt them!"

She wasn't ready to act. She didn't have a plan yet. But that didn't matter now. She had to move.

Everything seemed to happen in slow motion.

Billy turned toward Milo.

Quinn elbowed the door out of the way and lifted the sling-shot, the three-eighth-inch steel ammo ball tucked into the rubber sling, ready. She yanked it back, aimed at the back of Billy Carter's head, and released.

Billy sensed something and whirled at the last second. The ammo skimmed the side of his head rather than striking him in the center of the skull with bone-cracking force.

With a shriek of pain, he dropped the rifle on its sling and clutched at his head. Blood trickled between his fingers. "What the—"

Desperate to hit him again, she fumbled with the slingshot, rummaging frantically in her pocket for more ammo, but she wasn't fast enough.

He was on her in an instant.

Billy Carter was short, the same height she was, but every ounce of his small frame was hard and wiry muscle. He was incredibly strong.

He seized a hank of her hair and yanked her, stumbling and screaming, from behind the door. He dragged her to the center of the room beside the girls and struck her in the head with the stock of his rifle.

Hot white lightning exploded in front of her eyelids. Blinding pain. Her legs gave out, and she sagged to her knees.

"You little slut! You almost shot my eye out!"

Billy aimed a savage kick at her hand. Pain shot up her arm, thrummed through her fingers and palm. The slingshot went flying across the room. She didn't see where it landed.

Before she could react or move, he aimed the rifle muzzle in her face. The enormous black hole filled her blurry vision.

"Don't!" Milo knocked over the storage containers and ran in front of her, putting his tiny body between her and the muzzle of the AR-15. "Don't hurt her!"

Billy leered at her. Blood dripped from a rip in his ski mask. She couldn't see his face beneath that awful mask, only the black shining eyes. One eye glaring at her, the other staring off at something else.

"You're both gonna die tonight, kid," he growled. "Ain't nothing gonna change that now."

She managed to grab Milo around the waist and pull him out of the line of fire. He crumpled into a ball beside her, clinging to her arm. Behind her, Chloe and Juniper cried softly.

She tried to think clearly, to figure something out, but panic buzzed in her brain. She couldn't think a single coherent thought. There was only the fear. And the pain.

A second figure entered. Dressed in black like Billy, but taller and leaner. Black ski mask. An AR-15 balanced in his arms. He was shaky, twitchy.

The figure stopped short when he saw them. His head turned, taking in the little girls huddled against the clothing rack, sobbing. Quinn bowed on her knees with Milo before the man with the gun.

Billy let out an irritated curse and spat on the floor. "I know you got a soft spot for kids. You best turn around and leave right now."

"Not kids." The figure pointed at Quinn. "Just that one."

Time elongated. A staticky buzzing in her ears. A jolt went through her, all the way to her core.

Octavia. Quinn's mother was here.

47

QUINN
DAY SEVEN

Quinn stared at her mother in dread.

Octavia Riley was a part of this. This horror. All the death and carnage.

Ray had always been a shark, and Octavia had never questioned his brutality—or reined in her own cruel streak. But this?

Quinn felt like she'd just been gut-punched with a sledgehammer.

"How dare you?" Quinn asked. "How could you do this?"

"Shut up!" Octavia snarled, not even bothering to look at her.

Octavia shifted nervously, her movements jerky and frenetic. She was high as a kite. Quinn didn't need to see her hollow face to know that. It was in her twitchy limbs, in her scratchy, feverish voice.

"Your spawn nearly killed me," Billy said, gesturing at Quinn. "What the hell is she doing here?"

"Hell if I know. I'm not her keeper."

"You know what Ray would say. And Tommy." Billy's voice was low, a warning. "They said no witnesses."

Octavia didn't move. Quinn could hear her rapid, panting breaths, could smell the stench of sour sweat wafting off her.

"She's no problem," Octavia said finally. "I tell her, she won't say a damn thing to nobody."

Quinn bit her tongue. Hot coppery warmth flooded her mouth. She rarely did a single thing Octavia told her to, but this wasn't the time to get mouthy.

"She does, you're both dead."

"I'm not stupid. I know that."

Billy didn't move, didn't take his cross-eyed gaze off Quinn. "I should end her for what she did to my head!"

"She's my blood." Octavia scratched at her neck over her ski mask. "I'll owe you."

Billy's gaze roamed over Octavia's body in a sickening leer. He nodded, seemingly satisfied. "Yes, you will."

He swung the muzzle from Quinn to Milo.

"NO!" Quinn surged to her feet. "Don't touch him, or I'll kill you!"

"You might not want to kill that one either," Octavia said. "That's Sheridan's son. The cop. He could be useful."

"He's a freaking liability. They all are."

"So kill him later," Octavia said as easily as if she was discussing her next score. "Ray wants the girls. That's why I came to find you. You're taking too damn long."

"Don't you dare take them!" Quinn cried. "You can't have them!"

Juniper let out a horrible wail. Chloe moaned softly.

Octavia ignored them. "You're wasting time."

"No witnesses," Billy said. "That's the deal."

His eyes narrowed. His finger moved to the trigger. He was going to shoot Milo.

Quinn tuned out the pain pulsing in her skull. The world fell away—the supply room, her mother dressed in black, the sobbing girls and Milo shuddering beside her, Billy's vicious eyes, the barrel of the gun.

She pushed Milo to the floor. Almost in the same movement, the same breath, she flung herself at Billy. Sprang at him with a feral, frenzied cry, hands outstretched, fingers like claws.

"No!" Milo cried. "Quinn!"

The gun barrel struck her chest and was knocked aside. It didn't go off. She scratched at his face, going for his eyes, her fingernails scraping through the ski mask fabric. Her nails dug deep into the flesh over his nose and left cheek.

Billy let out a grunt of surprise. He staggered and fell back. Her momentum sent her falling on top of him, the rifle between them, but she couldn't get to it.

She didn't think. An animal fury coursed through her. She scrabbled at him, mauling him, tearing at his face with her fingers. The stupid ski mask kept her nails from doing enough damage. She growled in indignant, desperate anger.

Billy bucked beneath her, seized her shoulders, and threw her off him. She landed hard on her back. Pain spiked up and down her spine. He rolled on top of her, planted his knee on her chest, and punched her in the face, hard.

Agony radiated up her cheekbones straight to her brain. White spots flashed in front of her eyes as hot blood gushed over her lips and down her chin. She turned her head and retched from the blood and mucous going down the back of her nose into her throat.

Billy's oily black eyes flashed as he loomed over her. He grasped the rifle still hanging from the sling over his shoulder and pressed the barrel against her forehead. "You're gonna die now, you little—"

"You want the gold or not, Billy?" Octavia strode toward the girls. She dropped her rifle on its sling, grabbed the smallest one— Chloe—and hoisted the girl under one arm. "Bishop ain't talking.

Not even with Tommy working over the wife. Ray needs the girls, and he needs them now.

"Do you want me to tell him how you were jerking around over nothing? How long you think before the law gets here? We're running out of time. Lock them in. Let's do this, and we can come back for them. That kid could be our ticket out if things get hairy. You're the smart one, Billy. Come on. Put your dick back in your pants and think it through."

Billy cursed. He lowered the muzzle from Quinn's forehead and climbed off her.

Quinn barely felt relief. Darkness fringed her vision. She lay on her back, hardly able to move, blood in her mouth, on her face, dripping down the back of her throat.

"You watch them then," he said to Octavia.

"Whatever. Just go."

He grabbed Chloe from Octavia's arms. "I mean it."

Quinn tried to sit up, to go to her, but the nausea forced her back down. Her skull felt like an axe had just cleaved it in two. She spat a glob of blood and phlegm onto the carpet.

"Leave me alone!" Chloe screamed and batted uselessly at his face and shoulders with her tiny fists. Billy acted like he didn't even feel it, like she was little more than an irritating gnat.

He glared down at Juniper. "You come with me, too. You try to run or do anything other than what I tell you, I'm gonna break your sister's neck with my bare hands. I only need one of you. You understand?"

Juniper stared, hollow-eyed, face slack. She was going into shock. Her mind was shutting down to protect herself.

"Stop it!" Milo cried. "Don't take her!"

"Run, Juniper!" Quinn shouted. The sound of her own voice stabbed her throbbing head. "Don't listen to him! Run and hide!"

But Juniper didn't run. She walked obediently to Billy's side, her movements stiff and stilted, like a robot.

Billy turned and stalked from the room. Juniper trailed silently after him.

"Quinn!" Chloe cried. "Help! Quinn!"

Her terrible cries echoed down the corridor, seared into Quinn's brain.

Just like that, they were gone.

48

QUINN
DAY SEVEN

Octavia gestured with the AR-15. "Kid, get over there against the wall with all the clothes. Sit down with your legs crossed and your arms in your lap where I can see them. Quinn, come on. You have to get out of here."

Quinn didn't obey. Neither did Milo.

She blinked until her vision cleared and rose unsteadily to her feet. Dizziness slashed through her, but she remained upright.

She stood in the center of the room, Milo beside her, and faced her mother. "How could you let him take them! You know what he'll do!"

"That's none of your concern now. You got to think about you, baby girl. What the hell are you even doing here?"

"Don't call me that. Don't you dare call me that." Quinn started forward. Her breath came in shallow, guttural rasps. Her head ached with every movement. "We have to stop him. We have to save the girls—"

Octavia raised the rifle and pointed it at her again. "No."

Quinn halted. "What are you doing?"

"They aren't us! They're nothing like us. They're the ones

who judged us, turned their backs on us. Oh girl, I spent my entire life being judged and despised by these people. They hated you just like they hated me. You know I'm right. They're getting their due. They're getting exactly what they deserve."

And there it was. The cool indifference. The disregard for life. Her casual, dismissive selfishness. The way her own perceived mistreatment justified anything and everything.

Hot hatred erupted inside Quinn. "Move."

Octavia pulled the ski mask up over her face. Her skin was ashen, her gaze jumpy. "Forget about them. They're gone. You're the one in danger. I got Billy to leave so you could get out of here. You've got to go, honey."

"Move out of the way!"

Her face blanched. "I'm trying to help you!"

"Help? Is that what you think you're doing?"

"You get to leave. There's no one between here and the exit. I saved your life, baby girl." Her expression hardened. "Put my own ass on the line to do it too. A little thanks would be nice."

Anger thrummed through Quinn, overtaking the fear, the pain. She could barely keep her voice down. "You killed all those people!"

"I didn't pull the trigger," Octavia whined. Her eyes shuttered, went distant. "I didn't do nothing."

"You might as well have! You're just as guilty!"

"Guilty of what? All we want is what's owed us. That's what this is."

"Did you see the sanctuary? Did you see what they did?"

"I didn't see anything." Octavia gave a sharp shake of her head, her chin jutting defensively. "It's none of my business. Ray did what he had to do. He's not weak like most men."

That's what Octavia did. Spun lies and manipulated the truth to fit what she wanted. Pretended away reality if she didn't like it —or didn't want to admit it to someone else.

She didn't want to know. And so, she didn't.

Quinn licked the blood from her lips and spat on the carpet. She wiped the back of her arm across her face and took a step forward. She was done with this. Done with this woman who'd contributed DNA but little else. "Let us through, you waste of oxygen."

Octavia lifted the rifle. "Those girls aren't your business now. What is your business is Billy Carter. That man never lets a grudge go. Never. I know him. He's going to change his mind. As soon as he does what Ray wants, he's gonna come back here. And not with forgiveness on his mind neither."

"I'm not scared of him."

But she was. She knew exactly what Billy was capable of. She'd seen it firsthand. She scowled to keep her mother from seeing her fear.

"You should be, baby girl." Octavia's bloodless lips thinned. "Now move aside, or you'll make me do something I don't want to do."

"You won't shoot me. You don't have the balls."

"Not you." Octavia shifted her stance and adjusted the rifle in her shaky, twitchy hands. The muzzle wasn't aimed at Quinn. It was aimed at Milo.

Quinn's heart turned to ice. "Octavia—"

"I won't shoot you. I could never shoot you, baby girl. But I'll shoot the kid. Right in the leg."

Milo clung to her side, trembling like a leaf but still brave, so brave. "My Dad will come after you! He won't let you hurt us!"

Octavia snorted. "He doesn't need to be whole to be our protection. A hostage to make sure we get out of this place alive. See, those are the things I think of. *Me*. Ray never thinks down the line. He's not the smart one. I am."

Quinn stiffened. "Milo is coming with me."

"Like hell he is. He's my insurance. Get back, kid. You're staying right where you are."

"I'm not going anywhere with you!" Milo cried.

"They'll kill him," Quinn said.

"No, they won't." Octavia grinned, revealing her yellowed teeth, her face skeletal and garish in the eerie glare of the flashlight. "You don't need to worry about him, baby girl. This is about *us*. You and me."

Octavia was delusional. And she wasn't beyond killing Milo herself. Quinn believed that. Knew it in her bones.

Octavia Riley didn't care about anyone but herself. She never had.

A resounding *crack* echoed down the corridor. Muffled and distant. A gunshot.

Quinn and Octavia flinched.

Milo let out a dismayed whimper. "What was that?"

But they knew. They all knew.

Four more *cracks* followed the first one. Then silence.

Atticus and Daphne Bishop. Juniper and Chloe.

Quinn felt herself splintering. Breaking apart. Threatening to shatter into a thousand pieces.

No, no, no! This wasn't happening. Couldn't be happening. It had to be a dream. A terrible nightmare she could still wake up from.

Whatever lines or limits there were to sanity, she was past it, past anything a normal human being could endure.

But she couldn't crumple into a terror-stricken puddle of anguish and despair. She had to keep going, to keep pushing.

No way in hell was she dying here today. Not her. Not Milo.

Fury crackled through her like a forest fire. She let it burn through her, let it obliterate everything.

With a ferocious shriek, Quinn lunged forward and seized the barrel of the AR-15.

Octavia grunted and yanked back. The strap was still slung over her shoulder. Uncertainty flashed across her face. "What are you doing, baby girl?"

Quinn didn't bother to answer. She went for the gun.

She had always been strong, her muscles strengthened by climbing trees, shoveling the driveway, and helping Gramps chop wood. The drugs seething through Octavia's system made her strong, too.

They struggled over the gun in a silent, frenzied battle. Each grappling for the weapon, fingers clawing at the barrel, the hand-grip, the magazine and buttstock.

It wasn't working. Precious seconds ticked away. Every second that passed brought Billy Carter that much closer to this room, that much closer to killing her and Milo.

Billy wouldn't hesitate. Quinn didn't either.

She tensed her muscles, ducked in close, and kneed her mother as hard as she could in the gut. Blind panic fueled her.

Octavia collapsed in on herself, doubling over with a sharp gasp. She released the rifle.

Quinn wrestled the sling over her mother's shoulder and freed the weapon. She wrenched it from Octavia's grasp. Wielding it like a bat, she struck Octavia across the side of the head.

Octavia fell back, shock and betrayal registering on her face for the briefest second. Her body dropped like a marionette with its strings cut. She didn't get up.

Quinn didn't apologize. She felt no guilt. Maybe she would later. She couldn't think about anything, couldn't let the reality sink in or it would crush her.

The only thing she felt now was fear—and a fierce, primal determination to survive.

Blood pooled in the back of her throat with every swallow. It stuck tacky to her face, her hair. Her head pulsed; her nose felt broken. Adrenaline kept her on her feet.

Milo stood next to her. He looked at her, not Octavia's crumpled form. "Are you okay?"

"We're okay." She gripped the large, unwieldy weapon the way Gramps had taught her to shoot a .22, the stock butted up against her shoulder, like the madmen had as they unleashed death and destruction on the sanctuary.

She aimed straight ahead, her finger on the trigger guard but ready to shoot at any threat that came between her and Milo and escape.

"Come on, Small Fry." Quinn stepped over her mother's unconscious body. "We have to hurry."

49

NOAH
DAY SEVEN

Noah approached the rear entrance of Crossway Church at a crouch, his shotgun up and ready, muscles tensed, every sense on high alert.

The air was sharp and brittle. No wind stirred the trees. Their boots crunched dully through thick snow. An owl hooted from somewhere nearby.

He strained to listen, but the snow seemed to absorb all sound into itself. The wide, vast darkness absorbed all light and color.

The night was pitch black. No lights from the town. No red streaks from planes overhead. No street lights. No warm glow from the windows of neighboring houses. Only the narrow beams of their tactical flashlights pierced the darkness.

The cold penetrated straight through his department-issued coat. It seared his lungs with every frigid breath, burned every inch of his exposed skin. It was shocking in its violence. The cold was a brutal predator sapping their energy and strength, but not their resolve.

Julian and two other officers flanked him—Oren Truitt and

Clint Moll. One of their part-time officers, Samantha Perez, took up the rear and watched their six.

Chief Briggs, Hayes, and their team were approaching the church from the front, and Reynoso and a third three-man team of volunteer officers took the emergency exit on the west side.

All the officers wore standard body armor, which included ballistic vests. They had their department-issued Glocks holstered at their hips and carried Remington 870 12-gauge shotguns with tactical flashlights mounted on the barrels.

Normally, the response team would include county deputies and officers from various municipalities within the county. But tonight, they were only thirteen men against however many heavily armed, deranged maniacs lurked inside.

No backup. No choppers to call in for air support. No SWAT. No neighboring precincts to call for additional support. They didn't even have dispatch.

They were completely and utterly on their own.

Noah's stomach wound tighter and tighter with trepidation and dread. Dozens of innocent people were inside that church. One of his dearest friends and his beautiful wife and daughters. Quinn.

And Noah's own son.

Noah's entire life and purpose was trapped inside those stone walls. His pulse was a roar in his ears, his mouth bone dry. What was happening in there? Was Milo okay? Was he safe?

Or were they already too late?

Noah couldn't let himself think those thoughts. Couldn't let himself think about anything but the mission ahead. He was an officer of the law. It was his job to save people.

A whisper of doubt snaked through him. Who did he think he was? He was no superhero. He was just a small-town cop. Routine traffic stops. DUIs, tickets, spats between neighbors.

In the six years he'd been a cop, he could count the number of times on one hand that he'd needed to draw his service weapon. One of those times was right here in this parking lot only two days ago.

He wasn't ready for this. Wasn't prepared.

He had no choice.

With everything on the line, he had to step up. Had to get the job done.

For Milo. All of this, it was nothing if not for Milo.

They skirted the empty parking lot and moved in on the rear exit. Crouching shadows creeping through the darkness, weapons up and ready, their breath exhaling in silent crystallized clouds.

Noah kept his shotgun trained on the rear door. Julian would breach it, and Noah, Truitt, and Moll would rush in and secure the area. Hayes would strike with his team on the opposite side simultaneously.

When they were still ten yards away, the rear door burst open.

Adrenaline kicked his heart. Noah raised his weapon. Julian did the same.

A figure stumbled through the doorway. An AR-15 in his arms.

"Freeze!" Noah shouted. His body thrummed with tension, anxiety twisting his guts to water. His finger itchy on the trigger, ready to fire.

"On your knees!" Julian shouted. "Hands on your head! NOW!"

Noah's heart jackhammered as he moved forward, the Remington aimed at the suspect. "Get down!"

The suspect dropped to his knees and jerked his hands up. The rifle fell into the snow. The figure was covered in blood. Drenched in it.

Movement behind the first suspect.

His nerves raw, Noah's finger twitched on the trigger.

He almost fired. Almost, but didn't.

A second figure exited beside the first. Smaller, a child.

"Hold your fire!" Noah screamed.

Black curly hair matted red. A red-streaked face, the whites of the eyes showing. Huge dilated pupils contracting in the harsh flashlight beams.

His brain computed the information slow and halting. His breath caught in his throat. His lungs constricted. The barrel of his shotgun lowered an inch. "Milo?"

"Dad!"

Noah didn't think. He only reacted. He dropped his firearm, fell to his knees in the snow, and opened his arms wide. His son ran across the snowy parking lot and barreled into him.

Noah wrapped Milo in his arms, relishing the warmth of him, the *aliveness* of him, his heart flooding with overwhelming joy and relief.

"Stand down!" Julian shouted. "We have two civilians. Repeat, two civilian minors. Do not fire!"

Samantha Perez spoke rapidly into her radio, contacting Briggs' and Reynoso's teams, relaying information. The other officers stood guard, their weapons up and ready.

Noah didn't hear a word she said. The totality of his focus was on Milo.

He forced himself to pull Milo back at arm's length and examine him. The coppery stench of blood and death emanated from his very pores.

Noah's heart stuttered. His chest was too tight. He couldn't breathe. His child was standing right here in front of him, but there was so much blood. Too much.

Milo was wounded, maybe mortally wounded.

Despair welled inside Noah. He was too late. Too late to save him. He'd failed his most important job—to protect his child.

"Show me your injuries," he forced out. "Where are you hurt?"

"I'm okay," Milo said, his voice quavering. "Dad, I'm okay."

"Then where's the blood coming from?"

"It's not his," a young female voice said.

Noah's head snapped up. Quinn Riley still knelt in the snow a few yards away, her hands high in the air as Moll frisked her and Perez confiscated the AR-15.

Noah didn't even recognize her. Her blue hair was caked and matted to her skull. Her black eye makeup streaked her bloodied cheeks. Her clothes looked like someone had dunked her in crimson paint.

"I did that," Quinn said. "I covered us in blood. To play dead. To stay alive."

Noah's insides turned to ice. A chill that had nothing to do with the temperature settled over him. "Whose blood?"

"The people. The people in the sanctuary."

"How many are dead?"

She stared at him, hollow-eyed. "All of them."

50

NOAH
DAY SEVEN

Reeling, Noah staggered to his feet. Nausea wrenched his guts. He nearly gagged.

All those people staying with Bishop in the sanctuary. Families. Children. How could they all be dead? It didn't seem real. He didn't want any of this to be real.

"Who did this?" He already knew the answer, but he had to ask it anyway. "Did you see?"

"They were wearing ski masks. But I recognized their voices." Quinn sucked in a sharp breath as she stood shakily. "Ray Shultz and his thugs. Billy Carter and his brothers. And—my mother. They have automatic weapons."

"How many?" Julian asked tersely. "How many suspects?"

"Five or six from what I saw."

"Are you sure?"

Quinn swallowed. "My—Octavia is . . . unconscious. Or she was."

"She tried to hurt us, but Quinn wouldn't let her," Milo said.

Noah hugged him close. "What about Bishop? His family?"

"Ray and Tommy had them back in the food pantry, I think. I —I don't know if they're . . ." Quinn's voice trailed off.

She couldn't say the words out loud. None of them could.

"We have to get in there," Julian said. "Now."

Noah nodded tersely. He wanted nothing more than to hold his son tight and never let go. But he couldn't do that. Not yet.

This wasn't over. It was far from over.

"Sheridan, come in," Hayes said on the radio. "We've intercepted five or six suspects fleeing north along Elm Valley Road on snowmobiles. They escaped before we could close the net."

"We're going after them," Reynoso said on the radio.

Noah grabbed his radio with his free hand. "Copy. Sinclair and I will clear the church."

While Julian relayed their new information to Briggs' and Reynoso's teams on the radio, Noah turned to the kids.

They were both shivering violently. They weren't dressed for the bitter cold, and their blood-damp clothing made them more susceptible to hypothermia.

They were traumatized, their pupils dilated. They needed warmth, fluids, and medical care as soon as possible.

Noah felt Milo's forehead, checked his pulse. His skin was cold but not clammy, his pulse fast but steady. "Are you dizzy or lightheaded? Do you feel tired? Does your stomach hurt?"

Milo bit his lower lip and shook his head.

"Okay. Okay, good." Noah picked him up, gave him a fierce hug, and attempted to hand him to Oren Truitt. "Get him somewhere safe. He shouldn't be here for this."

Milo clung to him, grasping at his neck. "Dad! Don't go!"

"I'll be right there." Noah's voice cracked. "I'll be right back, I promise. I have to help Bishop. I need to help Juniper and Chloe. Okay? You're safe now, son. I promise."

With Milo still reaching for him, he forcefully placed his son in Truitt's arms. Truitt's face blanched, but he kept hold of Milo, tried to pat his back. "It's okay, little dude."

"No!" Milo screamed. Tears streamed down his face. They left clear tracks through the blood. He stretched his hands toward his father. "Don't go! Don't leave me! Daddy!"

Noah had never seen him so inconsolable. Not even after Hannah's disappearance. His son's despondent cries broke Noah's heart into a thousand pieces.

Milo had been so strong and brave to escape the church, and now that he was finally safe, his little eight-year-old body couldn't hold it together any longer.

Noah had never felt so torn. He longed to be there for his child, who'd just experienced a horror Noah couldn't imagine. He also knew that his skills were desperately needed to contain a deadly situation.

Milo was safe. Bishop wasn't.

This was his job. He had to do it.

He swallowed the lump in his throat and turned to Truitt. "Take them to Rosamond Sinclair's. Milo knows her. The superintendent will know what to do. Then find the nurse, Shen Lee. And Quinn's grandmother needs to be notified as soon as possible."

"Got it," Truitt said.

"Daddy!" Milo cried, his voice raw with despair.

Quinn stepped between them. She held out her hands. "Small Fry. I'm right here. I'm going with you."

Milo practically flung himself at her. Truitt let him go. Milo clung to her like a monkey.

She held him as tightly as he held her.

"The truck is parked behind the bank across the street," Truitt said. "It'll warm up fast, and we've got a first aid kit and some emergency space blankets."

Milo still in her arms, Quinn turned to trudge after him.

Noah touched her shoulder. "Quinn. What you did for Milo
—" His chest tightened. Tears pricked his eyes. He couldn't speak
the words aloud. They caught in his throat like stones.

She'd saved Milo's life. Risked her own life to protect his son.
He owed her everything.

She looked at him, her expression etched with sorrow. "I
didn't save the girls. I couldn't save them."

Noah's mouth went dry. "You did the best you could."

Quinn's face hardened. She looked like a savage Viking queen
fresh off the battlefield. Like she'd just walked through hell itself
to bring Milo out the other side.

"Just get the monsters who did this," she said. "Promise me
that."

Noah said, "We will."

51

NOAH
DAY SEVEN

C rossway Church was a massacre. Noah had never seen anything like it.

It looked like a battlefield. But this wasn't Syria or Iraq. This was the United States of America. This was rural southwest Michigan.

There were no words. No human language to communicate the horrors assaulting his senses. The sanctuary was still and utterly silent. It stank of death. Of blood and gore, bodily fluids, gasses, and human excrement.

The bodies his mind wouldn't—couldn't—describe.

Noah and Julian picked their way through the carnage, weapons up, sweeping their tactical flashlights back and forth slowly, their stomachs churning, both men shaken to their core.

They knew these people. Waved to them at restaurants or the gas station, chatted at Friday night football games and the barber-shop. Coached their kids in Little League. Pulled them over for tickets.

Tears streamed down Noah's face. He was barely aware he was crying.

Julian's face contorted in outrage. His eyes were red and wet.

There was no shame in their weeping. Only despair.

"They should've let us help them!" Julian said, anguish and fury in his voice. "This never would've happened if we'd been here!"

Noah's own guilt descended upon him, stifling and oppressive. "We couldn't have known they would escalate like this. We didn't know."

Julian didn't answer.

They kept moving, mentally cataloging the destruction like this was just another case, just another job. It was the only thing keeping them both from falling apart.

The overhead lights were shattered. So were the stained-glass windows, the blankets covering them pockmarked and shredded with bullet holes. More holes riddled the drywall, the pews, the organ and the pulpit. Here and there, a few overturned battery-operated lanterns glowed softly.

They had already cleared every room along the long L-wing of the church. They found the secretary collapsed across her desk in a pool of congealing blood, a flashlight knocked to the floor. They discovered the costume room with splatters of blood that told a violent story they didn't yet understand.

If this was where Quinn had left her mother unconscious, she was gone now. Ray must have found her and taken her with them when they escaped.

After they cleared the long L-wing and the sanctuary, they moved swiftly into the foyer. They would return later to inventory the crimes inflicted upon each poor soul, to investigate, to care for the dead and pay their respects, to mourn.

These victims were beyond the help of man. But if there was someone still alive in this hell, Noah and Julian would find them.

No masked men or women leapt out with guns drawn. No survivors crept out of hiding. Only more bodies. More corpses.

A few pistols lay near a couple of the men and women. They must have attempted to fight back but were overwhelmed by the firepower of their assailants.

In the short L-wing, several more bodies lay in the hallway or the fellowship hall where they'd fallen—most of them shot in the back as they'd fled the slaughter.

Noah recognized several of the volunteers: James McDill. Sandra Perkins. Ralph Henderson-Smith and his wife Lauren. Teachers. Bank Tellers. Restaurant managers. Mothers and fathers. Sisters and brothers, aunts and uncles, friends and mentors.

It was senseless. Unfathomable. There could never be a reason that could possibly encompass such an atrocity. The things people did to each other. The evil humanity was capable of inflicting.

Why did anyone need to believe in a devil when humans were evil enough?

A wave of raw, ugly emotion crashed through him. His throat went tight. His legs turned to jelly. He sagged against the wall next to a large framed photo of the Crossway congregation lined up in spring dresses and suits outside the church, smiling and happy.

He bent, forearms on his thighs, clutching the shotgun with trembling fingers and gasping for breath that wouldn't come. Vertigo lurched through him. The images of the dead flashed through his mind, one after another after another . . .

Julian came up beside him, weapon still up, alert to danger. "Don't lose it, brother. Not here. Not now."

"Milo—" Noah forced out. "He was here . . ."

"And now he's not." Julian's features were ghostly in the dim light. His mouth a thin line, his eyes bloodshot and haunted. "He made it. He's not one of them. You remember that."

"I'm trying."

"Keep it together and do your job. Do your damn job."

Noah sensed Julian was speaking to himself as much as to him. His shoulders were tense, his neck corded. A vein pulsed at his forehead.

Mentally, he shoved it all down deep—the horror and revulsion, the fear and anxiety. He knew how to do that. Knew how to keep all the feelings too dark and painful to contemplate somewhere below the surface, where he didn't have to feel them or think about them.

It was how he'd survived the last five years without Hannah.

Noah managed to nod. Someone had to keep going, had to make this right somehow. And that someone was him. Him and Julian. "You're right."

"We're the cops. The good guys. We're the ones who are gonna nail these scumbags to the wall."

"Julian . . ." This wasn't the right time. But here, surrounded by all this death, he had to say it. "Are we straight? You and me?"

Julian glanced at him. His eyes softened. "You couldn't lose me if you wanted to. It's you and me. Always has been. I have your back, Sheridan."

Noah pushed himself off the wall and forced his legs to straighten. He adjusted his grip on the Remington, his hands damp with sweat despite the chilly air inside the church.

"You good?" Julian asked him.

He nodded. "I'm good."

He wasn't good. Far from it. Nothing about this could possibly be called good.

But he was on his feet. It had to be enough.

Every sense on high alert, Noah followed Julian from the fellowship hall down the last hallway. Only four rooms remained uncleared. The three storage rooms and the main food pantry.

Four rooms to reveal his friend's fate.

They kept their weapons up, constantly sweeping back and

forth, the shadows shuddering and quivering, the darkness crouching just out of reach of their flashlight beams.

The dread was palpable. A living, breathing creature skulking behind him, prowling just out of sight, its rancid greedy breath hot on the back of Noah's neck.

He shuddered. The feeling didn't dissipate. If anything, it grew stronger.

A shuffling sound caught his attention.

Noah and Julian froze.

The soft scrape of a boot on tile. It came from somewhere ahead of them.

Julian gestured with the barrel of his shotgun. Noah nodded silently.

They lowered into crouches, weapons ready. Together, they crept down the hallway.

52

NOAH
DAY SEVEN

Noah eased along the wall, his weapon leading, his pulse a rush in his ears. Julian moved silently ahead of him.

The door five yards ahead on the right was open. A second door further up on the left led to the community pantry.

Noah and Julian stacked up on the left side of the doorway, Noah squatting, aiming low, Julian above him slicing the pie from the waist up.

Noah peered gun-first around the edge of the door frame and took in the scene.

Shelves of food and supplies. Rice, beans, and wheat spilled from bags and plastic containers punctured by sprayed rounds. Frigid air filtered from the broken window along the far wall.

In the back of the room next to the window, a man in a black ski mask hunched over a stack of storage totes.

He looked up, startled.

"Police! Don't move!" Julian shouted.

The suspect darted for the automatic rifle leaning against a shelf a few feet away.

Noah's adrenaline surged. He spun into the room, still keeping low, and fired at the man's feet. The retort exploded in the enclosed room. Tile shards flew up and sprayed the suspect's shins.

The man leapt back, cursing loudly.

"Hands up!" Noah shouted over the ringing in his ears, already racking another shell into the chamber. "Right now!"

The guy raised both hands. His ski mask was yanked up and bunched at his forehead. Grizzled acorn-brown beard. Sickly, pockmarked skin. Yellowed teeth. Randy Carter—thirty-two-years-old, drug addict, dealer, and ex-con. Went by the nickname Nickel.

Nickel had draped a blanket over the window frame and stacked several of the plastic storage bins against the wall. Through the window, Noah glimpsed a snowmobile parked just outside, the rear trailer packed with the church's food bins.

He'd been left behind. Maybe intentionally so he could steal more supplies. Or maybe inadvertently in the chaos.

Whatever the reason, he was here now.

"Ow! You shot me!" Nickel kept his hands up as he hopped on one leg. Several blood stains bloomed on his left shin from the tile shrapnel.

Anger and revulsion burned in Noah's gut. This lowlife scumbag was a mass murderer. The worst of the worst. He was responsible for the carnage in the sanctuary.

In that moment, Noah wished he *had* shot him. Right between the eyes.

"You look fine to me," Julian said. "Get on your knees."

He and Noah stepped into the room, firearms at the high-ready. Broken glass crunched under their boots, the floor sticky with syrup from ruptured cans.

"I work here! I'm a volunteer, helping give away all this crap," Nickel said frantically. His distraught gaze darted to the rifle.

"Just tryin' to protect myself from the crazies who attacked us. That's all!"

"We know exactly what you are!" Julian spat. He was shaking, his face red and blotchy with rage. "You think we're so stupid we wouldn't recognize you?"

Nickel's unfocused eyes narrowed. "Hey! I—"

"On the ground!" Julian shouted "Now!"

Nickel lunged for the weapon, simultaneously reaching behind his back.

Instinctively, Noah's finger moved for the trigger.

The retort of the gunshot splintered the air.

Nickel sank to his knees. He clutched at his chest with both hands. Blood bloomed and spread across his coat. The revolver he'd been reaching for—tucked into the back of his jeans—tumbled to the floor.

Noah's ears rang. Sound went tinny and distant. For an instant, he thought he'd pulled the trigger himself. His finger was still resting on the trigger guard.

It was Julian. Julian had fired at Nickel.

"You shot me?" Nickel asked, questioning, like he was so stunned this was happening to him, he wasn't sure it was real. "You shot me!"

Julian rushed forward and kicked Nickel in the chest. The man toppled onto his side.

"Julian!" Noah shouted too late.

His reactions were slowed, the horror of the night turning everything upside down and inside out, his overwhelmed brain struggling to process new stimuli.

Julian stood over the man, pointed his service weapon at his skull, and squeezed the trigger a second time. The suspect's head snapped back. His body went limp. A hole in the center of his forehead leaked a single bead of blood.

Randy "Nickel" Carter was dead.

"You killed him," Noah said in a choked voice.

Julian whirled to face him. His expression was grim, his mouth a flat line. His eyes blazed. "Did you not see what he did? Did you not see the dead little kids?"

Noah swallowed. "I did."

"Then you know what I had to do. It was a good kill. It was justified. You saw it. You saw him go for a weapon."

Noah *had* seen it. Of course, it was a good kill. He shouldn't doubt Julian, not even for a second. Hadn't Noah wished he'd killed the monster himself only moments ago?

But still, that faint, unsettled feeling niggled his gut. That voice whispering in his head. The first shot had been legit. The second one, though . . .

His eyes took in what he was desperate not to see. The suspect lying down, weaponless. The brain and blood splatter spray on the floor and shelves revealed the story the autopsy would tell. This was the point-blank assassination of an unarmed suspect.

He felt sick. His intestines cramped. He wanted to vomit the contents of anything he'd ever eaten. It was too much. Too much death.

It was this night. It was everything. All the dead bodies seared into his mind. His friends and neighbors. Murdered by savages. By monsters.

"We did what we had to do," Julian said fiercely. "We put down a rabid animal."

The country was in crisis. They had to protect the town. Julian had done what he had to do. What any good cop would have done.

"I know," Noah said.

"I have your back, brother. You know that. Family first, always." Julian touched his arm. "We need to clear the last few rooms. I'll take care of the rest. You go home to Milo. He needs you."

Noah nodded and forced himself to turn from the corpse.

A moan echoed down the corridor. Low and pained and full of despair.

Noah's heart stopped. *Bishop.*

"Noah, don't—"

Noah sprinted from the storage room, Remington pulled tight and ready to fire but only one thought on his mind. He dashed down the hall to the last door on the left. His thudding footsteps and pounding heart filled his ears.

Sensing Julian right behind him, he edged around the doorway, weapon leading, instinctively clearing the room.

He stopped and stood, stunned. He lowered his shotgun, his arms going numb with shock.

The metal shelving full of supplies lining the walls glinted in Julian's flashlight beam. Shredded cardboard and broken glass littered the floor. Dozens of leaking cans scattered everywhere. The sickly-sweet scent of peach syrup mingled with the coppery tang of blood.

Atticus Bishop knelt in the center of the pantry floor. Puddles of crimson stained the linoleum. His leather jacket and Hawaiian shirt were spattered and sprayed with blood.

Several frayed lengths of paracord lay on the floor behind him next to the bloody shard of a broken jar. Blood leaked from his right hand and dripped from the cuff of his jacket.

Bishop didn't look at them or acknowledge their presence. His broad shoulders were hunched in defeat, in grief, his head bowed.

In his strong, steady arms, he cradled his family. Kind, beautiful Daphne. Spirited Juniper. Spunky little Chloe.

All of them, dead.

53

NOAH

DAY EIGHT

It was three hours before Bishop spoke a word. Midnight came and went. No one even noticed.

Noah sat inside the pantry, his legs crossed, his back resting against the wall, the shotgun on the floor beside him. He hadn't moved in hours. Neither had Bishop.

No one had touched Bishop or tried to pry his family from his arms. Bishop had allowed Noah to cover their bodies with blankets. That was all.

It wasn't protocol. But protocol had died with the power grid.

They had left Bishop under Noah's watch.

Julian and the other officers were working the scene to the best of their abilities. It was grim work. Without power, they no longer had a means to analyze DNA or enter evidence into the databases, though they collected samples of fluids, blood, hairs, and cartridge casings as best they could anyway.

That was the job of the crime scene techs. Noah had no idea how things were being handled in the larger towns and cities, whether a skeletal crew of government and law enforcement still existed, or whether the system was crumbling everywhere without access to communication, transportation, computers, and high-tech equipment.

Everything was wrong, felt wrong. There were no multicolored plastic cones on the floor, no numbered pieces of tape on the wall to mark the different types of evidence. No technicians in Tyvek suits, collecting samples, taking photos, and making measurements, transforming a mass grave site into something alive with activity and purpose.

Noah shifted uncomfortably. His back ached and his glutes were going numb. Someone had brought in a kerosene space heater, a stack of donated blankets from one of the storage rooms, and a battery-operated lantern. At least he was warm.

He was thirsty but not hungry, though he hadn't eaten anything since before noon. He couldn't stomach the thought of food.

He sat with Bishop and he said nothing. He would wait for Bishop to speak first. He would wait all night if he had to. His friend deserved that, at least.

He wasn't stupid enough to believe he had a thing worth saying. *I'm sorry.* I'm sorry was a pebble hurled at a hurricane. Worse than worthless.

He'd heard a thousand *I'm sorry's* over the last five years, until he'd wanted to strangle every well-meaning stranger, acquaintance, and coworker who said it.

He touched his wedding band. His mind drifted back to thoughts of Hannah.

He had lost her. She had simply vanished into thin air. Like she'd been abducted by aliens or stepped into a parallel universe, leaving this one behind forever.

Someone had taken her. He believed that. Stolen her from their lives, erased her from existence. But believing and knowing were two different things.

He never had a body to bury. No funeral for closure, no communal grieving. No certainty.

Even five years later, the grief still hit him, sometimes out of nowhere. In the strangest places, at the worst times. The grocery store. One of Milo's Little League games. Or a certain song that Hannah had always loved to sing playing over the radio.

A few notes of "Hallelujah," "I Still Haven't Found What I'm Looking For," or "When Doves Cry," and it would all come back in an instant—Hannah curled up with Milo at bedtime, singing him rock songs as lullabies. The way she'd look when she sang, how the purity of her voice filled him with emotion, transported him somewhere else—almost like magic.

And just like that, the grief would hit him, a tidal wave, a tsunami pulling him under, swallowing him whole until he couldn't breathe, until he felt like he was dying. The anguish so overwhelming that death would be a relief.

Noah understood grief. But understanding it couldn't help him ease his friend's pain. His heart ached for Bishop, mourned with him.

He understood guilt too. Noah had almost lost Milo tonight. He couldn't reconcile his sorrow for Bishop with his own immense relief. Only chance—only blue-haired Quinn Riley—had kept Milo from sharing the same fate.

His child was safe. His child was bathed and sleeping in a warm bed with people who cared for him. Bishop's children were growing cold in his arms, his last memories of them the terror in their faces and the cries for help he could not answer.

Noah hated himself for it, for even thinking it, but he couldn't help himself. He would gladly endure the guilt of a hundred lost lives if that meant Milo got to open his eyes in the morning.

"I failed them." Bishop's strong baritone voice broke the stillness. It was ragged and broken. "I did everything I could to save them and it wasn't enough. It wasn't enough."

"Bishop—"

"I'm a husband without a wife. A father without children."

"You—"

"Leave me."

"I'm not leaving you."

"Go away."

"No."

"I want to be alone."

"You need a friend, Bishop. Whether you want one or not, you have me. I'm not going anywhere."

Bishop made a sound in the back of his throat, a wounded animal sound that wrenched Noah's heart and shattered it anew. Gone was his easygoing charm and infectious laugh, the kindness that warmed his features. Bishop was nearly unrecognizable.

He said nothing for several minutes.

Noah waited him out. He would keep waiting.

Truitt had sent him a message via the radio two hours ago. Milo was safe. He and Quinn were in Rosamond's care. The nurse was on his way. Noah longed to be with his son, but he couldn't leave Bishop. Not like this.

"It was Ray Shultz," Bishop said finally. He breathed heavily, in short deep gasps, every word costing him a great deal of effort. "It was them."

"They did this . . . for revenge?"

"Yes." Bishop raised his head and looked at Noah. His pupils were huge. His gaze distant. Blank and unseeing. "I thought the deacons would be enough. We had a guard on watch twenty-four-seven after what happened at the food pantry. I thought we were being smart. But we couldn't stop them. Our pistols weren't enough. They came in with automatic weapons, and we couldn't do anything . . . They wanted vengeance. They wanted blood. There was no reasoning with them. They were like . . . animals. Demons. Pure evil."

Bishop paused, stared off at nothing for a long minute. "They wanted a safe. Demanded to know where the gold was. They thought we were hiding something, something they wanted."

"Gold?"

"They . . . did things. They hurt Daphne . . . just . . . shot her. Shot them. Right in front of me. I was tied up. I couldn't help them. I couldn't do anything."

"What gold?"

"I don't know." He shook his head, brows furrowed in confusion, like he was trying to figure out the pieces of a huge and incredibly complex puzzle, trying and failing to fit them together. "There is no gold. There is no safe. There never was."

54

NOAH
DAY EIGHT

"We will get the people who did this," Noah said, his voice choked as he struggled to tamp down his own outrage. "That is the one thing I can promise you. We will get them, and they will pay the price for what they've done."

Bishop blinked. "Will they?"

"Yes."

"I thought they were already arrested. They were all in that old cell beneath the old courthouse. That's what you told me."

"It was an accident. A terrible accident."

"An accident that they got out?"

"We're still investigating. It never should've happened."

Bishop touched the blanket his dead wife lay beneath. His face contorted in agony. "You're better than that, Sheridan. 'Be harmless as doves, but wise as serpents.' I preach trust, compassion, and offering the benefit of the doubt. But this is too much to swallow, even for me. Even for you."

Noah was silent for a moment.

"There are things you don't see, Noah. Things you've never seen. Don't want to see."

"What do you mean?"

A muscle in Bishop's jaw twitched. "There are rumors. Some of the people in this town have skeletons in their closet. More than one."

Noah stared at him in disbelief. "This is the work of lunatics. Of madmen. Nothing else."

"Someone always profits from atrocity," Bishop said. "Who profits here, Noah?"

It was his grief talking. The seething, helpless anger below the surface. Bishop was spiraling down a black hole. Clinging to a life raft of desperation, slinging blame and responsibility wherever he could. Even places it didn't belong.

It was a natural response to trauma, one Noah had intimate experience with. He needed to help him, to bring him back from the brink.

"We need to take care of your family," Noah said in a gentle tone, changing the subject and steering it in a more useful direction. "It's time."

After a minute, Bishop nodded grimly. "Maybe you're right."

Carefully, almost reverently, Bishop slid his wife from his lap and placed her beside his two daughters. He rose to his feet and stood over the shrouded forms. Tears dripped down his cheeks. "I cried out to God, but He didn't hear me. 'Oh Father, where are you?'"

Noah had no answer to that. A crisis of faith was not a problem he knew how to solve. "Come with me. You're staying with us. We have a spare bedroom at the Winter Haven house."

A shadow passed across Bishop's features. "I'm not leaving."

Noah's mouth dropped open. "What? You can't stay here."

"This is my home. My church. My people."

"But—it's a crime scene. There are bodies everywhere."

Bishop's face turned a deeper shade of gray. He closed his eyes, his shoulders quaking.

"I'm sorry," Noah said. The very words he hated to say.

Bishop opened his eyes and rubbed at his face. "At dawn, hungry families will be lined up outside. If I am not here, they will have nothing to feed their children."

"Those families can go to the high school emergency shelter for help. This burden is not yours to bear alone."

"It is the burden I chose to bear. I will continue to bear it as long as I am able."

Noah stared at him, uncomprehending. "Why? Why do you even want to stay?"

"This is my calling. God put me here. God is still here, despite what you may think. He may have allowed my family to pass out of this world, but my faith is not shaken. I still believe. I will always believe. He has not forsaken me, and I will not forsake Him. I will not abandon my calling to help this town through its darkest days."

Maybe it made him a fool, but he'd always admired Bishop's unshakable faith in something larger than himself. Sometimes, Noah wished he had something more to rely on than his own frail, fallible self.

But this. This was something he couldn't understand.

"The food and supplies here belong to the church. If I'm not here, what will happen to it?"

Noah couldn't answer that question.

"The council will confiscate it. Maybe some will get to the people. But some will line the shelves of the rich and powerful. It is the way of things. It always has been. This is the Lord's tithe. One hundred percent of it belongs to those who need it—not in the hands of those who would steal it for themselves."

Noah shook his head. "Bishop, I don't want to say this. Truly I don't. But this is a crime scene. You cannot stay here."

Bishop's expression hardened. He loomed over Noah, his burly muscles tensed and bulging, the intimidating soldier in him coming out. "Unless you handcuff me and drag me out, I'm not leaving. Are you prepared to do that, Noah?"

Noah wasn't. He doubted anyone else was either. Not now. Not after all this.

"I'll sleep in the bathroom down the hall. There are blankets. I have all the food and water I need. I'm staying."

Noah blew out a frustrated breath. "Fine. I'll see to it you aren't bothered. We've been keeping the deceased at the funeral home. There won't be room for all these . . ." He almost said corpses but stopped himself. "The girls and Daphne will have a spot. They will. I'll contact—"

"I'm burying them. Tonight."

Noah balked. "You can't just—the ground is frozen."

"I'll soften the ground with a bonfire first."

"It doesn't matter. You can't just bury bodies in your backyard—"

"Don't you get it yet, Noah?" Anger warred with the sorrow marring Bishop's features. "It's all over. Everything's falling apart. What should I do? Call up the funeral home? Request an undertaker? They aren't at work. They have no electricity just like the rest of us. The only bodies they're worried about now are their own. They're worried about keeping themselves and their families alive. Whatever we need now is up to us. No government officials are wasting time handing out citations for improperly buried bodies. And if they do, let them come. I'll accept the consequences."

Noah wanted to argue. If he wasn't so utterly exhausted, so traumatized from this night of death and carnage, he might have. Instead, his shoulders slumped in defeat. "Let me at least help you."

But Bishop shook his head wearily. "This is my cross to bear. This I will do alone."

His tone brooked no argument. "Go home to your son. Hug him tight and tell him that he is loved."

Fresh guilt speared Noah. He could hardly look Bishop in the eye. "Do you need anything?"

Bishop shook his head wearily.

As Noah turned to leave, Bishop spoke one last time. "Keep your eyes open, my friend. The devil is a roaring lion, seeking whom he may devour. And he is not always who you think."

55

NOAH
DAY EIGHT

Noah and Julian finally returned to the superintendent's home well after two a.m., bone-weary and utterly exhausted.

Normally, they would just be one part in a massive cog of paperwork and processes. There was evidence to be compiled and collected, statements to take, witness canvasing, prosecutors and defense lawyers and court dates. Trials and verdicts and prison sentences.

Now he didn't know what was supposed to happen.

Hayes had radioed in two hours ago. They'd tracked Ray, Billy, Octavia, and the others to the Carter place, a sprawling forty acres across the river a few miles north of Fall Creek. The wooded property was located atop a hill that abutted the river, with a steep ravine along the western perimeter.

A half-dozen trailers littered the crown of the hill, along with several large barns, sheds, and other outbuildings. They had a well, access to the river and the woods for hunting and firewood. The location on top of the hill gave them the high ground.

Twenty to thirty people lived there at any given time. All lowlife criminals and their women, along with a few ragged, snotty-nosed kids.

Ray's crew had made it there ahead of the police. When Briggs attempted to arrest them, they were met with a barrage of firepower and driven back. Reserve Officer Clint Moll was injured—shot in the arm—before they were forced to retreat.

They needed to regroup and plan a raid of the property.

It would be far from easy. Ray, Billy, Tommy, and the others would be prepared. They would be ready for the law.

The confrontation would be bloody and brutal. The Fall Creek police department was vastly outnumbered. And from the reports of multiple semi- and automatic weapons at the church, outgunned as well.

But that was a problem for tomorrow. So was the conundrum of what to do with the victims' bodies. The cemetery vault at the Mercy Funeral Home was already overfilled.

As a temporary emergency measure, they'd wrapped the bodies in industrial garbage bags and transported them to Paul Eastley's large metal pole barn. The cold temperatures should preserve the bodies long enough to figure out a plan.

Tomorrow, volunteers would go out searching for more mortuary refrigerators in funeral parlors and health care facilities.

But he couldn't think about any of that right now. He was completely spent physically and emotionally. He had nothing more to give to the town right now. Milo was his only concern.

As soon as Julian unlocked Rosamond's front door, Noah went straight to the guest bedroom. It was dark, but the moon had appeared behind the clouds, and the faintest silvery light glimmered across two sleeping forms.

They were bathed and clean, wearing borrowed pajamas, their hair freshly washed—Quinn's blue again, Milo's black and curly and damp against the pillow. They were both half-buried beneath a mound of blankets. Quinn's body was curled around his son, enfolding him against her body, protecting him even in sleep.

Noah's chest squeezed, overwhelmed with the intensity of his love.

He let them sleep and returned to the sofa in the living room. Within five minutes, he'd passed out, still fully clothed.

Sometime after dawn, Milo padded out to the living room and clambered on top of him. Half-asleep, Noah wrapped his son in his arms and simply relished the feel of him, his warmth, the fresh smell of green apple shampoo in his hair, his little heart beating against Noah's chest.

An hour later, Rosamond finally managed to coax Milo from his father's arms and Quinn from the cocoon of the bed with the promise of an egg and pancake breakfast—with peanut butter and whipped cream topping for Milo.

The eggs were powdered, and the pancakes were from a box, but no one cared. Surprisingly, everyone had an appetite.

Maybe facing death made one ravenous for life. Even when the mind couldn't process the horror and trauma, the body knew what it needed. The body sought to live.

After breakfast, Noah and Julian cleaned up and did the dishes in silence. Noah gave Milo another double dose of his meds and checked him for symptoms.

Milo insisted he was fine.

He sat at one end of the island and worked on a coloring book. His shoulders were hunched, his expression closed. He colored in the same tree, over and over, with a red crayon. His face was pale and wan.

Quinn slumped beside him, staring off at some invisible point in the middle distance, her eyes far away. She'd hardly said a word. Neither had Milo.

Noah was worried about him, about both of them. Physically, but also emotionally. Both kids needed intense counseling. They'd endured a horrible trauma.

Normally, he'd have access to a slew of professionals to turn to for help. But now? There were no phone numbers to call. No electronic databases to access. He had no addresses to visit any child psychologists in person.

After a while, Quinn asked to return to her grandmother's house. Since the Orange Julius was still parked at Molly's, Rosamond offered to let her borrow one of the UTVs—utility terrain vehicles—that Tina Gundy had managed to get working again.

Quinn's quintessential sullen scowl had disappeared—for the moment. She looked younger and far more vulnerable without her heavy eye makeup. Even with the swollen purplish bruises and cuts marring her face, she could've passed for an elfin thirteen, not sixteen.

Noah marveled at this teenage girl. So young and vulnerable, so tough and resilient. She was a survivor. Stronger and braver than anyone gave her credit for.

Milo fiddled with his medical bracelet. He looked up. "Don't go, Quinn."

"I'm not going anywhere, Small Fry." Quinn jumped up from the counter, wrapped Milo in a tight embrace, and whispered something in his ear that Noah couldn't hear.

Milo didn't smile, but he nodded and let her go.

"I know a local therapist," Rosamond said after Quinn had left, quietly so Milo wouldn't overhear. "Last night, Officer Truitt went to Shen Lee's house and brought him over. He examined the children. Milo is untouched—physically. We can't test his hormone levels, but he recommended that you continue to double up on Milo's dosage for a few more days. Quinn sustained a blow to the head and has a mild concussion. Her nose looks broken, but it isn't. Physically, she'll be fine."

"Thank God."

"Yes." Rosamond managed a tight smile. "And I have something else for you."

She pressed a prescription pill bottle into his hands. He stared down at it in shock, turned it over, read the label and then read it again. "This is—this is hydrocortisone. Milo's medication."

"I know."

"Robert Vinson said the pharmacy was out."

"I know."

"Where in the world did you get this?"

She smiled tightly. "It's good to have friends in high places, Noah. Remember that. It's more important now than ever. This is from Mattias Sutter. My cousin. You'll meet him later. I told him about our needs, and he managed to find a nearby town with a pharmacy that had it in stock and bartered for it. He brought it to me as a gesture of goodwill."

"Goodwill for what?"

"You'll see soon enough. And there's more where that came from."

Noah pocketed the precious pills. Another month's worth. He could have wept with relief, with gratitude. "You're so good to us, Rosamond. How can I ever thank you?"

She squeezed his arm. "You and Milo are thanks enough, dear." She turned toward the kitchen for a moment and cleared her throat. When she faced him again, her eyes glimmered. Tears smeared her perfectly-applied mascara.

Noah stared at her, startled. He wasn't sure if he'd ever seen Rosamond Sinclair cry in his entire life. She prided herself on always keeping her cool, on maintaining absolute control of her emotions. But she wasn't in control now.

"Are you okay?" he asked.

Julian rose from his stool. He'd been unusually quiet all morning, his face drawn, his eyes bloodshot. "Mom?"

"You don't know how worried I was. Just frantic for you. For all of you." Her gaze flitted to the end of the island where Milo sat, then to Julian and back to Noah. "I said this to my son already, but I'm so very, very sorry. What happened last night . . . to think, it was almost Milo. I just . . ."

Her hands trembled as she rubbed her nose with a tissue. She wiped daintily at her eyes. "I thought I was doing the best I could to protect us, and then this happens. On my watch. Maybe I should step down. Maybe I'm not the right person to keep us safe."

"Mom," Julian said sharply. "Don't talk like that."

Noah hugged Rosamond. For such a formidable woman, she was short, only coming up to his chin. He pulled away. "Julian is right. You're doing everything you can, and then some. We all failed yesterday."

Rosamond nodded and sniffled. "Thank you, Noah. You always know what to say. That's why you're so important to me. You're all I have left."

Julian stiffened. A shadow passed across his face.

Noah knew she felt the disappearance of her eldest son keenly. He'd been her right-hand man. Her confidante. "He's just stranded somewhere like a million other people. He'll get home."

"I know." She drew herself to her full height and straightened her shoulders. "He's smart and resourceful. He'll get here when he gets here. I could sure use his help, though. Gavin's always been the dependable one." Her gaze settled on Julian. The corner of her mouth twitched. "You're going to have to step up now."

Julian's expression flattened. "I already am."

"Of course, dear." Rosamond smiled a strained smile, already dismissing Julian, and turned to Noah. She smoothed the sleeves of her lavender pantsuit. "The rest of the council will arrive shortly for an emergency meeting."

"I promised Atticus Bishop we would get justice for his family," Noah said. "For all the families."

Rosamond pursed her lips. Her eyes flashed with a dark anger. "I will take care of Fall Creek. Trust me."

56

NOAH
DAY EIGHT

"This is not my first choice, nor my second," Rosamond said gravely.

She sat on a tall stool in the living room, the rest of the council arranged around the living room. Noah and Julian sat on the couch next to Hayes. Dave Harris stood on the other side of him, next to Annette King and Mike Duncan.

A stranger sat on the stool in front of the island beside the superintendent. A big white guy wearing green camo fatigues with SUTTER emblazoned across the patch over the left side of his chest, a US MILITIA patch over his right, an AK-47 slung over one shoulder.

He looked to be about six-foot-three and two hundred and fifty pounds, a brute of a man, all bulging thighs and arms. He had a barrel chest, a thick neck, a bald shiny head, and pale blue eyes sunken into his fleshy face.

Mattias Sutter of the Volunteer Militia Brigade of Southwest Michigan sat still and silent, unmoving, his eyes slowly sweeping the room, taking everything in.

Noah felt the tiny hairs on the back of his neck rise slightly. The man hadn't said a word, and he was already unnerving.

"My heart is broken by the atrocity that happened last night," Rosamond continued. "Utterly broken. Forty-seven souls. Eighteen of them children. Eighteen! They went to school with us, shopped with us. They were our coworkers and friends. It is unconscionable. We must do everything in our power—everything!—to prevent this from happening again."

Tears glistened in the corners of her red-rimmed eyes. "None of us were expecting this. No one was prepared. The power went out, and we thought things could continue much like they had been. But we were wrong. We can't do the same things we used to do because our world is changing on us, and not for the better.

"I don't know how long it'll take for the power to be restored. Six months. Maybe six years. If we are going to survive until then, we must change. We must adapt. Otherwise, it is those willing to be more brutal and savage than we are who will survive, not us. And I will not see that happen. I will not allow it to happen in Fall Creek."

The room filled with low, tense murmurs. Sorrow, anxiety, and fear strained every face. And anger. Everyone was simultaneously terrified and outraged.

Several council members wept openly. Chief Briggs looked grim and shaken. Annette's face was pinched and white. Even Darryl Wiggins slumped in his seat, his hair mussed, his face unshaven, looking appropriately devastated.

Everyone knew a victim. Everyone affected by this tragedy.

Mike Duncan's neighbor. Jose Reynoso's sister-in-law. A half-dozen of Annette King's students and former students. Two of Dave Farris's employees.

The mood of the council had shifted since their last meeting only a few days ago. Their sense of security had just been ripped out from under them.

The idea of safety had disappeared the moment the EMP hit, but people were finally starting to understand how drastically everything had changed.

Rosamond cleared her throat. "I took the liberty of inviting Mattias Sutter here to speak with you. He has agreed to marshal the fifty-three men under his command to join the Fall Creek Police Department in a raid on the Carter compound tomorrow at dawn. They will help us bring Ray Shultz and the Carter brothers to justice. For we demand justice. And we will not rest until we get it."

Rosamond took a breath, seeming to compose herself, and gazed around the room. "In exchange, we have offered to host the men as well as their families, those that have them, at the remaining homes in Winter Haven."

Noah did the math in his head, his gut a block of ice. That was two or three militia families or several single men per house.

How would the rest of the townspeople take this? Strangers warm and cozy while they went hungry and shivered in the dark.

He couldn't think of that now. That was a problem for another day. They had to overcome this lethal threat first.

"We're not here to take over." Sutter's voice was quiet but commanding. He had an air of authority about him, a natural confidence. "We're not here to trample on anyone's toes. We want to help. And yes, I won't lie. A warm house with electricity and hot showers is a mighty fine temptation. We're getting something out of this, too. But that will not prevent us from working together in a symbiotic relationship.

"We are ready and willing to put our lives on the line to protect the fine people of Fall Creek. We'll be setting up and manning roadblocks into and out of town starting tomorrow. You've been lucky this far since you're small and off the highway.

We're going to make this town safe. Starting with wreaking vengeance upon a bunch of mass murderers."

Annette King nodded in weary resignation. "We have to be safe."

"We can't allow anything like this to happen again," Dave Farris said.

"Rosamond was right all along," Wiggins said darkly. "We should have voted her way last time, and we sure as hell better do it now."

Noah rose to his feet. "I agree."

Everyone quieted. They all watched him, listening intently. Everyone knew he'd worked the Crossway Church massacre. Everyone knew Milo Sheridan was one of the only survivors.

"The superintendent is right. The world is changing on us, and we must be ready to change with it. We're not only struggling to survive the elements, to provide food and shelter for our loved ones, but we're also facing threats like we've never encountered.

"I think we can all agree that this has been the longest week of our lives. The stores are running dangerously low. Pantries are empty. People will start starving. They'll see their kids going hungry, and what will they do? We have to make sure we can protect ourselves from that contingency."

He took a breath, thought of Milo. "For me, I'm willing to do anything for my son. Anything. I think we'd all do the same. If that means welcoming the Volunteer Militia Brigade as a support to local law enforcement, then that's what I'm prepared to do."

Mattias Sutter tilted his chin at Noah in acknowledgment.

"Thank you, Officer Sheridan," Rosamond said. "He's said everything I would say to you, and better."

"We do what we have to do," Wiggins said imperiously. "Whatever it takes."

"We have to protect the town," Annette said, her voice hoarse.

"I think we're ready for a vote." Rosamond clasped her hands together in front of her stomach. "What say you?"

In only a few seconds, the vote was completed. A quick show of hands showed the majority in favor of the militia moving in.

Only Chief Briggs kept his hands in his lap, his expression tense.

"And the yeas have it." There was no trace of victory or excitement in her voice—only her usual calm, measured tone. "Thank you, everyone. And thank you, Mattias."

Noah squelched his own anxiety. The militia would keep Fall Creek safe. They would keep Milo safe.

In the end, wasn't that what mattered?

"Tomorrow, this will all be over," Rosamond said. "We will mourn our dead, but we will be secure. We can put our children to sleep with the confidence that they will wake in the morning, safe and protected. We have an arduous task before us, but the people of Fall Creek are made of tough stock. We will survive. And we will rebuild. We will make it through this!"

"Here, here," Wiggins said.

The others nodded.

Rosamond cleared her throat and surveyed the council. She waited until all eyes were on her. Until it was so silent you could hear a pin drop.

"You are family to me. Each one of you. I hope you know that." She smiled that warm, grandmotherly smile, tears still shimmering in her eyes. "We have thirty empty homes in Winter Haven. We cannot let such a valuable resource go to waste. And each of you—the leaders of this community, right here in this room —those homes are for you and your families. For all that you've sacrificed and will sacrifice to keep this town safe and united, you deserve it."

Everyone rose to their feet, broke into applause. Their weary faces shone with grief and fear and worry, but also hope. They were desperate for it.

From the back of the room, Chief Briggs got up silently and moved to the front door. He pulled his coat off the hook, tugged on his boots, and left without saying a word.

Rosamond barely glanced at Briggs as the door shut behind him. The corner of her mouth twitched. Noah knew her well enough to know what she was thinking. She had the council. They were with her all the way. She didn't need the police chief's support, not this time.

Noah clapped along with everyone else. Still, he couldn't erase the unease tangling in his belly. He couldn't get Bishop's words out of his head.

This feeling, deep in his gut. One he loathed but couldn't escape.

That whatever this was, it wouldn't end with the death of Ray Shultz and the Carter brothers.

This was far from over.

57

NOAH
DAY EIGHT

That night, Noah left Milo with the Sinclairs.

He was drained, spent, his soul weary, but he couldn't rest. Any sleep he sought would be full of nightmares, of blood-drenched pews, Daphne and Chloe and Juniper calling out to him, plaintive ghosts demanding to know why they were dead, why he hadn't protected them.

Instead of sleeping, he took the Kawasaki, topped it off with a jerrycan stashed in Rosamond's garage, and hooked it up to one of the large trailers Julian had borrowed from the townspeople. He packed a shovel, a tarp, and a long, rectangular sled he'd also found in the garage.

He headed north out of Fall Creek toward Kalamazoo via Old 31 and I-94. The temperature hovered well below zero. Darkness encroached on every side.

Above him the sky was immense, flooded with stars. They'd never felt so bright. Sharp splinters of ice scattered across black velvet. The moon was full and round and reflected blue light off the unbroken snow.

He forced himself to focus straight ahead. The guard rails had disappeared beneath massive snowdrifts. Only the humps of snow smothering the abandoned vehicles and occasional road signs poking out of the endless field of white alerted him to the location of the road.

The highway wasn't plowed. Hadn't been in the last eight days. Since the event. Black Christmas, people were calling it. He didn't care what it was called.

When he reached Bittersweet Ski Resort, he pulled into the parking lot, switched off the snowmobile, and transferred the shovel, tarp, and rope to the sled. He removed his helmet and left it with the machine. He pulled on a balaclava to protect his face, flicked on the headlamp he'd brought, and started walking.

The brutal cold tunneled straight through his gear. His eyebrows and eyelashes felt frozen. His movements already stiff and awkward, but he kept moving.

The burned and blackened husk of the lodge loomed out of the darkness. He veered around it. The snow muted the ugliness, just like it muted sound. The silence was loud in his ears. His breath escaped his mouth in a pale white mist.

He felt like the only human being alive for miles. It wasn't a pleasant feeling.

He liked people. Needed them around. He'd never been great at being alone. Too many dark thoughts and haunting memories to wriggle inside his brain and take up residence.

He'd made a promise. He'd promised Quinn. He wasn't a hero. He wasn't a great man. He failed. He was flawed. He'd made too many mistakes to count. Mistakes that had cost lives.

But he loved his son. And he was a man of his word. He hoped it would be enough.

Pulling the sled burdened with supplies behind him, Noah began the long, arduous trek to the top of Rocket Launcher run.

He climbed. And climbed. Plowing doggedly through thigh-deep snow, his boots breaking through the crust, his breath ragged, his lungs burning with cold fire.

Once he'd nearly reached the top of the hill, it wasn't hard to find their chairlift.

He'd had hours to memorize the particular shapes of the trees, the way the slope veered sharply to the left just past that jutting stump. The break in the red fencing he and Quinn had used to rescue Milo and Phoebe.

He counted the chairlifts between the towers, found the correct ones. The chairlifts were empty. He sighed with relief, something loosening inside his chest. The blizzard must have blown the old man's body down.

He hadn't known how he would get the body from the chairlift. He just knew he had to come up here. He had to try.

He took the shovel out of the sled and started digging through the deep snowdrifts. Noah didn't stop to rest until he'd found and uncovered them both—Brock Mason and Dương Văn Dũng, Quinn's grandfather.

He stared at the bodies with a pang.

He was law enforcement. He should've done a better job. He should have saved them. Just like he should've saved the victims in the Crossway massacre. He should've been smarter, better, faster. Some cop he was turning out to be.

He couldn't even protect his son. Couldn't protect his best friend's family.

He didn't cry. His face was too frozen to cry.

He hadn't been prepared enough. Once, he'd allowed himself to be lulled into complacency. But he wasn't that person anymore.

Five years of grief had taught him that. The last week of chaos and suffering had taught him more.

Reality was ugly, brutal, and dangerous. He couldn't blindly believe that he and Milo would be okay. He had to make sure of it. It was his responsibility.

His muscles straining, groaning and huffing from the effort, Noah rolled each stiff, ice-covered body into a tarp, loaded them onto the sled, and bound them in place with the rope.

The return trip would be more difficult than the ascent. The path before him would only become more difficult, in more ways than one. He understood that now.

Surviving this new EMP-ravaged world would demand everything from him. And then it would demand more.

Whatever trials and hardships he'd already endured would be nothing compared to what lay ahead.

But he would do it. He had no choice.

"I'll do whatever I have to," Noah vowed aloud, speaking into the endless icy silence. "Whatever it takes."

The End

ACKNOWLEDGMENTS

Thank you as always to my awesome beta readers. Your thoughtful critiques and enthusiasm are invaluable. As I embark on a brand new series, your support and encouragement meant everything to me.

Thanks to my readers for their excellent character names! Please do not judge these wonderful people based on the actions of the characters named after them in this book. I took their names only and made the characters do what I wanted, as is an author's prerogative.

To Rachel Watts Mitchell for Brock.

To Mike Smalley for Phoebe.

Chris Doenges for lending his name to the weed-smoking liftie.

Annette King Cairl, the dedicated principal of Fall Creek High School.

Tina Gundy, the adorable Fall Creek mechanic.

Dave Farris as the ham radio guy.

Jose Jaime Reynoso as a Fall Creek police officer.

Robert Vinson as the local pharmacist.

Bonnie Smith for the name "Maxine Hammond" a local of Fall Creek.

Oren Truitt, Samantha Perez, and Clint Moll as part-time police officers.

And Paul Eastley, local farmer.

Thank you so much to my awesome, amazing, and fantastic BETA readers: Fred Oelrich, Melva Metivier, Wmh Cheryl, Annette Cairl, Jessica Burland, Sally Shupe, Becca and Brendan Cross, Robert Odell, and to George Hall for his keen eye and military expertise.

To Mike Smalley for Noah's cop skills.

To Angela Martignetti Baez for patiently answering all my questions in regards to Milo's Addison's Disease. Any mistakes are my own.

To Michelle Browne for her line editing skills and Nadene Seiters for proofreading.

And a special thank you to Jenny Avery for catching those last pesky errors.

To my husband, who takes care of the house, the kids, and the cooking when I'm under the gun with a writing deadline. To my kids, who show me the true meaning of love every day and continually inspire me.

Thanks to God for His many blessings. He is with us even in the darkest times.

And to my loyal readers, whose support and encouragement mean everything to me. Thank you.

AUTHOR'S NOTE

I hope you enjoyed *Edge of Madness*! I hope you weren't too upset that Liam, Hannah, and Ghost were missing from this part of the story.

They will be in book #3, *Edge of Darkness*, I promise!

When I tried to combine the two main storylines together in the first book, it didn't work. Hannah and Liam needed to tell their beginning uninterrupted. Noah and Quinn wanted their own book, too. Sometimes, the story dictates the form.

While the setting of Southwest Michigan and the surrounding towns are real, Fall Creek is my own invention. Bittersweet Ski Resort is a real place, but I added the Rocket Launcher ski run— and Milo's favorite giant peanut butter cookies.

The task of safeguarding an entire town in desperate need of pretty much everything is a challenge for both the characters and the author. I don't envy Noah the arduous task ahead of him!

I hope you'll continue to follow Noah, Quinn, and Milo as well as Hannah, Liam, and Ghost on their journey throughout the *Edge of Collapse* series.

Thank you for reading!

ABOUT THE AUTHOR

I spend my days writing apocalyptic and dystopian fiction novels, exploring all the different ways the world might end.

I love writing stories exploring how ordinary people cope with extraordinary circumstances, especially situations where the normal comforts, conveniences, and rules are stripped away.

My favorite stories to read and write deal with characters struggling with inner demons who learn to face and overcome their fears, launching their transformation into the strong, brave warrior they were meant to become.

Some of my favorite books include *The Road*, *The Passage*, *Hunger Games*, and *Ready Player One*. My favorite movies are *The Lord of the Rings* and *Gladiator*.

Give me a good story in any form and I'm happy.

Oh, and add in a cool fall evening in front of a crackling fire, nestled on the couch with a fuzzy blanket, a book in one hand and a hot mocha latte in the other (or dark chocolate!): that's my heaven.

I mean, I won't say no to hiking to mountain waterfalls, traveling to far-flung locations, or jumping out of a plane (parachute included) either.

I love to hear from my readers! Find my books and chat with me via any of the channels below:

www.Facebook.com/KylaStoneAuthor

www.Amazon.com/author/KylaStone

Email me at KylaStone@yahoo.com